BURN

JAMES PATTERSON is one of the best-known and biggest-selling writers of all time. Since winning the Edgar™ Award for Best First Novel with *The Thomas Berryman Number*, his books have sold in excess of 300 million copies worldwide and he has been the most borrowed author in UK libraries for the past seven years in a row. He is the author of some of the most popular series of the past decade – the Alex Cross, Women's Murder Club, Detective Michael Bennett and Private novels – and he has written many other number one bestsellers including romance novels and stand-alone thrillers. He lives in Florida with his wife and son.

James is passionate about encouraging children to read. Inspired by his own son who was a reluctant reader, he also writes a range of books specifically for young readers. James is a founding partner of Booktrust's Children's Reading Fund in the UK.

Why everyone loves James Patterson and Detective Michael Bennett

'Its breakneck pace leaves you gasping for breath. Packed with typical Patterson panache . . . **it won't disappoint**.'
Daily Mail

'It's no mystery why James Patterson is the world's most popular thriller writer. Simply put: **Nobody does it better**.'
Jeffery Deaver

'No one gets this big without **amazing natural storytelling** talent – which is what Jim has, in spades.'
Lee Child

'James Patterson is the **gold standard** by which all others are judged.'
Steve Berry

'Patterson boils a scene down to the single, telling detail, the element that **defines a character** or moves a plot along. It's what fires off the movie projector in the reader's mind.'
Michael Connelly

'James Patterson is **The Boss**. End of.'
Ian Rankin

Have You Read Them All?

STEP ON A CRACK

The most powerful people in the world have gathered for a funeral in New York City. They don't know it's a trap devised by a ruthless mastermind. Despite battling his own tragedies, it's up to Michael Bennett to save every last hostage.

RUN FOR YOUR LIFE

The Teacher is giving New York a lesson it will never forget, slaughtering the powerful and the arrogant. Michael Bennett discovers a vital pattern, but has only a few hours to save the city before things get too close to home.

WORST CASE

Children from wealthy families are being abducted. But the captor isn't demanding money. He's quizzing his hostages on the price others pay for their luxurious lives, and one wrong answer is fatal.

TICK TOCK

New York is in chaos as a rash of horrifying copycat crimes tears through the city. Michael Bennett cuts his family holiday short to investigate, but not even he could predict the earth-shattering enormity of this killer's plan.

I, MICHAEL BENNETT

Bennett arrests infamous South American crime lord Manuel Perrine in a deadly chase that leaves Michael's lifelong friend dead. From jail, the prisoner vows to rain terror down upon New York City – and to get revenge on Michael Bennett.

GONE

Perrine is back and deadlier than ever. Bennett must make an impossible decision: stay and protect his family, or hunt down the man who is their biggest threat.

BURN

A group of well-dressed men enter a condemned building. Later, a charred body is found. Michael Bennett is about to enter a secret underground world of terrifying depravity.

BURN

JAMES PATTERSON
& MICHAEL LEDWIDGE

arrow books

Published by Arrow Books in 2015

3 5 7 9 10 8 6 4 2

First published in Great Britain in 2014 by Century

Arrow Books
Random House, 20 Vauxhall Bridge Road,
London SW1V 2SA

www.randomhouse.co.uk

Addresses for companies within The Random House Group Limited can be found at: www.randomhouse.co.uk/offices.htm

The Random House Group Limited Reg. No. 954009

A CIP catalogue record for this book
is available from the British Library

ISBN 9780099574040
ISBN 9780099574057 (export edition)

Typeset by SX Composing DTP, Rayleigh, Essex
Printed and bound by CPI Group (UK) Ltd, Croydon, CR0 4YY

Penguin Random House is committed to a sustainable future for our business, our readers and our planet. This book is made from Forest Stewardship Council® certified paper.

For Kevin and Blaithin Durkin and family

Prologue

CALIFORNIA LEAVING

One

LOS ANGELES

THE WORK VAN WAS a new Mercedes, white and high roofed, with the bloodred words TURNKEY LOCKSMITH hand-painted on its side.

At a little before 7 a.m., it was winding through the Hollywood Hills northwest of LA, the steady drone of its diesel engine briefly rising in pitch as it turned onto the long climb of Kirkwood Drive in Laurel Canyon. Two hundred feet below the intersection of Kirkwood and Oak, the van coasted to a crackling stop on the gravel shoulder of the secluded road and shut off its engine. A minute passed, then two. No one got out.

As the bald Hispanic driver flipped down the visor to get the sun out of his eyes, he spotted a mule deer nosing out through the steep hillside's thick underbrush across the street.

Go for a lung shot, he thought as he imagined getting a bead on it with the new compound hunting bow his girlfriend had gotten him for his birthday. *Track the blood trail down between the infinity pools and twenty-person funkadelic hot tubs before lashing it to the van's front grille. See how that would go down with George Clooney and k. d. lang and the rest of the Laurel Canyon faithful.*

He was feigning a bow draw when the elegant deer suddenly noticed him and bolted. The driver sighed, leaned slightly to his right, and depressed the intercom button under the drink holder.

"How's this? Line of sight OK?" he said.

"Yes. Maintain here until the hand-off, then head for position two," intercommed back the sharp-featured, copper-haired woman sitting directly behind the driver in the sealed-off back of the high-tech surveillance van.

There was a dull mechanical hum as the woman flicked the joystick for the high-definition video camera concealed in the van's roof. On the console's flat screen in front of her, an off-white stucco bungalow a hundred and fifty feet up the canyon slowly came into view.

She panned the camera over the bungalow's short, steep driveway of bishop's hat paver stones, the broken terracotta roof tiles above its front door, the live oaks and lemon trees in its side yard. She'd been here several times before and knew the target house as well as her own at this point.

She was halfway through the tea-filled Tervis tumbler from her kit bag when a truck slowed in front of the target house. It was a new Ford Expedition SUV, glossy black with heavily tinted windows. After it reversed up the driveway almost butt-up against the garage, the passenger-side door opened and out stepped a lanky middle-aged white man in a gray business suit. He adjusted his Oakley sport sunglasses for a moment before he reached into the open door and retrieved what appeared to be a military-issue M-16.

Then, up on the porch above him, the bungalow's front door opened and Detective Michael Bennett came out of the house.

The woman almost spilled the tea in her lap as she quickly panned the camera left and zoomed in on Bennett and the crowd of people coming out behind him. His kids were in cartoon-character pj's, their tan and striking blond nanny, Mary Catherine, in a bathrobe, drying her hands with a dish towel. One of the Bennett boys—was Trent his name? Yes, Trent—immediately started climbing out over the stair's cast-iron rail, until Mary Catherine pulled him back by his collar.

The cacophony of the family's calls and laughter rang in her earphone as she turned up the volume on the van's shotgun mike.

"*Arrivederci*," Bennett said playfully to his rambunctious family as he went down the stairs. "*Sayonara, auf Wiedersehen*. And, oh, yeah. Later, guys."

The woman in the van watched silently as Bennett smiled and crossed his eyes and stuck his tongue out at his family. He was pushing forty, but still tall and trim and handsome in his dark-blue suit. Biting at her lower lip, she didn't stop focusing until his dimples and brown eyes slid out of the bottom of the frame into the SUV.

As the Ford rocketed out into the street, the copper-haired woman had already put down the joystick and was wheeling the captain's chair around toward the three men in bulky tactical gear sitting and sweating on the steel bench behind her.

If it hadn't been for the glistening snub-barreled Heckler & Koch machine guns in their laps, the large men could have been professional football players. Wide receivers in the huddle waiting for the quarterback to call the next play.

“To repeat one last time,” she said calmly as the work van’s engine suddenly roared to life and they lurched into the street. “Front door, side door, back door. When the doors pop, you will stay low until you are in position.”

The poised woman quickly lifted her own submachine gun from the foam-lined hard case at her feet. Easily and expertly, she worked the H&K MP7’s action, slamming the first HK 4.6x30mm cartridge into the gun’s chamber with a loud snap.

“This isn’t a drill, gentlemen,” she said, looking up at the Bennett safe house growing rapidly now on the flat screen.

“Welcome to life and death.”

Two

"SO-OO," I SUDDENLY CALLED out into the SUV's dead silence after five minutes of zigzagging up and down and hither and yon over the roller-coaster roads of the Hollywood Hills. "Anybody read any good books lately?"

I smiled encouragingly at each of the four large gentlemen sitting around me. But try as I might, I couldn't get the conversational ball rolling. Not one of the armed-to-the-teeth business-attired behemoths I was riding with smiled back or even said a word. I thought briefly about trying to start up a hearty round of "Ninety-Nine Bottles of Beer on the Wall" to break the ice, but then I finally dropped my grin and shrugged.

"Yeah, me neither," I mumbled as I turned back to the bulletproof window. "Exactly. Who reads?"

I guess I couldn't really blame the fellas for ignoring me. My US Marshal buddies were busy at work, busy keeping their eyes peeled for things like snipers and machine-gun ambushes and IEDs as we made our way from my Hollywood Hills safe house toward downtown Los Angeles.

I was being accompanied by the marshals so early this Monday morning because of a trial. The DEA had tried and convicted five of the recently deceased Manuel "the Sun God" Perrine's Tepito cartel pals in a huge coke bust and were about to sentence the drug soldiers today.

I was involved because, in addition to the drug charges, the cartel death squad had already been convicted in absentia of the murder of a federal ADA in New York, a woman named Tara McLellan who had been a very close friend of mine.

I'd spoken to her still-devastated family and, death threats or no death threats, I was going to the courtroom today to speak for her at the victim impact statement.

On a happier note, after the trial, it was going to be checkout time for me and the Bennett clan from the Hotel California. The Golden State had been a nice place to visit, but we were finally going back home to the Big Apple where we belonged.

Myself, and especially my stomach, really couldn't have been happier. The four corners of my carb-jonesing Irish heart—real pizza, real bagels, real rolls, and especially real Italian bread—were a mere day away.

As was our freedom from all this aggravating hiding and security, I thought, glancing at the marshals, who had been nothing but expert in their care of my family during our time in the witness protection program.

In twenty-four hours, we'd finally be home in New York with our lives back.

Now all I had to do was get through them.

"Ninety-nine bottles of beer on the wall," I hummed to myself as I stared out at the insanely blue California sky.

Three

I WAS IN THE midst of a daydream where I was locked in overnight at an Arthur Avenue bakery with several tubs of Breakstone's lightly salted and a butter knife when we pulled off the 101 and approached the white stone pile of the Los Angeles Federal Court in downtown LA's Civic Center.

That was when my gluten-filled fantasy came to an end. Abruptly.

Forward through the windshield was a huge commotion. A large crowd of civilians was assembled in front of the august court building. They stood behind metal sidewalk barricades and a line of nervous-looking uniformed LA cops holding plastic shields and wearing full face-masked riot helmets.

"What the heck is this? OJ can't be on trial again, can he?" I said.

As we came closer, I could see that the crowd consisted of about a hundred fifty young people clustered on the sidewalk. More than a few in the crowd were wearing blue-and-white bandannas, bandit style, over their faces. There was even a muscular guy in a wife-beater wearing one of those spooky antiestablishment Guy Fawkes masks.

People began yelling and chanting and pumping their fists as someone struck a tom-tom over and over. Signs being shaken to the beat read,

NO JUSTICE! NO PEACE!
RACIST SEGREGATION!!!!
DOWN WITH THE KKKops!

Having become quite rudely acquainted with the LA gang culture in my time here searching for Perrine, I knew the blue-and-white do-rags meant MS-13. I also knew that MS-13 was an LA-based ally of the Tepito cartel scum I was about to help get sentenced.

It made me sit up straight, seeing fired-up gang members amassed in some sort of halfhearted political protest. I knew full well that some of these gangsters weren't exactly your peaceful protester types. In fact, the cartel affiliates didn't have qualm one when it came to incredibly bloody violence.

Perrine's people had actually killed a federal judge in New York *at the courthouse in the middle of Perrine's trial!*

Remembering that, I felt my stomach drop as I watched shaved heads on the sidewalk turn toward our SUV. Some of the tattooed young bangers were elbowing each other, pointing our way as we slowed.

Oh, boy. Here we go. Though I hadn't advertised that I was going to make an appearance at the courthouse today, my face had been in the media before. There was the odd chance that one of these guys might recognize me and want to collect on the multimillion-dollar contract that was currently hovering over my head.

It can't be helped, I thought, bracing myself as we finally came to a halt by the court entrance on North Spring Street. Nothing—no gangbangers, no fake protest or anything else—was going to stop me from standing up for Tara today.

"You know, we still have some time, Mike," Big Joe Kelly, the US Marshal team captain, said beside me as the crowd shifted and approached the SUV. "We could go for some Starbucks or something. Come back when it looks a little calmer."

"Nah, Joe," I said with a casualness that was all show. "Let's just do this quick before I ruin the nice clean underwear I wore for the courthouse security strip search."

Doors opened and Joe and the other big marshals got out. Joe went over and spoke to one of the cops, who quickly came over with two other uniformed riot cops, and then my door opened.

Stepping out from the sealed vault of the bulletproof SUV into the loud whooshing buzz of the jeering crowd was like coming out of a pool. A pool I felt like diving back into when more and more people in the crowd started rushing over.

"I smell pork!" some girl kept saying as the muscle head in the Guy Fawkes mask suddenly rushed up and snapped a picture of me with his cell phone.

"Got your picture, pig!" he yelled from behind his mask. "I'm gonna find out who you are and where you live and pay you a visit! Pay your pig family a visit!"

I was doing pretty well up to that point, but at the mention of my family, I lost my composure a little. In fact, I lunged at the stupid son of a bitch. Unfortunately, Joe stiff-armed him away before I could get my hands around his throat.

Then the marshals half-led, half-shoved me forward in a tight phalanx toward a break in the metal barrier. I was just through it and had set foot on the first marble step when it happened.

Pop-pop-pop-pop!

A string of explosions suddenly ripped the air all around us, and Joe was turning and shoving me back as the crowd churned.

In the mad rush, my ankle caught the edge of one of the metal barricades and the next thing I knew, I was knocked off my feet facedown on the cement sidewalk. Smelling gunpowder, I looked down at myself, my jacket and slacks, scanning for holes. Peeking up through a forest of legs, I saw some LAPD uniforms rush into the swaying, screaming crowd, throwing people out of the way. A K-9 unit German shepherd started barking to wake the dead, sending people running.

"It's OK! It's OK! It's firecrackers!" came a loud, tinny voice out of Joe's radio. "No gun! I repeat, no gun! Some ass in the crowd just tossed a pack of lit firecrackers."

The crowd started laughing their collective faces off. Sarcastic clapping began and about fifty people gave me the finger as Joe helped me to my feet. Unbelievable. And they called this the *Civic* Center?

"You OK, Mike?" Joe yelled, grabbing my arm.

"Well, about that clean underwear," I said as I peeled myself off the concrete.

Four

THE WITNESS WAITING ROOM adjacent to the second-floor federal courtroom where I was going to give my statement was a happy surprise after the fireworks show and my unexpected sidewalk rugby match. It had leather furniture and piped-in slow-dance Muzak and a rack of magazines next to the coffee machine.

For twenty minutes, I sat in it alone, humming to Michael Bolton as Joe and his guys stood vigilantly in the hallway outside the locked door. The little stunt downstairs had fired them up beyond belief. Even with the tight courthouse security, they weren't taking any chances.

I'd just finished pouring myself a second cup of French vanilla coffee (which I probably didn't need, considering my already frazzled nerves) when the door unlocked and a middle-aged blond court officer poked her friendly face inside and said it was time.

All eyes were on me as I followed the officer's blond ponytail into the bleached-wood-paneled courtroom. The line of orange-jumpsuited convicts sitting at the two defendants' tables peered at me curiously with "haven't I seen you someplace before" expressions as I made my way to a podium set up beside the witness box.

Alejandro Soto, the highest-ranking of the Tepito cartel members in attendance, seemed especially curious from where he sat closest to the witness box. I recognized his gaunt, ugly features from the video of the Bronx motel where he had brought my friend Tara to rape and kill her.

I stared directly at Soto as the court clerk asked me to state my name for the record.

"My name is Bennett," I said, smiling at Soto. "*Detective* Michael Bennett."

"Bennett!" Soto yelled as he stood and started banging his shackled wrists on the table. "What is this? What is this?"

No wonder he was shocked. His organization was out to get me and suddenly, presto, here I was. *Be careful what you wish for,* I thought as two court officers shoved the skinny middle-aged scumbag back down into his seat.

The violent crack of Judge Kenneth Barnett's gavel at the commotion was a little painful in the low-ceilinged courtroom. Our side could set off some firecrackers, too, apparently. Tall and wide, Barnett had the build of a football player, bright-blue eyes, and a shock of gray hair slicked straight back.

"Detective Bennett," he said as I was about to take my prepared statement from my jacket pocket. "Before you begin, I would just like to gently remind you that the victim impact statement is not an occasion for you to address the defendants directly. It is a way for me, the sentencing judge, to understand what impact the crimes in this case have had on you and society and thereby determine what appropriate punishment to mete out to these convicted men. Do you understand?"

"Perfectly, Your Honor," I said.

Especially the punishment part, I thought, glancing at Soto again.

I took my written statement out of my pocket and flattened it against the podium as I brought the microphone closer to my mouth.

Five

"MY NAME IS MICHAEL BENNETT," I said. "I am a twenty-year veteran of the NYPD, the last nine working as a first-grade detective. Tara McLellan, who these men have been convicted of killing, was a colleague of mine and a very close family friend. I was asked to come here today by her devastated family in order to address the court."

Someone in the crowded courtroom coughed in the silence as I paused to take a deep breath.

"Tara was an extremely beautiful and bright young woman who loved life more than almost anyone I've ever met," I started.

But as I said those words, I did what I'd sworn I would not. I locked up, choked up as I pictured her. Her raven-black hair and bright-blue eyes. Her smile. A tear rolled off my cheek and landed on the page with a tiny splat. I clenched my jaw as I wiped my face and then, with an outrush of breath, forced myself to continue.

"Tara loved gardening at her small house in Westchester, loved to travel. Her numerous nieces and nephews looked forward to every birthday for the moment when Aunt Tara would arrive with the ridiculously elaborate character cakes she would bake them, charting the landmarks of their childhood from Elmo to Justin Bieber with food coloring and frosting and love."

I took another breath in the now-dead silence.

"But what she loved most of all in this world was delivering justice as an assistant United States attorney of the Southern District of New York. Tara stood in courtrooms just like this one. Stood before the worst that humanity has to offer—killers and mobsters and con men. She stood before these predators of the innocent, looked them in the eye, and with a conviction and courage few will ever know, she said simply, 'No. You will not get away with what you have done. You will not get away with the pain you have inflicted.'

"Tara's loss in that dim Bronx motel where she was inhumanly violated before being beheaded isn't felt just by her grieving parents, Camille and

James, or her two sisters, Annette and Jeanie. Nor just by all her nephews and nieces and cousins and friends.

"No, Judge Barnett. Tara's loss is your loss as well. It is everyone's loss. There are very few people on this planet who never back down from evil. Tara was one of them. The light of this world has been dimmed without Tara McLellan in it anymore. Thank you."

I'd folded my paper and was about to leave, when Judge Barnett motioned me to stay.

"Detective Bennett, wait," he said. "Thank you so much for those words. I myself had gleaned most of your impression of Ms. McLellan from these proceedings, but to hear you put the tragedy of her loss in so personal and poignant a way has helped clarify this court's decision."

He swiveled to the seated defendants.

"Will the convicted please rise.

"Alejandro Soto?" Judge Barnett said.

Soto's defense lawyer tugged his sleeve.

"What?" Soto said, staring at his ankle shackles.

"This court and the federal government, representing the people of these United States of America, hereby sentence you to die by means of lethal injection."

Judge Barnett cracked the gavel again at the audible gasp that rose in the courtroom.

"Tomás Maduro," the judge said, turning immediately toward the next defendant. "This court and the federal government, representing the people of these United States of America, hereby sentence you, too, to die by means of lethal injection."

And down the line Judge Barnett went, handing out death sentences. I couldn't believe it. It was only under the rarest of circumstances when the federal courts handed out capital punishment. Only sixty-nine people had been sentenced with it since 1988, and only three, including the Oklahoma City bomber, Timothy McVeigh, had actually been executed.

Now, not one, not two, but all five of these vicious, evil men were going to get the needle. The cartels meted out death like it was water, and apparently, Judge Barnett wasn't going to take it anymore.

That was when I did it. What the judge had asked me not to.

I turned to the baffled, raging defendants and addressed them directly. As the drug-dealing murderers were surrounded by court officers, I gave each one a smile along with a happy little wave good-bye.

Six

I WAS BACK IN the hallway outside the still-turbulent courtroom when Joe and the rest of my US Marshal bodyguards rushed over.

"Looks like the stooges outside on the plaza are going wild after the verdict, Mike," Big Joe said with concern. "I already radioed down to Larry Burns. We're going to take you out back through the prisoner paddock."

"Sounds good, Joe," I said, walking past him toward the corner of the hallway. "Just let me hit the boys' room and I'll be right with you."

Actually, I didn't need to use the restroom. I was still massively keyed up after sitting across from Tara's killers and the last thing I needed was to get back into the coffin of the SUV, no matter how safe it was.

That was why I decided to do what I did next. It was time to cut the apron strings and leave the prisoner entrances to the prisoners from here on out.

I passed right by the bathroom and found the stairwell door and used it and headed down.

Joe was right, I saw immediately when I approached the main entrance in the downstairs lobby. The quote unquote protesters seemed spitting mad where they milled around behind the aluminum sidewalk barricades at the bottom of the courthouse steps. I was just in time to see the action begin. One of the gangbangers knocked one of the barricades over and then there were several loud bangs as the LA riot cops broke out the tear gas. The crowd scattered like leaves on the business end of an air rake, running back out into North Spring Street and the corporate plaza on its opposite side.

"Hey, buddy, you know there's a side entrance you can use," one of the court officers manning the metal detectors said to me as I picked up my gun and headed for the front door. "Looks a little hairy out there."

"That's OK, friend," I said, winking as I flashed my shield. "I'm a barber."

Coming down the steps, I smiled as the LA cops pushed the punks back farther into the corporate park. You could see from the signs lying in the gutter that the protest was pretty much over. The crowd was already breaking up into little groups and going home.

Evildoers had been brought to justice upstairs, and now order had been restored down here. Score one for the good guys. It looked like we'd won. Well, today's battle, at least.

I walked up Temple Street behind the courthouse. It really was a nice day, temperate, not a hint of a breeze, the intense California light bright and unmoving on the bleached-looking white buildings. My native New Yorker's impression of LA was that it was beautiful, even perfect in some ways, yet slightly off-putting, like an austere, alluring blonde wearing a slightly strange expression that makes you suddenly wonder if maybe she might be completely out of her mind.

My cell phone went off as I made the corner. It was my US Marshal buddy Joe Kelly. I was about to pick it up, but then I decided to text him back instead.

I'm fine, Joe. I decided I'm going to get back home on my own. If I need you I'll call.

Seven

I FLAGGED DOWN A gypsy cab and headed home.

The whole way back up the 101 to Laurel Canyon, I listened to the Mexican driver behind the wheel play a type of music called *narcocorrido*. Having become familiar with it in my recent investigations into the cartels, I knew the traditional-sounding Mexican country music had gangster-rap-style lyrics about moving dope and taking out your enemies with AK-47s.

Though it had a nice, sad sort of rhythm, considering the fact that the story of my life had recently pretty much become a *narcocorrido*, I didn't think I'd be adding it to my iPod playlist anytime soon.

Finally standing in the street out in front of the safe house thirty minutes later, paying the driver, I heard a sudden shriek of rubber. Just south down the curving slope of Kirkwood, I stood and watched as a white Eurostyle work van fishtailed off the shoulder and barreled straight toward me.

No, was my weary thought as I watched it come. This couldn't be happening. The van shrieked again as it came around the closest curve and hit its brakes.

Forgetting the cabdriver, I palmed the stippled grip of my Glock and drew as I hit the driveway, ducked my head, and ran up the steps of the house two at a time.

"Mary Catherine! Seamus!" I yelled as I pounded on the screen door with the pistol barrel.

My shocked-looking nanny, Mary Catherine, had just opened the front door when I heard the rattling metal roll of the van door opening at the bottom of the stairs.

"Mike, Mike! It's OK! Stand down! It's OK. It's me!" came a yell.

I turned. Down the stairs, a large bald guy with a gun was standing over my taxi driver, now lying facedown on the street. Also standing now in the open side doors of the white van was a woman. A very pretty woman in blue fatigues with copper-colored hair.

"Agent Parker. Long time no see. Are you out of your mind?" I screamed.

I should have known, I thought. It was a friend of mine. Emily Parker, special agent of the FBI. I guess I shouldn't have been surprised. Emily and I had taken down Perrine together less than a month before, and I knew she was still working in LA. I just didn't know *I* was her work.

I racked my weapon to make it safe as I came back down the stairs.

"I mean, Emily, you of all people should understand how paranoid I am these days about things like, I don't know, mysterious vans racing up on me. Is this some kind of practical joke? Why didn't you tell me you and the FBI were watching my house?"

"It was just a precaution for your court appearance today," she said as three drab-fatigue-clad FBI agents with large guns suddenly emerged from the foliage along the side of our house.

"Additional security was ordered," she said. "I kept it low key because you guys have been through enough. I didn't want to get you upset."

"In that case, I guess I'm not having a heart attack," I said.

"Listen, you should be the last one to talk about jokes, Mike," Emily said. "You know how many people are looking for you? Ditching the marshals after that verdict was beyond childish. We thought the bad guys got you. We've been worried sick."

"Ditched? I texted Joe. Besides, I'm a grown man, Parker," I said. "A grown man who needed some fresh air."

"During a gang riot?"

I shrugged.

"Taking my life back needs to start somewhere. I'm tired, Emily, of the death threats, all the worrying. I came out here because of Perrine, and now he's in the ground, and I'm done hiding. You and I both know the cartels are too busy killing each other for Perrine's turf to bother coming after me. Perrine was a monster. Monsters don't get avenged, last time I checked. Judge Barnett has seen to that. What was it that BP oil spill CEO guy said? 'I want my life back.' "

I walked over and knelt down and finally paid my cab-driver, still facedown on the asphalt.

"What's the quote, Emily? 'Those who would sacrifice freedom for security deserve neither and will lose both'?"

"What's that other quote about a well-balanced Irishman?" Emily said, hopping from the van. "'They have a chip on both shoulders'?"

Then she surprised me for the second time in two minutes. She walked up and wrapped her arms around me and pressed her face hard against my neck.

"I going to miss you, Mike... working with you. Just working. Don't get the wrong idea," she whispered in my ear.

"Good-bye yourself, Parker. It was fun strictly and platonically working with you as well," I whispered back as she broke it up.

She hopped back into the fed van with the rest of the agents. As they pulled away, I looked up to see Mary Catherine standing at the top of the stairs by the iron railing of the porch.

I immediately gave her my brightest smile. The on-again, off-again relationship I had with Mary Catherine had most definitely become on-again during our close-quarters California exile. She'd actually had to kill a cartel hit woman to protect the kids. We'd talked about it, cried about it. I don't think I'd ever been closer to this incredible young woman. Or more attracted.

I thought her dander might be up a little at seeing me share a hug with Parker, who I'd once or twice almost had a romantic relationship with, but to my happy surprise, Mary Catherine's slim hand slid easily into mine as I got to the top of the stairs.

"Time to go home, Detective Bennett," Mary Catherine said in her musical brogue as she suddenly broke my grip and playfully pushed me toward the door.

Eight

IT SEEMED LIKE EVERYBODY in LA had decided to come to see us off at LAX that evening.

There were people just about everywhere, packing the garish fluorescent-lit corridors, riding in humming golf carts, escalating up and down escalators, floating along on those George Jetson moving sidewalk thingies. Undeterred, our Bennett troupe trekked onward—under, over, and around the billboards and luggage carts and mobs of distressed-looking travelers.

I was a little distressed myself as I watched a tatted-up young street hoodlum in a flat-brim Dodgers cap saunter up from the opposite direction. I know it's not polite to stare, but I did so anyway, keeping my eyes on the illustrated young gentleman's hands until he was well past us.

Even in the airport on the opposite side of the TSA security checkpoint, I guess I still wasn't completely over my fear of our being attacked by some gang fools looking to get in good with the cartels.

We kept rolling. Somewhere ahead in the crowd, Mary Catherine was on point, trying to get us to Terminal 4 and our American Airlines flight home. Seamus and I were taking up the rear to keep track of the laggards.

Public Lollygaggers One and Two, respectively, were Eddie and Trent, who, when they weren't screaming and chasing each other around the banks of pleather seats, wanted to stop to get something from every Wendy's and Starbucks and gimcrack souvenir stand we passed.

I knew the box of Mike and Ike movie candy I'd let them purchase at the gas station on the van ride over would come back to haunt me.

"Dad, can we get Lakers caps?" Trent said.

"No," I said.

"Dad, can we at least get a Kobe bobblehead?" said Eddie.

"No, there are enough bobbleheads in the Bennett family, thank you. I'm talking to two of them right now, in fact."

"Dad, can we at the very least use the bathroom?" Trent cried.

"No, no, no," I said.

"Well, actually, that might be a good idea," Seamus said, smiling sheepishly beside me.

"Lollygagger Number Three, I presume," I said, rolling my eyes.

I pinched two fingers together and put them in my mouth and whistled up ahead to halt our rolling army.

"Pit stop!" I yelled.

I stayed by the massive mound of our carry-ons as the sexes split up into the restrooms. As I nervously checked and rechecked the time on my phone, I heard some excited yelling that at first I thought might be a flash mob or something. Then I saw some teenage Asian guy walk by on the concourse with an entourage, followed by a gaggle of screaming girls trying to snap cell phone pictures of him.

Was it the Chinese Justin Bieber? I wondered with a shrug. I had no clue. This LA Asian stuff was way beyond my Bronx Irish Catholic sense and sensibilities. The good news was I wouldn't have to worry about all things Hollywood once we made our flight.

That is, *if* we made our flight, I thought, frowning at my phone again. American Airlines had bent over backward to accommodate all thirteen of us on the red-eye on short notice. If we missed our plane, I feared we'd never escape from LA.

I took a quick head count as my family spilled back out onto the concourse.

Eleven, twelve, and lucky number thirteen.

"OK, boys and girls and um . . . priests, is everybody, um, unhydrated now? Excellent. OK, let's move, people. Forward march."

We were all on the plane and somewhere in the night sky, probably over Colorado, an hour and a half later when I finally was able to calm down. Socky, our now-tranquilized cat, was purring peacefully in his travel box between my feet. Mary Catherine, who probably could have used a tranquilizer or two herself after getting everyone ready for our coast-to-coast trip, was sleeping beside me in the window seat.

It felt good when she shifted toward the aisle and rested her head on my shoulder. It felt *very* good there, just right, in fact. We'd had our ups and downs, but it felt like we were settling in now, finally. At least I hoped so.

Just as I closed my weary eyes and was about to

follow Mary Catherine's lead, we hit the turbulence. The two-footed kind.

As if on cue, I heard some commotion behind me. There was a sweet-voiced yell of "No!" followed by the distinctive loud and wet sound of a child tossing his or her cookies. The retching sound fired three times in quick succession, and then Fiona and Bridget were standing in the aisle beside me.

"Daddy, Bridget threw up in the seat pouch! Bridget threw up all over the magazines!" Fiona called out excitedly.

I sat up and hugged the poor kid as Mary Catherine shot awake and quickly thrust some napkins into my hand.

From somewhere up ahead in the wall-to-wall-crowded cabin, I heard a male voice moan, "Oh, the stench! Oh, for the love of Pete!"

My sentiments exactly, fella, I thought as I sopped up the mess with one hand and rapidly hit the button for the flight attendant with the other.

For the love of Peter and Paul and the rest of the apostles, may we get back to New York in one piece, I prayed.

Part One

HARLEM SHUFFLE

Chapter 1

HARLEM
3:12 A.M.

THERE WERE ONLY TWO tonight to start off the season in New York. Though there were a total of a dozen in the group, the members, all being at the highest echelons of wealth and power, had busy lives, charities to chair and companies to acquire, so attendance was sporadic and often fluctuated. Four, including the two founding members, were from the US, four were from Europe, and there were two each from Hong Kong and Russia. They were considering two new members, one from India and one from Brazil, but the jury was still out.

The young New York financier who hosted all the NYC events was a founding member. The Brit, whose real estate baron family owned a large chunk of Notting Hill and most of Manchester, had a fortune in the upper hundred millions, but he was a pauper compared with the New York financier. Though the American kept his name off the *Forbes* list by choice, his hedge fund-acquired wealth was rumored to be mind-boggling.

So it was more than a little ironic that the financier and the well-heeled Brit were riding like a couple of schmucks in an ugly metallic-brown Mazda CX-9 crossover as they cruised up Lenox Avenue in East Harlem.

The Brit didn't mind. Slumming, roughing it, enhanced the manly intimacy and esprit de corps that the organization had been formed to engender. Besides, as they all knew, discretion was entirely necessary.

The building where they finally pulled to the curb was at Lenox Avenue and 145th Street, in front of a subway pit for the 3 train. It was a broad, three-story prewar structure that probably had once been a luxurious apartment house. Now its high windows were sealed with cinder blocks and its once-grand arched doorway held an ugly spray-painted steel shutter.

The Brit, who had just been elected an executive director at the IMF, gazed up at the curious structure.

Having briefly flirted with becoming an architect at Warwick before coming to his senses, he detected a golden-mean, Parthenon-like quality in the well-constructed building, slightly wider than it was tall. He also picked up a faint flavor of French classical style in the building's quoins and the porthole-like oculus window beneath its open cornice. It made one think of ruins, he thought. Of rituals.

Something stirred deep in the pit of his empty stomach. Might the French aspect of the location denote tonight's fare? he wondered, licking his thin lips. Was there a little haute cuisine on the menu tonight? Hmmmm. It was always a surprise, per club rule, and the anticipation was killing him.

"I hate to admit it, but you nailed the venue this time," the Brit said, turning toward the financier sitting directly behind him. "This is like coming upon a temple in the middle of a jungle."

The tall American hedge fund owner smiled as he patted the driver on the shoulder.

"Don't thank me. It was Alberto who found it, of course."

The Brit, who was sitting in the front passenger seat, smiled at the hulking chauffeur, Alberto Witherspoon, beside him. Alberto smiled back, a twinkle in his brown eyes as he nodded proudly.

"Least I could do," he said.

The Brit had heard all about Alberto. The story was that the handsome, six-foot-four-inch gentle-seeming black man from Oakland had once been a bodyguard to the infamous cult leader Jim Jones. He'd been there from the early days when Jones was still a darling of political figures like First Lady Rosalynn Carter, California governor Jerry Brown, and gay rights activist Harvey Milk. Alberto had been off on a supply run when Jones had persuaded the nine hundred Americans who had signed up for his socialist agrarian paradise in Guyana to raise a glass of cyanide-laced Kool-Aid.

Or at least that was what the deviant claimed, thought the Brit. One could only happily imagine the kinds of unholy things the not-so-gentle giant had seen and done.

Chapter 2

THE BRIT WATCHED AS Alberto gazed up and down the darkened street, listening to the police radio in the drink holder. The placard he removed from his jacket and placed on the dash denoted the car as on official NYPD business.

The Brit shook his head and smiled gleefully at the official-looking document. It looked real, it probably *was* real. The financier was supposed to have connections virtually *everywhere*.

That was what he loved about this club, the Brit thought as Alberto handed him a flashlight. Its reach was something altogether new. Literally nothing was prohibited. There was nothing they couldn't do.

A clatter of steel from the subway pit sounded like some far-off torture in a dungeon as they crossed the deserted sidewalk to the building's steel-shuttered entrance. Before he unlocked the gate, Alberto set down the large suitcase he had taken from the crossover's trunk. Then he rattled the gate up and lifted the case again.

The first thing the Brit noticed was that it smelled like fire inside—rich, fragrant wood smoke. He thought of rituals again as he looked up at the cracked, blistered black walls and ceiling in the beam of his flashlight. Marble steps appeared in the light, an iron balustrade heading up.

Everything was set up on the third floor in a large room broom-swept of rubble. The grill was top-of-the-line and massive, its stainless steel gleaming from the moonlight that fell in through a ragged basketball-size hole in the ceiling. Beside the grill was a large sheet of thick plastic, rattling in the cold wind that came in with the moonlight.

The Brit thought it looked like a dinner setup at one of the high-end safaris his wife had dragged him to in Botswana. *Nothing but the best,* he thought, accepting a warmed brandy glass from Alberto as he took his seat.

"That's not what I think it is, is it?" the Brit said as Alberto brought over a dark, heart-shaped bottle and poured a careful measure.

“I remembered how much you liked the Courvoisier last month in Tokyo, so I thought I’d blow the dust off some of the Jenssen Arcana I received for my fortieth,” the financier said as he leaned back in his chair and lit a cigar.

“That was incredibly thoughtful of you. I mean that,” the Brit said, touched. He took a sip of the fifty-five-hundred-dollar-a-bottle hundred-year-old brandy.

“I have incredible respect for you, Martin. The others don’t seem to fully appreciate what I’ve set up here as much as you. You get it. I can’t explain how important that is to me,” the financier said as Alberto tied on a simple white chef’s apron and fired the grill to preheat.

The financier passed over some Ecstasy and then a large bag of coke. As the excellent drugs started to work their glittery magic, there was a squeak, and Alberto was rolling over an empty gurney he’d produced from the shadowed corner of the room.

When Alberto brought over the suitcase, the Brit’s stomach churned again deliciously. He felt the hair on the back of his neck stand on end as a heady cocktail of narcotic- and alcohol-enhanced emotions swirled through him. Anticipation, joy, fear.

He swallowed as Alberto slowly zipped open the suitcase and took out what was in it. Though he knew what was coming, the Brit watched as the brandy in his hand wavered, and his eyes almost bugged out of his head. The dust between his feet darkened in coinlike shapes where the expensive liquor splattered upon the floor.

This was far better than the Marquis de Sade he had slavered over after lights-out at Beau Soleil, he thought, gazing on the stunning scene before him. Better even than the parties he had attended in Libya that time with the sultan. For so many years, he had wrestled with what he was. Now, with the help of his comrades, he could finally accept it, relish it, worship it, as the thing that made him truly superior to other men.

This is real, the Brit thought, making eye contact with the bound, wide-awake, nude young woman Alberto easily lifted above his head.

Dear me, this is so very, very real.

Chapter 3

IT WAS LIKE SLIPPING into a favorite old pair of shoes that first Monday morning back in New York.

As I woke in our West End Avenue apartment, I smiled at everything, the ceiling that needed painting, the traffic sounds out the window, the tick of Mary Catherine's teakettle from the kitchen. Even the sound of the kids fighting and teasing and slamming bathroom doors and clomping around on our big old apartment's worn oak floors was like music to my ears.

Mary Catherine had the troops lined up and ready for inspection as I came into the dining room. I scanned all the happy, scrubbed, bright-eyed faces. I'd never seen my guys so happy to be geared up with backpacks and lunch bags in their plaid Holy Name uniforms.

"Hey, everybody. Did Mary Catherine tell you the good news?" I said to them. "Homeschooling went so well in California, we're going to continue it here. Only with uniforms. So sit down, children, and take out your math workbooks."

"No! Ughhh! Wrong, so wrong! Never! Please, no!" they cried with accompanying Bronx cheers.

Ricky dropped and lay on his back with his eyes closed and his tongue stuck out. "Can't homeschool!" he gasped. "No friends. Need teacher. School. Need school!"

"Oh, well. If that's the way you feel about it, I guess we could try regular school on a day-to-day basis. But if there are any problems, you know you always have a place here all day with Teacher Daddy."

"Daddy!" Chrissy said, laughing as she tugged on one of my pockets. "Stop teasing and being so silly!"

"Yes, Daddy, please do," said Seamus, appearing in the doorway of the kitchen with my favorite DAD: THERE IS NO SUBSTITUTE coffee mug in his fist. "I mean, bad enough you have 'em traipsing off to the ends of the earth like a pack of tinkers. Do you have to make them late on their first day back?"

"Good morning to you, too, Father," I said

merrily as Mary Catherine finally got the Bennett train rolling out the door.

"And you're welcome for the coffee," I said. "And my mug."

Chapter 4

AFTER WAVING EVERYONE GOOD-BYE in the lobby and getting into the unmarked Chevy the department had dropped off for me on the corner the day before, my first stop was a no-brainer.

I rolled down West End Avenue to Ninety-Sixth and double-parked and went into the no-name deli-grocery on the corner. I could have hugged the Middle Eastern gentleman behind the counter when he gave me his regular gruff "Hey, boss," along with my too-hot, probably-not-fair-trade coffee and my buttered roll.

As I sat in the double-parked cop car eating my breakfast, I stared out, fascinated at the passing crosstown buses and Verizon vans and town cars and taxis. It was overcast, the September wind wafting the few trees West End still had lining the block to the south. I guess absence really does make the heart grow fonder, because all of it—the awnings on the buildings, the handymen hosing the sidewalks, the Sanitation Department street sweeper scraping the curb—seemed fresher, somehow more vibrant, more there.

The kids aren't the only ones excited about their first day back, I thought as I tightened my tie in the rearview. I had a morning meeting with the police commissioner down at One Police Plaza. After my western adventures, I was more than eager to go back to my desk at Major Crimes, but my old boss, Miriam, had explained that the commish wanted to talk to me about a brand-new position opening up.

Is it a new homicide squad? I wondered as I drink-holdered my coffee and dropped the tranny into drive. *An antiterror assignment?* I didn't care what it was as long as it was something juicy, something I could sink my teeth into.

After half an hour of threading my way around delivery trucks and suicidal bike messengers on the narrow downtown Manhattan streets, I pulled around a bomb barrier and up to the security booth at NYPD headquarters at One Police Plaza.

Only VIPs got to park in the front lot, but since

I was meeting with the commissioner, I thought, what the hey? I'd give it a shot.

"Yeah?" the old cop in the booth said, thoroughly ignoring my shield.

"Got a meeting with the big guy," I said. "The commissioner."

"Yeah, right," the craggy-faced lifer said, trading his *Post* for a clipboard. "Name?"

"Bennett," I said.

He flicked up a sheet, flicked it back down, and then relifted his *Post*.

"Sorry, Charlie. You need to park on the street because I guess you ain't on the A-list this morning."

Chapter 5

AS IT TURNED OUT, the old cop in the parking lot was righter than rain about me not being on the A-list. The only list I was on that morning, I was about to learn, was one of those four-letter ones that start with the letter *s*.

My not-so-warm welcome back into the bosom of the department family continued in the marble HQ lobby after I told one of the cops at the formidable security desk that I was there to see the commissioner.

"Are you sure?" said a tall, gray-haired black cop beside the security turnstile. "I was told the commissioner was on his way down to Washington this morning to testify before Congress about gun violence."

"Well," I said, "my boss told me to come down for a nine-o'clock meeting with him."

“Maybe I’m wrong,” the congenial cop said, lifting his phone with a smile. “Wouldn’t be the first time. What’s your name? I’ll check with his secretary.”

The veteran cop hung up a minute later.

“The secretary said the commissioner apologizes about the last-minute change of plans, but your meeting has been shuffled over to Chief of Detectives Starkie. He’s on the tenth floor.”

“Chief of Detectives Starkie? Raymond Starkie?” I said.

“That’s the man,” the cop said with a nod.

“What happened to Ronnie Child?” I asked.

“Child retired three months ago,” he said.

I nodded as I headed for the elevators, trying to think.

Dealing with any COD, the NYPD’s second-in-command, was notoriously hazardous. The Chief of Detectives was usually the commissioner’s hatchet man, the court strangler, the guy who assigned the kinds of unpleasant tasks that the commissioner didn’t want to dirty his hands with.

But the fact that the new one was Raymond Starkie was particularly worrisome, since he and I had some history. Back when we were rookies, we had been friendly rivals of sorts, working the same evening shift at the Bronx precinct where I started my career. Both of us ambitious and gung-ho, we'd competed to see who could come up with the most collars.

But that wasn't our only competition. Starkie had been first to meet my wife, Maeve. Long before Maeve lost her courageous battle against ovarian cancer, she had been an emergency room nurse at the Bronx hospital near the precinct. In fact, Maeve had agreed to go out with Starkie before she met me, and I made her cancel on him.

Starkie never forgave me for that or for the fact that I was named Bronx rookie of the year over him, and our rivalry became a lot less than friendly. It got physical once at a retirement party at a bar on Norwood Avenue, where he gave me a cauliflower ear and I gave him a chipped tooth.

After that painful parting of ways, Starkie had gone the administrative route in the department. He attended NYU law school and had risen quickly through the ranks. He was an effective and efficient manager, they said, if a tad heavy-handed.

As I stepped into the elevator and hit ten, it suddenly occurred to me how out of touch I'd been. The power structures and politics in the department could change in a New York minute, to borrow a cliché, and here I'd been away for nine months.

After all my morning's enthusiasm at being back, it suddenly occurred to me that I was a man without a country, with no turf, no rabbi, and maybe no immediate prospects.

Chapter 6

EVEN AFTER ALL THESE years, Starkie was still a tall, strapping, good-looking guy. He had short-cropped white-blond hair and twinkly blue eyes. When I spotted his friendly, open smile at his office door, I was actually hopeful, for a beat, that maybe Starkie was ready to let bygones be bygones.

But then his smile soured as he elaborately checked his watch. It was a Rolex, gold and shiny as the four spit-shined brass stars winking from his tailored dress uniform's shoulder.

"Late, huh, Bennett?" he said, shaking his head instead of my hand. "But I guess, what's a few more minutes after nine months, right? This way."

Bennett? I thought, following him into his spacious office. By using my last name, Starkie was immediately letting me know that history or no history, he was my superior. *Uh-oh.*

There was a bank of computers behind Starkie's walnut desk, a flashing six-screen array like an investment banker's. Staring at the monitors, I suddenly remembered that Starkie was a vocal champion of CompStat, the computer- and statistics-based method of policing that the NYPD had first spearheaded in the '90s. Because of this, his nicknames included Numbers, Compstarkie, and HAL 9000 for his sometimes emotionless, single-minded devotion to the computer-driven stats.

There were stacks of paper on another desk in the corner, obscuring a commanding view of the Brooklyn Bridge. There was a chair opposite his desk, but he didn't offer me a seat, so I just stood there.

As Starkie sat, he lifted a white file folder off his desk and leaned back in his big tufted leather chair, licking a thumb as he leisurely went through it. It was my file, I realized. It wasn't too hard to pick up on his ham-handed theatrics. My career was literally in his hands.

"So, how was California? Did you enjoy your leave of absence?" Starkie said, glancing at me over the edge of the file after a long minute.

Leave of absence? I thought, perplexed. Why did

he somehow make my being forced into witness protection with my family seem frivolous, like I was trying to take a stab at landscape painting?

"Busy," I said.

Between tanning sessions, I teamed up with the feds and helped bring down the cop-killing Mexican drug cartel kingpin Manuel Perrine, I thought but didn't say. *Maybe you heard about it?*

"Well, since you haven't been around," he said, finally setting down the file, "you'll find that there are a lot of new things happening here in the department. I know in the past you've benefited from loosened departmental guidelines, from superiors looking the other way. So let me be the first to inform you that those days are over.

"This is the new NYPD, Bennett," he said, gesturing at the computers behind him. "That's why I'm here. To shake things up, to usher in a new era of accountability and a new emphasis on chain of command."

He knocked twice on my file with his chunky NYU law school ring before smiling again.

"That's why, in the spirit of shaking things up, I've ordered your transfer. Let me congratulate you on your new assignment, running the NYPD's brand-new Ombudsman Outreach Squad at a Hundred and Twenty-Fifth Street in Harlem."

Chapter 7

I STOOD THERE BLINKING, trying not to topple, as I sifted through the rubble of the ten-story building that had just collapsed on top of me.

I'd thought I would be getting a plum assignment after my hard work of bringing down Manuel Perrine. At the very least, I thought I'd be returning to my desk with the Major Crimes Division. What the heck was an Ombudsman Outreach Squad? I didn't know. And definitely didn't want to find out.

"The ombudsman squad is the mayor's idea," Starkie said, reading my mind. "Its mission is simple: to help the city's most vulnerable victims. It's a second chance for the department to laser-focus on victims whose concerns have fallen through the bureaucratic cracks. It's up and running, but there are still some glitches that need ironing out."

Starkie blinked at me elaborately to show how badly I was being screwed. "But nothing that a veteran investigator like yourself can't handle," he said, smiling. "When I heard about the fledgling squad's challenges, and the fact that you'd just come back, I couldn't think of a better match."

I stood there staring at Starkie. We both knew what was going on. This wasn't a promotion. If anything, my new assignment, some mayoral pet project that sounded like a disaster in the making, was a massive demotion, a bald, backhanded slap right across my face.

I'd put in over twenty years on the job racking up collars, crushing case after complicated case. I'd risked my life, the lives of my family, and now, as a reward, I was being ramrodded to some backwater political pet project?

Over what? A silly twenty-year-old rivalry? One little chipped tooth?

I kept staring at him across the desk. Starkie stared back serenely with his cold, twinkly blue eyes. He wasn't smiling now, but I could tell he wanted to. I could also tell he wanted me to freak out and scream bloody murder about my transfer. I definitely wanted to. I would have loved nothing better than to chip another tooth for Starkie, or maybe resign.

Instead, I took a deep breath. I wasn't about to give him the satisfaction. It took everything I had to cool my engines, to keep my powder dry, but I managed it. Barely.

"So, any questions?" he said in a pleasant voice as he reached across the desk and handed me my transfer papers.

"None, Chief," I said, accepting the sheets.

I folded them neatly and tucked them into my jacket pocket before I extended my hand. I even put a happy salesmanlike ear-to-ear grin on my face that hopefully masked the fantasy of crashing a chair over his head that I was having.

"In fact, I'm raring to get started serving the department in my new capacity, with your permission, of course, sir," I continued, offering my hand with a happy wink of my own.

After a long, puzzled moment, Starkie stood. He finally took my hand warily.

"OK, then. Um, carry on, Bennett," he said.

"Will do, Chief. Thanks for meeting with me. Bye now," I said before turning and walking out the door.

Chapter 8

THERE WAS A TICKET on my cop car when I got back to it.

Of course there was. I'd parked it in the only free spot available in Lower Manhattan during a workday, namely in front of a fire hydrant. If I hadn't put my police business placard on the dash, it would probably have been towed.

I was kind of sorry it hadn't been, I thought as I got in and started it. At that point, a day at the tow yard seemed preferable to dealing with the rank garbage Starkie had just gleefully dumped into my lap.

Harlem is toward the north end of Manhattan Island, a pretty direct shot from southern Manhattan, where I currently was. But since this was the *new* NYPD, as Starkie had described it, I decided to take an alternate route over the Manhattan Bridge into Brooklyn.

I drove around on the BQE and then around the maze of Queens side streets, weighing my new situation. My first and most tempting option was retirement. Having over twenty years in, I could easily put in my papers and just wash my hands of the whole thing.

Because I had accomplished what I had set out to do in life: be a pretty damn good cop. Like my father before me, I'd sent some monstrous people away to prison, a few of them even to the graveyard.

Maybe this was it, I thought. Maybe it was time to hang it up.

But after a while, I started thinking about it, about Starkie and his petty bullshit. I couldn't let him win that easily. I had outmanned him when we were rookies, and I would outman him now. I'd take anything and everything Starkie could dish out and throw it back in his face. Somehow. As with our little head-to-head in that Bronx bar, I definitely wasn't going down without a fight.

I was actually a little excited, at least about the idea of the new squad. Despite the glitches Starkie had mentioned, and the fact that the mayor was involved, the idea of a squad devoted solely to helping the city's most vulnerable people sounded somewhat intriguing.

I looked around for a sign back to Manhattan to find out what exactly was an Ombudsman Outreach Squad.

Chapter 9

WHEN I ARRIVED A little before lunch, 125th Street, Harlem's version of Main Street, was busy with people and activity.

There were sidewalk vendors and bustling clothing stores and lines of people in front of curbside food carts. There was also a lot of scaffolding and cranes from new construction and building renovations. I even saw a Times Square-style double-decker bus go by filled with wide-eyed tourists.

It was nice to see the historically run-down area busy, I thought as I parked. At least Harlem's future was looking up.

My new work location was the ninth floor of a new stone-and-glass government building on the corner of 125th and Adam Clayton Powell Boulevard. There was a surprise waiting for me when I got through lobby security and walked off the elevator onto the ninth floor. And it wasn't a happy one by any stretch.

It was even worse than I'd thought. Which was saying something, since I didn't even really know what to think yet.

There was a long line outside the office. We're talking waiting-on-line-for-Yankees-playoff-tickets long. But instead of elated fans, this one was filled with quite pissed-off-looking citizens. The crowd ran the demographic gamut of New York's working-class whites and blacks and Hispanics and Asians. There were a lot of young women, a lot of them single moms, I'd be willing to bet, with squirming preschool kids in tow.

Instead of storming up front and immediately demanding to find out what the insane holdup was, I decided to take another tack. I got on the end of the line. Heck, I was pretty pissed off, too.

When I turned the first office corner twenty glacially slow minutes later, I saw the office's official name for the first time. A long plastic banner on the wall said WELCOME TO THE SPECIAL PROJECT OFFICE FOR COMMUNITY RELATIONS WITH THE NYPD. Underneath it in smaller type was the peppy assurance, IT'S A BRAND-NEW DAY.

The SPOFCRWTNYPD, I thought, shaking my head. *Rolls right off the tongue.* I mean, even a Polish radio announcer couldn't pronounce that one.

"This is bull," said a young black woman in a red hoodie in front of me as she shifted the bright-eyed two- or three-year-old girl she was holding onto her other arm.

"You can say that again," I said.

"You taking off work?" she said, turning back toward me.

"No, not really."

"You're lucky," the mom said. "I'm wasting a personal day on this."

"I wouldn't call it lucky," I mumbled. "Why are you here?"

"Drug gang just moved into my next-door neighbor's apartment, an eighty-three-year-old woman. Just took it over. I told the local precinct three times but ain't nothing been done. They told me to come here. I been standing here has to be an hour now. This city. I should have known."

I spoke to some other people. It seemed like every aggravating case the local precincts didn't want to deal with was being sent here to my new world.

And what a not-so-wonderful world it was.

What I saw firsthand over the next hour of

waiting was unbelievable, unforgettable. There was one female clerk behind the DMV-like counter. One!

Not that there weren't more personnel present. On the contrary. Through an open doorway behind the clerk, I saw a wide-assed male cop first sleep, then read the newspaper, then sleep again. The only other cops I could see were sitting at desks as far away from the reception desk as they could get, heads down, idly clicking at computers, shopping sites probably.

Everywhere phones were ringing. Everywhere no one was answering them. *What a completely maddening New York bureaucratic disaster,* I thought. *No, worse,* I remembered.

This was apparently now *my* completely maddening New York bureaucratic disaster.

Chapter 10

THE BETTER PART OF an hour later, I finally got to the head of the line.

"Here you go," said the clerk as she shoved a sheet of paper at me in greeting.

Her shirt was unbuttoned low enough to show a lot of cleavage, and there was an earring in the lower of her DayGlo-pink lips. Or a lip ring, I guess you'd call it. Whatever it was, it was absolutely not up to the NYPD's professional-appearance standards.

Who was running this asylum? Oh, yeah. Me.

"Hi, I need to talk to someone," I said, ignoring the paper. "I just moved to Harlem four months ago, and I was robbed three times by the same street-corner kid. Nothing's been done about this. The kid is still out there. He put a gun to my head, for God's sake."

The lip-ringed clerk nodded sympathetically a couple of times. Then she shoved the paper at me again.

"That does sound like a problem, sir," she said. "But instead of telling me, you need to tell it to this Departmental 313-152 Form."

"Then what?" I said. "Aren't those police officers back there behind you? Can't one of them come with me? The kid's on the corner right now. Or he was two hours ago when I got on line. I'll point him out."

"They're currently working on other cases, sir," the clerk said, blinking at me.

"Please, I need help," I said. "I don't mean to be pushy, but I'm afraid for my kids."

"Put it all down on the form, sir. We can't do anything without the proper paperwork," she said, glancing down at her lap, where I'd bet my paycheck she had a cell phone. Without looking at me, she gestured with a hand off to the right.

"There's pens on the table over there," she said.

The clerk checked her Facebook page or Buzzfeed or whatever for a second before looking up and then through me.

"Next!" she bellowed.

They say you can catch more flies with honey.

But unfortunately, I wasn't trying to catch flies.

I was trying to restore order in a land in which chaos was currently in full ugly reign. Fortunately, having ten kids, I had been to this place before and knew what to do. Desperate times called for desperate measures.

It was break-glass-in-case-of-emergency time, also known as completely freak out.

As it turned out, I didn't go to the table with the paper. Instead, I stood rooted to the linoleum and glared at the clerk until she once again acknowledged my existence. Then I turned around to the old Asian grandmother with two little boys coming up behind me.

"I'm sorry, ma'am," I told her. "But as it turns out, you're actually not next."

"Hey! What are you, crazy?" said the clerk when I faced her again.

I lifted the Departmental 313-152 Form off the counter and slowly tore it in two. Then tore it in two again.

"Why, yes," I said. "Apparently I am. Who wouldn't be crazy trying to deal with this lousy excuse you call a police squad?"

She pursed her DayGlo lips.

"You best stop poppin' off," she said, wagging a

finger at me ghetto-style. “This is a police facility. You want to get locked up? Now, you can either go over there and fill out your form or I can reserve you a room at the Rikers Island Hilton, *comprende?* Your choice. Last chance.”

“No,” I said, glaring at her. “I don’t *comprende.* I have no idea what’s going on here. And it seems like neither do you.”

Chapter 11

"HEY, WISE GUY. YEAH, you. You looking for trouble?" said a burly young white cop as he got up from one of the desks in the corner.

He was a six-foot-tall, broad-shouldered guy in dark slacks and a white dress shirt with the sleeves rolled up over his thick forearms. He was smiling and chewing on a piece of gum as he quickly came out from behind the counter straight at me. His pepper spray was already out, I noticed, and he had a twitchy finger on its trigger, ready to go.

"You doing a little drinking this morning, buddy? Lookin' for some trouble?" he said almost hopefully.

"No, cowboy, but you and everybody else in this unit just found a whole bunch," I said as I took out my shield.

The cop and the clerk stared at each other, then at me.

"Allow me to introduce myself. I'm Detective Mike Bennett, the unlucky SOB who just got assigned to CO this wreck."

First I pointed at the clerk.

"You," I said. "Button that shirt, take that thing out of your neon lip and your butt out from behind that counter, and go on home until you read the NYPD uniform policy and realize this isn't a circus sideshow."

Before she could protest, I pointed at the aggressive cop.

"You," I said.

"Me?" the strapping twenty-something said.

"Yeah, you. Go back to your desk and turn off the Tetris, and while you're there, tell the rest of the mopes in this unit that Daddy's home and he wants everyone standing in line in the hall by my office until further notice. Everyone except for you, that is. You can take off for the rest of the day, too, Dr. Pepper Spray."

As he reluctantly walked off, I turned toward the line of exhausted, frustrated people behind me.

"I'm sorry, everyone, but this office is closed for the day," I announced.

If I thought the people were pissed off before, they were twice as steamed now. There was a lot of groaning and cursing. Someone kicked the wall hard enough to shake the banner. I wondered for a scary second if I was going to need to call for some real cops.

"This is bull!" someone called out loudly.

Yes, it is, I thought. "This is bull" was today's theme. It was New York City's theme pretty much every day, when you came to think of it. If the politicians were honest, they'd put it on billboard-size signs at the city line.

WELCOME TO NEW YORK. IT'S BULL!

"Sorry, but it can't be helped," I called back. "Hopefully, we'll be open tomorrow, but I can't make any promises. The Project for Outreach Relations with the NYPD apologizes for any inconvenience."

"Man, you even got the name wrong," a thin black man in a UPS uniform said, pointing at the wall banner with a loud "Tsssk."

"My mistake," I said, going over and ripping the banner off the wall. I crumpled it loudly in my hands as I stepped behind the counter and methodically stuffed it into a wastepaper basket.

"Whatever we are, we are now under renovation!" I called out. "Thank you and I'm sorry and good-bye."

Chapter 12

I SPENT THE NEXT hour in my new office trying to get my bearings.

The office itself was a nice surprise. It was a recently redone, roomy corner space that had new furniture and an extensive view of tree-lined Adam Clayton Powell Boulevard to the north. It even had a washroom and a coffeemaker, which I promptly filled and got percolating before I started stacking the massive pile of in-box files on my desk.

First order of business was to read through the squad's operational details folder. In some ways, the unit was like a mini-precinct. In addition to a locker and interview rooms, the office space had an on-site armory, cruisers in the underground lot, Kevlar vests and radios. Coordination had been set up with the Twenty-Eighth Precinct house a couple of blocks away for backup and lockup as needed.

But in other ways, the unit was like a much more agile, roving detective squad consisting of a handful of officers and a couple of clerks. The officers were what was known as white badges, plainclothes cops recently taken from patrol to see if they had the wherewithal to become permanent detectives.

Managed correctly, the squad could be an effective tool, I realized. It would just be a matter of prioritizing cases and laser-focusing on a few cases at a time like any other squad. Maybe this wouldn't be so bad after all. I was actually a little excited.

Until I got to the assigned officer personnel files.

"OK, now I get it," I mumbled to myself as I skimmed through the records.

It wasn't just the most frustrating cases that were being shunted here, I realized. It seemed that some of the department's most frustrating *cops* had been sent here, too. Instead of confusing myself further, I decided to put names to faces and meet my new charges one by one.

"Arturo Lopez!" I called out to the cops lined up outside the door.

A friendly-seeming young Puerto Rican officer came in. I recognized him as the big-boned cop who'd been sleeping at his desk. Arturo was about five-ten and about five hundred pounds. Well, maybe not five hundred, but easily thirty pounds overweight.

"Lopez, are you interested in being a good cop?" I said after I introduced myself.

"Yes, I definitely am, sir. It means everything to me."

"Good deal. Let me ask you a question. How fast are you?"

"How fat am I?" he said, hurt. "C'mon, that's pretty cold, sir."

"Not fat, Lopez," I said. "Fast. *F-A-S-T.*"

"I don't know. Sort of fast, I guess. Who's to say?"

I raised an eyebrow at him.

"If I said, 'Hey, Arturo, let's you and me have a race to the elevator,' would you have a chance of winning?"

"Maybe?" he said, wincing.

He finally lowered his head. "No, not a chance."

"See, it's not really the weight, Arturo. It's the ability to get around. Things go down fast on the street, and we have to watch each other's backs out there. No one is going to want to partner up with you if you can't catch up. If you really want to be a detective, you need to lose some weight, dude. You need to start running and working out or you're going to be working somewhere else."

"I get you, Detective. I will. I promise," he said as he left.

"Noah Robertson!" I called out.

A good-looking blond guy walked in. He was impeccably dressed in a modish soft-gray bespoke suit with a white silk shirt and silk navy tie, with a matching pocket square. His gelled hair was sharply parted à la Cary Grant, and on his feet, I saw, were fancy euro shoes that looked a lot like black velvet slippers. He was tall and tan and slim and looked more like an actor or a Hollister model than a cop.

I'd already read that there had been some kind of sex harassment deal at his last assignment, which explained his presence here. I didn't ask about it. He was just another of the problem children I'd inherited, as far as I was concerned. All I cared about was here and now. It was *A Brand-New Day,* after all.

"Robertson, why are you here?" I said, squinting at him.

The elegant young man stared at me for a beat.

"I want to be a detective, obviously," he said.

"Yes, but why?" I said. "Let me guess. Because you're a clotheshorse and the uniform doesn't live up to your high sartorial standards?"

"Well, I am a clotheshorse," he said with a canny little smile. "But I only want what you want, Detective. To help people who need helping. Get bad guys off the street. Maybe get a chance to use my brain in the process."

I nodded. I liked his answer. But I wasn't finished.

"If that's the case, Robertson, then why were you hiding in the corner with everybody else when I came in?"

He looked out my window for a moment, thinking, then gave me his little smile again. "I was waiting for an inspirational leader to arrive," he said, holding up a finger.

Elegant and able to bullshit on his feet. That might come in handy, I thought.

"Be careful what you wish for, Robertson. Now go back out in the hallway."

"Naomi Chast!" I called out after he left.

Chast was a pretty, medium-height young woman with tightly tied-back strawberry-blond hair and an almost too lean, wiry triathlete's build. She was wearing a crisp NYPD polo over her department-issue navy tactical pants.

She seemed professional and kind of normal, I thought as I thumbed through her paperwork. But that was impossible. If she were normal, why would she have been sent here?

When I looked up from her file, she was suddenly glaring at me.

"Oh, I see. You're cleaning house, huh?" she said with her hands on her hips. "Well, let me save you the trouble. Transfer away. You think I want to be in this chickenshit outfit, you're crazy. You don't think I know how all this political crap works? Let me tell *you* a few things."

As she continued to rant, I flipped another page of her file and found a note handwritten by the squad's previous leader.

Impulse control? it said. *ADD? Anger management issues?*

Yes. Yes. Yes, I scratched next to it, and underlined it twice.

Chapter 13

AFTER I GOT CHAST to calm down and go back out into the hallway, I decided to make my first command decision.

I stood and stuck my head out of my office door.

"Listen up, people. I'm hitting the Reset button," I said. "So whatever nuttiness has been going on around here is over now, OK? I have one rule. I only work with driven, dedicated cops. If you came here to hide out and push pencils and wait for Thursday's check to clear, I'm sorry, but those days are over.

"Now I want you to go home and get some sleep and decide if you want to keep working here. Because tomorrow, we're starting from scratch."

They were leaving when a well-dressed thirty-something black woman came running into my office.

"Hi, Detective Bennett, is it?" she said. "I'm Ariel. Ariel Tyson."

I looked up at the woman, at the serious brown eyes behind her red-framed eyeglasses. I had already learned from the files that she was the other clerk.

"I was just at lunch," she said, "and I heard you sent everybody home, and I just want you to know I'm good at my job. I love my job. End of story. I live six blocks from here, and I have three kids. I'm bringing them up the best I can."

"You show up every day for work, Ariel?" I said.

"Every day. On time. Don't even put in for overtime."

"Then I have just one question," I said, rubbing my eyes. "How did you wind up here?"

"Bureaucratic screwup. What else?" she said with one of the widest, most likable smiles I'd ever seen.

That was when it happened. I finally had a laugh. The first one of the day.

"How are you doing, Detective?" she said, starting to laugh with me. "You look like you're having yourself a real long day."

"I've just been assigned to coach the Bad News Bears on the Island of Misfit Toys, Ariel. Isn't it obvious that I'm having the time of my life?"

As Ariel was leaving my office, I heard someone coming down the hallway. It was the aggressive young cop, Dr. Pepper Spray. His file indicated that his name was Jimmy Doyle. He was a young "gunslinger" cop who already had two kills on the job, which was probably why he'd been assigned here. So his old CO wouldn't have to fill out the paperwork when he shot numero three.

Doyle held up his hands as he came past my door.

"I know, I know. Calm down, boss," the spunky cop said. "I'll only be a minute. I left my wallet in my locker, and I can't walk home to the Bronx."

I smiled at his back as he went past. The young cop reminded me of someone. Oh, yeah. Me. About half a lifetime ago.

Chapter 14

I WAS POURING MYSELF a coffee refill when the police-band radio in the corner of my office crackled.

"Twenty-seven," a dispatcher said. "Come in. We have shots fired. I repeat, shots fired. Corner of a Hundred Twenty-Seventh and Eighth Ave."

"A Hundred Twenty-Seventh and Eighth? That's two blocks away. It's where we buy coffee," Doyle suddenly said from where he was now standing in the doorway of my office.

I hopped up immediately and grabbed some vests and radios out of the locker in the corner.

"What gives?" Doyle said when I handed him his vest. "The other squad leader said we shouldn't respond to local calls."

I pushed the young cop out of my doorway and toward the office exit.

"Yeah, well, he's not here right now, is he?" I said. "C'mon, Doyle. What are you waiting for? Those who dare, win. Lead the way."

Down on the street, we bolted diagonally across Adam Clayton, ran two quick blocks, and hooked a left up 127th. There was a project complex on the right-hand side of the street, a row of old brownstone houses on the left. Some howling teenage girls came out of one of the brownstones as we were running past.

"Get back inside!" I yelled as Doyle and I sprinted for the corner.

Doyle and I both had our service weapons drawn when we arrived on the corner of Eighth. Two people were down. Two young black men, neither of them older than twenty. One was facedown in the gutter between two parked cars, not moving. The other one was sitting, leaning up against the doorjamb of the corner bodega, bleeding heavily from his chest and mouth.

A large, older black man with short dreads and Carhartt coveralls was down on his knees beside the victim, holding a dirty towel to the kid's chest with his left hand while holding the kid's hand with his right. The gasping youth had on a Dodgers hoodie and had a pale-blue bandanna tied Tupac-style around his head.

Gangs, I thought immediately, seeing the rag. *Pale blue. Crips.*

"C'mon, c'mon," the man said to the bleeding youth in a Jamaican accent. "C'mon, son. Stay awake, now. They're comin' to help ya."

I went and squatted by the kid in the gutter. He was stocky, wearing a pristine white-and-light-blue-striped polo and oversize jeans. But there was no helping him. There was a large-caliber bullet hole the size of a bouncy ball just above his right temple, and blood and brain matter covered the left leg of his pants.

I saw a gun tucked at the back of his waistband, some type of Taurus semiautomatic. I retrieved it carefully and unloaded it as I stood.

"What happened?" I said to the Jamaican guy.

"These two was comin' out the store," the man said, "and it was 'blam blam blam.' Some fools shootin' a long rifle gun from the window of a green car right there on the corner right in the middle of the damn day."

"What kind of car was it?" I said.

"Like a Honda maybe, or a Nissan. With the loud muffler on it. You know? It was like a teal green."

I was about to call it in on the radio when I saw that Doyle had beaten me to the punch. He was also moving back the growing crowd of people. The kid took control well, I noticed. He had an easy, convincing authority for such a young cop. I was immediately impressed.

I knelt and clapped my hands by the face of the young man, who was now bleeding out, as his eyes started to flutter. The kneeling Jamaican looked at the kid and shook his head before he pointed his sad and stunned face at me.

"This young, young man," the Jamaican said, staring at me furiously. "Over what? What?"

A Twenty-Eighth Precinct squad car shrieked up a moment later, an ambulance right behind it.

"What is it? What's up?" said the thin sergeant who leaped out of the car. He had one of his black-gloved hands on his gun and Ray-Ban sunglasses propped on top of his shaved head.

"Drive-by," I said, handing him the Taurus, watching the EMTs hurry the teen wearing the Dodgers hoodie into the back of the ambulance. "Two down. One gone, the other likely. Crips gang-bangers, looks like."

"What are you guys? Gang squad?" the

sergeant, whose name was Gomez, said, staring at us as he called it in.

"No, we're the, um, ombudsman squad over on a Hundred and Twenty-Fifth," I said.

"The what?" Gomez said, utterly confused. "Wait, you mean the mayor's thing? Are you frickin' kidding me? You heard the call and just came running, huh? Or did you zipline out of the building like Batman and Robin?"

"Yeah, we ran," Doyle said, immediately squaring up on the skinny wise guy. "What did you do, Gomez? Crawl?"

The screaming ambulance pulled away.

"Good job, do-gooder squad, but wait," the sergeant said as he pretended to answer his cell phone. "That was Commissioner Gordon," he went on, lowering his phone. "He said your new orders are to go back and deactivate the bat signal."

"C'mon, Doyle," I said, getting between him and Gomez. "Let's leave the paperwork on this one to the Joker." I turned to leave.

Chapter 15

THE BUILDING AT 793 West End Avenue looks a lot like the rest of the prewar buildings on the Upper West Side. Its brick-and-limestone-trimmed facade is worn and probably due for a power wash, but there's no denying that its lines are still grand, its hunter-green awning and polished brass poles still classy and stately.

The words *sight for sore eyes* could have been added to its description as I scored a rare parking spot across from my apartment house that afternoon after work.

I sat for a moment and just stared up at the dusty windows of my apartment on the eighth floor. There were so many memories there. My mind spun at all the christenings and birthday parties and anniversaries. All the happy faces lit by candlelight around the table.

How my deceased wife, Maeve, had put the calculus of all those dates together in her head and never missed a one, I will never know. She never forgot an occasion to celebrate all of us, the people she loved so dearly, with a card and a cupcake, with a book, with a prayer.

"We'll be starting on all the graduations soon enough, won't we?" I said to Maeve as I sat there in the car. *Weddings someday, too,* I thought, and then new christenings and new birthday parties and on and on and on. I smiled as I got out onto the sidewalk. It was good to be home.

I crossed the tree-lined street and went under the awning into the lobby.

I was expecting to say hi to Ralph, the evening doorman, but there was a new guy standing by the mailroom in the wood-paneled lobby. A short, stocky thirtyish guy with black hair who I'd never seen before. He reminded me a little of the old-school tough-guy actor Charles Bronson. *He must have been hired while we were away,* I thought. *The New York minute strikes again.*

"Yes, may I help you?" he said with a thick foreign accent. *Albanian?* I thought. *Polish?*

"I'm Mike Bennett. I live in eight A. I've been away for a while."

The guy checked the board.

"Oh, yes. Bennett. Hello, Mr. Bennett. I am Joseph. I am new."

"Nice to meet you, Joseph," I said as the door opened behind me and I heard peals of laughter.

"It's Dad!" somebody screamed.

I turned around to see Fiona and Bridget and Jane and Ricky and Eddie and Trent running like a bunch of manic dwarves at me across the lobby. They were still in their Holy Name uniforms, dragging backpacks and lunch bags.

"Group hug!" the girls screamed as they crashed into me.

"Oh, yes, and group kissy-wissys, too!" Ricky said, making kissing sounds as he piled onto the scrum.

I smiled as I shrugged at Joseph. My guys seemed even loopier than normal, which was saying something. They must have had a long day, too, by the looks of it.

Joseph seemed a little overwhelmed as I introduced my large, boisterous family.

"So many children," he said, smiling. "Incredible."

"Don't worry, Joseph," I said, winking at him as the kids dragged me toward the elevator. "All the others should be along any minute now."

Chapter 16

THERE WAS AN AMAZING surprise waiting upstairs.

My first clue that things were looking up was the heavenly aroma of roasted meat that washed over me as I opened my front door.

Could it be? I thought as I stopped in my tracks and closed my eyes and inhaled. I smiled widely as I nodded. *Why, yes, it could!*

It was a pot roast, the comfort food to end all comfort food, at least for me. Not just any old pot roast, either. I could tell it was pot roast à la Mary Catherine, made with roasted garlic and red wine. As I locked up my Glock, the scent was suddenly accompanied by some serious sizzling from the direction of the kitchen. My mouth instantly watered. There was some sort of deglazing action going on in there, some sort of luscious homemade gravy being made.

After the day I'd had, God, or at least his angel here on earth, Mary Catherine, was finally taking pity on me.

After I washed up, I walked into the dining room to spot most of my kids seated around our massive dining room table. As I high-fived and tickled everyone hello, I noticed that the nice linen tablecloth had been set out along with the Bennett family heirloom mismatched china and silver.

"What's up with the Sunday dinner on Monday?" I whispered to Shawna as I sat. "Don't tell me I missed another birthday."

"I wouldn't be surprised," Seamus said across from me as he tucked a napkin into his Roman collar.

A moment later, Mary Catherine, Jane, and Juliana, who'd all apparently been working their fingers to the bone, came in, carrying the beautifully prepared feast. In addition to the roast, there was a mountain of mashed potatoes to rival Everest, I noted with amazement.

"I have just died and gone to Irish heaven," I said to Mary Catherine as Jane set the gravy boat down in front of me like a sacrifice. "What's the fancy occasion? Please tell me we had a visit from the Publishers Clearing House people."

"No occasion, really," Mary Catherine said with a little smile as she sat. "Call it the First Supper."

"The First Supper?"

"It's the first chance we've had since we got back home to have a real supper together," Mary Catherine said. "I thought we should celebrate."

"I like the way you think," I said as I forked pot roast onto my plate.

"Eh-hem," Seamus said loudly as he put his hands together and closed his eyes.

I reluctantly put my fork down and followed suit along with everyone else. After a second, I peeked, scanning all the cute, solemn faces around me, and smiled.

It's good to be home, I thought for the second time that evening.

"Bless us, O Lord, and these thy gifts, which we are about to receive from thy bounty through Christ Our Lord. Amen," Seamus said.

"Especially the gravy," I said.

"Amen," everyone agreed.

Chapter 17

AFTER OUR HOME-RUN DINNER, Mary Catherine and I left Seamus and the big kids to do the dishes while we went out for a walk.

First stop was all the way down at Seventy-Ninth and Amsterdam, at this ice-cream place I was addicted to called Emack & Bolio's. We got the ice cream to go and took the slow roll back to the apartment through Riverside Park.

It was a beautiful night, a little cool but clear, with a three-quarter moon shining up the silky surface of the Hudson off to our left. On the right were Riverside Drive's famous whimsical, grand, rambling apartment buildings straight out of a New York fairy tale.

You couldn't have asked for a more romantic moonlit stroll, which was precisely why I'd brought us this way. Mary Catherine and I had our ups and downs in the relationship department, but like I said, lately we'd become closer than ever.

As we walked, I glanced at Mary Catherine's elegant profile beside me, the elfish upturn of her tiny nose, the pale of her throat. It was almost embarrassing how much I was feeling for her. Like a damn teenager.

She busted me staring at her a second later.

"Can I help you, Mike?" she said, smiling.

"I was just wondering how your exposé was going," I said between bites of my peanut butter Oreo.

"My what?" Mary Catherine said.

"Don't be coy with me, Mary Catherine," I said. "I know you're working on your nanny diary. I mean, that's why you've stayed on all this time, isn't it? To reveal all the juicy *Sex and the City* truth that is working for the family of a Manhattan single-dad cop with double-digit adopted kids?"

She gave me a playful shove as she rolled her eyes.

"Fine. You got me, Mike. It's true," she said with a mischievous smile as she spooned up her raspberry chip frozen yogurt. "In fact, just today I wrote a really juicy entry. Do you want to hear it?"

"Yes, very much so," I said.

"Hope you're ready," she said. "It goes, 'Dear Diary, I must tell you this. Today I went down into the steamy basement of my handsome employer's luxury prewar coop.' How's that for a start? Juicy enough for you?"

"Oh, yes. Very mysterious and provocative," I said. "Especially the handsome employer part. Please, by all means, keep going."

"'Upending the spilling sack in my aching hands, I stood there breathless, having never in my life experienced such a heaving sea as the one bared before my eyes. There they were in front of me. Fifty shades of gray . . . socks.'"

It was my turn to give her a playful shove as I started laughing.

"You naughty girl," I said.

" 'As if in a fevered dream,' " Mary Catherine continued, "'I finally tore my eyes away from the socks, lifted the bulging orange bottle of Tide, and slowly poured the thick liquid into the detergent dispenser. That is all for now. I will write more later.' "

"What!" I yelled. "Come on, don't stop now. Dripping detergent? You can't leave me hanging like that!"

Mary Catherine shook her head as she pointed her plastic spoon at me.

"Sorry, Mike, but like the rest of my adoring fans, you'll have to wait for my book tour, when I'll reveal the rest of the raw, steamy, stiletto-heeled New York City truth."

Chapter 18

WHAT HAPPENED NEXT WASN'T planned by any means.

Blame it on the fairy tale, I thought.

My hands found Mary Catherine's waist and I was kissing her.

"I don't deserve you. You know that, right?" I whispered as we came up for air. "You're one of the best things that's ever happened to me. Hell, to anyone."

"You mean that, don't you?" Mary Catherine said, staring point-blank into my eyes.

She suddenly broke away from me and jogged a little bit ahead.

"Come on, now. Hop to it. Let's work off some of that ice cream, Detective!" she called back to me. "We need to get moving. We definitely don't need to get a desk appearance ticket for another flagrant PDA like that one!"

"Don't worry, I'm a cop, Mary Catherine," I said, chasing after her. "You'd be amazed at what a flash of my badge can do."

We passed something I'd forgotten all about as we were coming up on Ninety-Third Street. Up a set of park stairs on the street was the Bennett family van.

I started leading Mary Catherine up the stairs.

"What are you doing?" she said.

"You're worried about public displays of affection, right? Well, I have a solution," I said as I unlocked the van's front door. "Let's remove the public aspect."

"In the van!" she said. "You're crazy. The van isn't what I would call private. People will see us!"

"No, they won't. The back windows are tinted, sort of," I said as I yanked her hand. "Anyway, we'll lie down low."

I kissed her.

She laughed.

"We are not doing this," she said.

"Yeah, well, you're the one who had to start everything up with all that naughty detergent talk."

A screaming siren went by as we continued to kiss, followed by what sounded like the rattle of a homeless guy's shopping cart filled with returns.

"Wow, talk about setting the mood," she said, taking a step back from me and leaning against the side of the van.

"What can I say? I'm an incurable romantic," I said. "This sucks. I don't like being such a cad, but with my ten kids and your new nanny roommate from ten A, there in your room on the top floor, it's hard to find a place to be alone. In fact, it's pretty much impossible."

"Well, you'll have to try just a little harder, Casanova," she said, smiling.

I snapped a finger.

"I know," I said, taking her hands. "We'll plan a weekend, or at least a Friday night. We'll go away—or no, we'll stay in town. That's it. We'll paint the town red at a French bistro and then get a place somewhere special. Have you ever been to the Plaza?"

"The Plaza," Mary Catherine said. "Oh, sure. My sister, Eloise, and I grew up there."

"C'mon, I haven't been there, either. It'll be a panic, I promise. What do you say?"

"I say you're out of your mind," she said, smiling.

I kissed her.

"That goes without saying," I said. "The question is, are you game, Lady of Erin?"

She kissed me back.

"I'll believe it when I see it, Man of Blarney," she said.

Chapter 19

"REMEMBER, NOW," I SAID, kissing Mary Catherine one last time in the elevator as I stepped out onto my floor. "The town. The color red. The finest French restaurant in the city, then the Plaza. We're going to do this."

Mary Catherine laughed as the elevator door closed.

A strange sound greeted me as I tiptoed through the darkened apartment and opened the door of my bedroom. Someone was crying. What the heck? What could be wrong now?

It was actually two someones. I threw on the light to find Chrissy and Shawna camped out on my bedroom chair in their pajamas, cheeks tear-soaked, whimpering.

"What is it, girls?" I said, rushing over to them. "What happened? Are you hurt?"

"No, Daddy. It's not that," Shawna said, sobbing. "It's just so sad."

"What's so sad? Why are you crying?"

"We miss them, Daddy. We miss them so much," Chrissy said.

"Who?"

"Flopsy, Mopsy, and Desiree," said Shawna.

"And Homer," Chrissy said. "Poor, poor Homer. He must be so lonely."

I shook my head. Of course. If it wasn't one thing it was another. My nutty kids were missing Mr. Cody's farm animals from our California safe house.

"It's OK, girls," I said, sitting down between them. "I'm sure the animals are fine. Maybe tomorrow we can e-mail Mr. Cody and have him send us a picture."

"Or a FaceTime?" Shawna said, wiping at her brightening eyes.

"Hooray, yes! Can we FaceTime with Homer, Daddy? Can we? Can we?" Chrissy said.

FaceTime with a chicken? I thought, rubbing my temples. *Will this day never end?*

"We'll see. Now, please, back to bed. You have school in the morning."

"No, Daddy. We can't sleep in our beds,"

Chrissy said. "The big girls sent us away when we started crying."

"And the door is so creaky," Shawna said. "They'll just be mad again if we wake them up."

"Where are you going to sleep, then?"

They sat there blinking up at me with their sugar-frosted-cupcake eyes.

"No," I said, knowing that look. "Don't worry about the creaky door. Go back to your room and your own beds."

But it was no use. They kept staring, kept twinkling.

I let out a breath.

"Fine," I growled. "Just this once because you're so sad, I guess. Go get your pillows."

"We already brought them," Shawna said, pulling them out from the other side of the bed.

"Of course you did. How convenient. Anyway, now, here's the rules. No nugglance or poking or combing Daddy's hair, and most of all, no giggling and tickling. If you wish to sleep here, we will sleep. Do I make myself clear?"

They stared at me, biting their little lips to stifle the giggles that had already started. How did I get myself into these things?

I washed up and got into my pj's and lay down.

Then I sneezed as something furry scrubbed up against my left nostril.

"What the—!" I said as I shot up to a barrage of hysterical giggling.

I clicked on the light. It was the stupid cat!

"Put Socky out of this bed, Chrissy. This bed has a strict no-cat policy. No means no. Get him out of here!"

"But Socky misses Touchdown and Flopsy, Mopsy, and Desiree, too," said Chrissy.

"No, Socky misses the rodents, and most of all, those delicious birds," I said as I placed the cat on the floor and put the pillow over my head.

"That's so mean, Daddy," Chrissy said. "Homer is a bird and Socky is my friend. Socky would die before he hurt even one feather on Homer's head."

Wanna bet? I thought.

"Mean Daddy," Shawna agreed with another giggle.

"Please, girls. Mean Daddy has work tomorrow and just wants some sleep, OK? Just a little sleep, pretty please," I said as I felt the cat leap back up onto the bed and use the back of my left leg for a scratching post.

I shook my leg free and was about to get rid of the cat again but then wisely resigned myself. I closed my weary eyes and pictured room service breakfast at the Plaza. As I fell asleep, I pictured Mary Catherine in a white bathrobe raising a mimosa as the sun came up over Central Park.

Chapter 20

I GOT OUT OF the house at an extra-early six-thirty the next morning to beat the traffic.

Not the commuter traffic in the street so much as the always-heavy bathroom traffic in my apartment on weekday mornings.

From the corner deli, I grabbed a breakfast sandwich and a coffee and the paper. The *Post* wasn't in yet, but the *Daily News* was, so I picked up a copy, which I perused in the front seat of my Chevy as I ate my ham, egg, and cheese.

After I read the sports section, I flipped the paper over. I skimmed through what Kanye was up to these days, and then I read something interesting on page four.

There was a story about a jewel heist at some high-end jewelry shop out in Brooklyn.

The criminals seemed sophisticated. Rushing in wearing ski masks and brandishing handguns, they'd forced the store staff to the ground before smashing display cases with ball-peen hammers and grabbing the most expensive items. The smash-and-grab gang had struck thrice and was always in and out in minutes and got away without a trace.

It really did sound like an interesting case, I thought as I put down the paper and started the car. A crew of professional thieves was something a cop could really sink his teeth into. I imagined the stakeouts and suspect interviews, the adrenaline-laced thrill of the hunt.

Then I stopped fantasizing as I reminded myself that my involvement with high-profile cases was now a thing of the past.

I was first one in at the ombudsman office at 125th in Harlem. After I keyed myself in, I turned on the lights and parked myself at my desk. I was drinking a coffee to the sound of a soothing Mozart horn concerto from YouTube and going through more complaints when a woman poked her head in the doorway.

"Detective Bennett?" she said.

It took me a few seconds to realize that it was the clerk I'd sent home yesterday. It was hard to recognize her, what with the long-sleeved blouse and tailored pants and no gaudy makeup. The only earrings she wore were in her ears this morning, I noted happily. She looked quite respectable and professional. Well, what did you know? Day two and I was already making some headway.

"Yes, Ms. Ramirez?" I said, taking note of her name tag.

"I just wanted to apologize for my appearance and behavior and stuff yesterday. I read the manual like you said, and I'm going to follow it. I actually like my job, and I'd like to try to show you that I'm actually really good at it if you give me another chance."

"Sounds good, Ms. Ramirez," I said.

"Oh, please call me Roz," she said, smiling.

I didn't smile back. The last thing this tattooed young lady needed was to be more casual in the workplace.

"That's OK," I said. "I'll just stick with Ms. Ramirez for now, Ms. Ramirez."

Chapter 21

FIRST UP ON THE day's agenda was a squad meeting I called and held in the small conference room next to my office.

By a little after nine, around the battered laminate table that was almost too big for the room sat the squad's full retinue of *un*usual suspects.

Gung-ho Jimmy Doyle was present and accounted for on my left, beside a happy Arturo Lopez and the stylish Noah Robertson. On my right was wired-a-little-too-tight Naomi Chast, sitting beside a new female cop who'd been in court testifying the day before.

The new cop's name was Brooklyn Kale, and she was a nice-looking and very tall young black woman. I'd read in her file that the six-three Brooklyn had played basketball with the University of Connecticut Lady Huskies and was one of the point guards on the 2009 NCAA championship team. She was also a Harlem native who'd grown up six blocks north up Adam Clayton Powell Boulevard.

Which I liked. Brooklyn knew the area, the community, had some skin in the game. I just hoped her policing skills were comparable to her accuracy from the three-point line.

I started off the meeting by handing out the current docket of complaints I'd had Ms. Ramirez print up.

"Now, before we get started looking these over," I said to everybody, "I think it's important to let you know what I expect out of this squad. What I expect is nothing short of doing this job absolutely as well as anybody can possibly do it, OK? We prioritize the cases and we work 'em and work 'em and work 'em until they're done.

"So I don't want to hear excuses. We set our goals, and we methodically accomplish them. And then we go home and go to sleep and wake up and do it again."

I looked everyone over. They mostly seemed to get what I was saying. Arturo even gave me a happy little thumbs-up.

Was I being too harsh? Too drill sergeant? Maybe a little, but that was probably better in the beginning with these newborn baby cops. I could show them my good cop side once the ground rules were laid down and I started seeing some results.

I looked over the complaint list. At the top were a lot of strange but not really police-related complaints. People were wondering things like why weren't their radiators working and what school district were they in and what was up with their food stamp application.

"Ms. Ramirez, Ms. Tyson," I said to the two clerks, who were hovering in the conference room's doorway. "Do you see all these housing complaints and whatnot at the top of this list? Can I put you two in charge of redirecting non-police complaints to the proper city agencies?

"I'm not trying to diminish these issues. I might want to call the cops if rats were infesting my building, too. But we don't fix streetlights or fill in potholes. We just deal with actual crimes. Help out people who are in danger, that sort of thing. If you have something questionable, by all means leave it on the docket, but my boss is a nut about numbers, and we can clear a lot of these by proper redirection."

"On it," Ariel Tyson said, leaving the room with Ms. Ramirez.

I quickly kept reading until I found something valid.

"OK. Look here on page two, folks. The third complaint from the top. A woman named Holly Jacobs is being harassed by her ex-boyfriend. She states that her boyfriend threatened to murder her, cut her up, and feed her to the seagulls out at Coney Island. See, this is a police matter. Just threatening to murder someone is a crime called—"

"Yes, simple assault. We know. We learned this at the academy. Have mercy," said Naomi Chast testily beside me.

"Very good, Naomi," I said after a long wide-eyed moment. I nodded at her calmly before licking my thumb and turning the page. "It is called simple assault. You're right. Now, see, we're starting to get somewhere."

Chapter 22

"DETECTIVE? MIKE? I MEAN, SIR?" Arturo Lopez said, raising his hand like a very overgrown third grader.

"Yes, Arturo?"

"Did you happen to see this strange, um, cannibal thing down on the bottom of page three?"

I went down the list. At the bottom, there was a complaint. And Arturo was right on the money. It was pretty strange, all right.

A complainant with the curious name of Hudson Du Maurier III claimed that early in the morning Thursday last, he observed something odd from his sixth-story apartment window on Lenox Avenue. He was looking out the window when a brown hatchback pulled up in front of an abandoned building on the corner of 145th.

He said several men exited the vehicle and entered the premises. He also said that through a large hole in the roof of the abandoned establishment, he made out a large, blazing grill. He said he also spied a large black man in chef's whites, and what looked like a girl bound like a "leg of lamb."

Du Maurier concluded his account by stating that he was afraid the girl had been eaten by these men, and that he could be contacted at his apartment to provide more details, such as the vehicle's license plate number, which he'd jotted down.

"And then Mr. The Third woke up and rolled over and finished his last rock of crack and lived happily ever after," said Doyle from the other end of the table.

"Actually, I think I know this man from when I was on patrol," Naomi Chast piped up. "He's got some mental issues, schizophrenia, I believe, but he's not a crackhead."

"Oh, he's just schizo," Doyle said, nodding. "Sorry for doubting his addled, er, I mean riveting account."

"He sold books on the street, I think," Chast said, ignoring Doyle. "No, wait. He was a sketch artist. One of those sidewalk people who will draw your caricature for ten bucks. He was a pleasant enough character. Definitely not a troublemaker or attention-seeker. We saw plenty of them, believe me."

"Wait, I think I heard of him, too," Brooklyn Kale said. "Always wears, like, a dirty tuxedo kind of getup, right? Like a magician or something. He used to be a children's book illustrator or something in the seventies. A community activist, too. Chast is right. He's odd but not nuts. At least not completely."

"I want this case," Naomi said as she started tapping the table hard with her bit-to-a-nub fingernail. "I have the most seniority here, and I deserve first pick."

"Fine," I said, leaning back in my chair. I was a little afraid not to give her the case. She might bite off my head.

"Chast, go with Kale," I said. "You two can go and see if there's anything to what Mr. Du Maurier is saying."

Chast stared at me with a hard, pissed-off look, her specialty, apparently.

"I don't think so," the strawberry blonde said, standing and slipping on her Windbreaker. "In fact, no way."

"No? What do you mean, *no,* Chast?" I said.

"I don't need a partner. I don't want one. I work better and move faster alone," she said. Then she turned and walked out the conference room door.

"Whoa, Chast. Are you kidding me? Get back in here," I yelled as I stood up.

"Don't bother on my account, Detective Bennett," said Brooklyn. "You probably noticed by now that Officer Chast doesn't exactly play well with others."

"Brooklyn's right, Detective. I'd just as soon let her go," Arturo said. "Officer Chast isn't exactly easy to work with."

"Make that impossible," said Noah Robertson, drumming his fingers on the table.

"Now, c'mon, guys," said Officer Doyle. "Our colleague isn't even here to defend herself. Besides, there was that one fugitive case two weeks back where she helped me get that guy under control. Remember that big dude outside the Duane Reade on Lenox?"

"That was me, you idiot," Brooklyn said.

"Yeah?" Doyle said, squinting across the table at her.

Doyle turned to me with a shrug.

"I guess it's unanimous, Detective Bennett," he said. "Chast completely sucks as a partner."

Chapter 23

I DECIDED TO LEAVE Doyle, Robertson, and Kale to man the office and took Arturo Lopez with me to check on Holly Jacobs, the woman with the pyscho boyfriend.

Holly Jacobs's place turned out to be a dozen blocks to the south, across the street from Morningside Park near 116th Street. She lived in a beautiful six-story brownstone building that she buzzed us into after we arrived and gave her a call.

Holly Jacobs was a striking, well-dressed and well-put-together middle-aged black woman with a short *Vogue*-ish asymmetrical bob haircut. Her white-on-white apartment was sleek and modern and immaculate. The books on her shelves were those coffee-table artsy ones. Edward Weston, Magritte, *The Drawings of Peter Paul Rubens.*

She sat us down in her sunken living room on a couch near the bay window that overlooked the leafy park.

"So tell us, Holly," I started. "You're having some problems with your ex-boyfriend?"

Holly stood and folded her arms over her flat stomach and stared out the window for a few moments before she nodded. She took a photograph off the coffee table and handed it to me. It showed a handsome, smiling, wiry young black man with a shaved head.

"This is Roger. I met him at a club about a year ago. I thought I'd put my clubbing days in the rearview, but I'm a marketing consultant for a fashion company, and I was celebrating a deal with some young clients. He looked like a model when he came up to me at the bar. Still in his twenties, chiseled-looking. You know, somebody special."

She took a long breath.

"We started dating. I knew it was too early when he said he wanted to move in. I mean, he didn't even have a job, but I was flattered, I guess. He was charming, attentive, younger. The first time he hit me was when I came home from work about a week after he moved in."

She paused for a moment.

“I was putting down the groceries at the counter, and he had his head in the fridge. When he closed the door, out of nowhere, he slapped me hard enough to give me a bloody nose. He had this far-off look in his eyes. I don’t know what the hell he was on, but after a second or two, he went into the bedroom and passed out.

“When he woke the next morning, he said he had blacked out after partying with some old friends, and that they must have put something in his drink. He had some really great excuses, couldn’t stop apologizing. He cried. So I let him stay.”

She started crying then.

“After that—after he bloodied my face and my clothes—I let him stay. Imagine? He started hitting me pretty regularly then. I’m supposed to be this fashion guru, and I was so stupid.”

Chapter 24

ARTURO STOOD IMMEDIATELY AND gently held the woman's elbow.

"No, Holly. It's OK. Don't do that. We're here, OK? We're going to help you now. This man tricked you. It could have happened to anyone. Don't blame yourself. He's in the wrong, not you."

She sniffled, composed herself.

"Eventually, about a month later, I just woke up one morning and realized how crazy my life had become, and I threw him out. The super is a good friend of mine, and he and a couple of guys who work here came up and backed me up when I told Roger to get his stuff and get out.

"That very next night when I came home from work, I saw him through the glass of the front door, sitting in one of the lobby windows, holding a bulging laundry bag and a butcher knife. I ran back and got into my cab and called the cops, but he was gone by the time they showed up. He took everything. My jewelry, my computer, a bunch of my financial records."

"When was this?" I said.

"About a month and a half ago," she said. "I reported it to the precinct, canceled all my credit cards, changed the locks. I thought it was over until he started leaving all these anonymous threats on my social media page. He told me how he's been following me, waiting for the right moment. Biding his time. 'You can't just throw me away,' he said.

"He started calling my cell and landline in the middle of the night. Sometimes both at the same time. He's even called and harassed some of my coworkers, people I introduced him to. The things he says."

She shook her head rapidly.

"It's like a nightmare. I've been to court three times, but I still can't get a restraining order because I don't even know his real name."

"Holly," I said. "Do you have any time at work that you could take off? Maybe two weeks or so?"

"No," she said. "We're swamped with a new client, a celebrity fragrance that's just getting ramped up. Why?"

"This guy seems pretty impulsive and obsessed. If you took a trip, if he noticed you weren't around for a consistent stretch, it might take the thrill out of it for him, and he might move on."

"But I can't. I just told you," Holly said as she started crying again.

While Arturo continued to comfort her, I took a cell phone photograph of the suspect and sent it to the local precinct captain's e-mail address. Then I made an actual phone call to the precinct captain to fast-track the case.

He told me he'd let the shift commanders know what was up and gave me the desk number for Holly to call instead of 911 in case she spotted this wacko. I wrote the precinct number on the back of my card along with my cell phone.

"Holly, listen to me, OK?" I said. "I don't care if it's day or night. I live pretty close by downtown. You see Roger, you call the precinct, then you call me, and we'll come running right away, OK? You have friends close by now. You don't have to face this alone."

Holly nodded. She finally looked relieved.

"Thank you so much for coming by and taking my situation seriously, Detectives," she told us as she led us back out into the hallway.

Chapter 25

FOR THE NEXT HALF hour, we drove around the Morningside Park area, looking for Roger.

"Good work comforting that lady up there, Arturo. She was pretty shook up. You're good with people," I said as we circled the block.

"Poor lady," Arturo said, shaking his head. "Least I could do. Imagine some fruitcake stalking you like that?"

"This guy is more than just a nut," I said. "A lot of stalking cases are just bluff by spurned jerks, but Holly's account is definitely concerning."

"How can you tell the difference?"

"The fact that this Roger guy seems to have some psychiatric issues, that he's a physically abusive substance abuser, and that Holly had been intimate with him are some very serious red flags when it comes to the potential for violence."

I suddenly stopped the car as we were sweeping around Holly's block for the second time. I took a pair of binoculars that I keep in the glove compartment and pointed them into Morningside Park.

"What's up?"

I handed Arturo the glasses.

"Female on the bench off to the right by the playground," I said.

"The white girl with the glasses?" Arturo said, focusing in.

"She's directly opposite Holly's building, and she's got a camera with a telephoto lens."

"Birdwatcher?" Arturo said.

"She's watching something," I said, pulling over. "This Roger guy is quite the ladies' man, right? Well, maybe he got himself a new friend to keep an eye on Holly. Let's go see what she has to say."

Only having been in it a few times, I had almost forgotten how nice a park Morningside is. Built by Frederick Law Olmsted, the famous nineteenth-century landscape architect who designed Central Park and Prospect Park, it had meandering walkways and grand stone staircases and even an elaborate waterfall beside one of its pathside ponds.

Too bad I wasn't there to sightsee.

"Hey there," I said, showing the woman on the bench my shield as I approached. The pale woman stood up, quickly stuffing the camera into a bag and gathering her things. But before she could take off, Arturo was already coming up the opposite side, blocking her way along the curving tree-lined path.

"What do you want?" the woman said. "I'm not doing anything."

It was hard to tell how old she was. Besides the granny glasses, she had studs in her pierced cheeks, a men's vintage-shop gray raincoat and badly dyed black hair peeking out from under a ragged tweed cap. She'd been pretty once, probably not too long ago. Now she looked as hard as the old concrete she probably slept on every night.

"Sit back down," I told her.

"What is this about?" she said as I sat down next to her and took out my binoculars and pointed them at Holly's building. I knew it. She had a straight shot to the front door.

"This is about him," I said, showing her Roger's picture on my phone. I stared at her face as I showed it and caught a brief flicker of recognition.

"Hey, Mike, watch her," Arturo called out as the

young woman thrust her hands into her bag.

I waved him off. She wasn't going for a weapon, I knew. She was just busy thumbing the Delete button on her camera. It was a Sony, a three-or-four-hundred-dollar digital SLR. Which made little sense, considering she was homeless. Probably stolen by Roger, I thought. I let her thumb away at it.

"What's your name?" I said.

"Piss off," she said.

I looked at her glassy eyes. It looked like she was on something.

She didn't say anything as I went into her tattered backpack and took out a wallet. She had a Connecticut driver's license. Rachel Wecht. I couldn't believe she was only twenty-one. Thanks, drugs. Thanks, broken families. I was also right. She had been pretty once.

"Listen, Rachel," Arturo said. "This guy Roger, or whatever his name is, who's got you doing this, he's really not as exciting as you think he is. In fact, he's trouble. Like you'll-end-up-dead kind of trouble. We have a warrant out for his arrest."

"We could lock you up right now for aiding and abetting a known criminal," I said. "But I'm going to go on the assumption that he lied to you, OK? I'm going to cut you some slack. If you tell me where he is."

She sneered at me as she took off her tattered cap and spun it on her finger.

"As if I knew what the hell you're even talking about," she said.

"This lady you're watching. She was Roger's old girlfriend," Arturo said. "What do you think happens to you when he gets sick of you?"

She rolled her eyes and shrugged before she stood up and shouldered her pack.

"I'm leaving," she said with a dreamy smile.

I let her walk. She'd called my bluff. There was nothing to hold her on. Not yet, at least. If anything, I was even more concerned about Holly now. Roger was recruiting people to help him stalk her.

"This Roger really is a ladies' man, huh?" Arturo said as we watched her leave. "Maybe that's what I'm doing wrong. I need to drop my nice-guy routine and act more like I just escaped from the nuthatch."

Part Two

ONE OF OUR OWN

Chapter 26

THAT EVENING AFTER WORK, instead of heading straight home, I did something pretty out there. Something fairly nuts even for me. Which was saying something.

I drove up into the Bronx near Yankee Stadium and made a purchase. Two purchases, actually. I hid them under my coat as I made my grand entrance that night around seven p.m. into the Bennett family abode.

"Ladies and gentlemen and children of all ages. I have an announcement. A neenie-neenie-nouncement!" I bellowed, quoting Chrissy, as I barged my way through the front hall into the living room.

Mary Catherine came in from the kitchen, giving me a wink as she wiped her hands on a dish towel. I'd already made her privy to the surprise. I'm by no means the sharpest knife in the drawer, but even I was smart enough to know to run something like this by her first.

Seamus appeared behind her with a folded *New York Times* crossword puzzle clutched in his hand.

"And what's going on here with all this ruckus?" he said.

"I'm sorry, Seamus. You'll just have to wait until the masses are amassed and everyone is present and accounted for. This is a four-alarm family surprise. Maybe a five-alarmer."

"Let me guess," Seamus said excitedly. "You've finally checked yourself into Bellevue?"

"Not yet, old-timer," I said, hefting my surprise. "But you may have a point after you see what I have behind curtain numero uno."

The kids rushed in. Even the big ones. Earbuds were removed. I definitely had their attention.

"Now, are you ready?" I said.

"Yes!" they yelled.

Well, the little ones, at least, with a beaming Chrissy and Shawna leading the chorus.

"I can't hear you!" I said. "Are you ready!?"

"Dad, enough, please, would you?" Brian said. "I have a Latin test tomorrow."

"Well, then, without further ado, I present to you..."

I pulled the coat away like a magician, revealing the hamster cage I was balancing on my forearm.

And the puppy I was holding in my palm.

"AWWWWWWWWW!" said everyone.

And I mean everyone. Even most of the boys.

No wonder. In the palm of my hand was the cutest little border collie puppy in the history of the world. He was mostly white, with some almost tigerlike black stripes on his back and a black patch over his left eye.

"A puppy!" the little girls yelled as they hyperventilated and hopped up and down.

"And a hamster!" Chrissy shrieked. "Put them down! Put them down! I need to touch them now!!!!"

"Why, yes. A puppy and a hamster," I said, continuing to hold them aloft. "The two newest members of Clan Bennett are here. On one condition."

"Anything, Daddy!" the girls squealed.

"That little hands pitch in to take care of our family's newest members, especially walks. Dogs need walks with people attached to the other end of the leash."

"And pooper scoopers," said Seamus.

"I'll walk the hamster," Eddie said.

"You *are* a hamster," replied Ricky.

"We promise, Daddy," Shawna said. "Can we touch them now? Can we, please? Please?"

"I suppose," I said as I finally placed the puppy and the hamster cage on the floor and wisely backed out of the way.

Chapter 27

I WAS COMMUTING UP to Harlem the next morning and had just turned south on Adam Clayton Powell when my phone rang.

“Hi, Detective. This is Doyle. Jimmy Doyle.”

“Hey, Jimmy. What’s up?” I said.

“I just had a phone conversation with Officer Chast’s stepmother down in Florida.”

“Officer Chast’s who?” I said.

“Exactly,” Doyle said. “That’s what I said. Anyway, I got in ten minutes ago, and there were a bunch of messages left here from her, and she’s really worried about Naomi. Apparently she and Naomi are close, they talk three, four nights a week. Been doing it for the last ten years, since Naomi moved up here and became a cop. Anyway, she was waiting for Naomi’s phone call all day yesterday because it was the stepmom's birthday. But she didn't call."

"Have you tried calling Naomi?" I said.

"It just kicks into voice mail. Chast is pretty good about getting back to you day or night, so it's pretty weird."

"Where does she live?"

"Central Park West in the hundreds."

"OK. I'm about two blocks from the office. I'll pick you up on One Twenty-Fifth and we'll head over and see what's going on."

Chast's building was at 109th and Central Park West, a block south of the northwest corner of Central Park. It was about twelve stories, red brick trimmed in pale limestone, one of those anonymously beautiful prewar structures that you never get tired of seeing in and around New York.

But when we parked in front of it, I could see that despite its good bones, the building had gone to seed a little. There was some choice graffiti here and there along its base, some broken glass next to a broken pay phone kiosk on the corner. When we reached the door, instead of the doorman that the old building probably once had, there was a buzzer system. First we pressed for Chast in apartment 4H. There was no response after a minute, so we pressed for the super. No dice on that front, either.

I then did what every New Yorker does when confronted with a buzzer system and a locked lobby door of a building to which they need access. With both hands fluttering like Liberace playing a solo, I rang every button in the box.

"Who is it?" said a woman's rough voice after thirty seconds.

Doyle rolled his eyes. The woman sounded almost exactly like the "Do your paperwork" lady, Roz, from *Monsters, Inc.*

"NYPD," Doyle said. "Open the door, please."

"Yeah, and I'm Hillary Clinton, you jerk," replied "Roz," then added, "You kids get outta here before I call the cops. And stop pissin' in the elevator! What are ya? Dogs? Go piss in the park, you filthy animals."

"I want to shoot this thing. Can I, please? Just once?" Doyle said, pounding on some more buttons.

Fortunately, before he could take out his service weapon, the door's buzzer went off, and we went up the stairs to Chast's apartment door. After knocking on it pretty hard for a few minutes, I started getting worried. If Chast was sick or hungover, she would have woken up. If she was in there, she was in trouble. I truly hoped she wasn't.

Chapter 28

I SENT DOYLE DOWN to the basement to see if he could find the building's super. He came back up five minutes later with the super's wife, an attractive fiftyish redheaded woman in flannel pajamas, named Meg Hambrecht.

"I knew it," she said, fumbling with a huge set of keys at Chast's door. "Every time my husband goes on jury duty something like this happens."

"You hear anything out of the ordinary in the building last night, Ms. Hambrecht?" I said.

"Not a thing," she said, finally spilling the keys into my hands. "Here. I'm useless. You try."

The second key I tried worked. Doyle and I looked at each other nervously as I swung the door open into the dead-silent apartment.

Dear God, I prayed silently. *Please let Chast not be here.*

"Could you wait out here, Ms. Hambrecht?" I said.

"With pleasure," she said.

"Hey, Naomi? Hello? Naomi, it's Detective Mike Bennett and Jimmy Doyle. You in here? You OK?" I said as we entered the apartment.

We passed by a galley kitchen and a sunken living room. Doyle and I exchanged a concerned glance when we spotted the closed back bedroom door.

I turned the door's paint-flecked glass knob and pushed it open.

Naomi was sitting slumped over at a cluttered home office armoire. Immediately, we could see her open eyes, the blood splatter among the pencils and notebooks, her chunky black service Glock on the carpet between her feet.

Officer Naomi Chast was gone.

"No," Doyle said, groaning as he started to walk over to her. "C'mon! This isn't right. How is this possible?"

I grabbed his shoulder and pointed him toward the door.

"Go call it in, Doyle," I said. "Call it in."

Chapter 29

AS WE WAITED FOR the local precinct detective to arrive, I went over to Naomi and knelt beside her.

"Mike, what are you doing, man? Aren't we supposed to let the precinct DTs handle this? I can't stand seeing her like that. I feel like it's somehow my fault."

"Doyle, get over here," I said as I peered into Naomi's face.

"No, man. I don't want to," Doyle said.

"Now," I said.

"What?" he said as he finally arrived behind me.

"Look, her front tooth there. It's chipped."

"Uh-huh."

"And here, look at her left hand. Her nails are neat and polished, but on her right hand, there are three broken fingernails."

“What are you saying?”

I suddenly snapped my fingers as I glanced in the closet and under the bed.

“Doyle, listen. This is important. Where did Naomi wear her service weapon? On her right or left hip?” I said as I looked over the contents of her desk.

Doyle closed his eyes.

“Left,” he said.

“That’s what I thought,” I said. “She was left-handed, but her bullet wound here is more on the right.”

“You’re right,” Doyle said. “That doesn’t make any sense.”

“No, it doesn’t,” I said. “And also look at this computer cubby. It’s got everything, right? Except the computer. Where’s her computer? It’s not in the living room or the closet or under the bed. It’s not anywhere.”

“You’re right,” Doyle said. “What’s going on? You think she didn’t do this?”

“Hey, what are you doing in here?” said a voice from behind us.

“Glad you’re here,” I said, extending my hand to a bald, skinny, pale, thirtyish detective in a brown golf shirt. “I’m Mike Bennett. This is Jimmy Doyle.”

“Fred Evanson,” the cop said, shaking hands.

"Nice to meet you, Fred," I said. "We worked with Naomi. Her stepmother said she wasn't answering her phone since yesterday, so we decided to check in on her."

Evanson frowned over at her.

"I'm sorry about your colleague. Damn, I hate to see that. So young. Real tragedy. This job can really chew you up," Evanson said.

"That's just the thing, Detective. I don't know if it was the job. There're signs of a struggle. Chipped fingernails, a chipped tooth. Also, her computer is missing and—"

"Whoa. What the—? What the hell are you doing here, Bennett?" said an older Hispanic cop, stepping in.

I restrained myself from rolling my eyes. I knew the cop, unfortunately. His name was Freddy Abreu, and he was known in the department as a creep and complete hack who for some unknown reason kept getting promoted. Actually, the reason was known. It was because he was a good friend and even better minion of Chief of Detectives Starkie.

"Get the hell out of here now, Bennett, before I have you written up for messing with my crime scene. Wait out in the hall. Now," Abreu said.

Chapter 30

WE DID AS WE were told. We sat out on the steps in the building hallway as more uniforms and more detectives and the crime scene unit arrived. I got the call I was expecting right after I sent Doyle to get us some breakfast.

"Bennett," I said.

"One question, Bennett," Starkie said. "Just one. Are you effing kidding me? Five seconds ago, I put you in charge of that unit, and now one of your guys is a stiff? What kind of manager are you? This officer meets her new boss, then goes home and blows her brains out?"

"That's just the thing, Starkie. There are signs of a scuffle. I don't think she committed suicide."

"Already heard about your little conspiracy theory, Bennett. You're thinking maybe she was shot from a black helicopter, huh? Or the president put her on the drone kill list? Or maybe it had a teensie weensie bit to do with the fact that several of her prior assignment evaluations rated her as excessively emotional?

"She was unstable, Bennett, and you pushed her right over the edge. So if I were you, I'd get my think box humming to deal with that, because don't be surprised if that's the media narrative coming your way. Because if you think I'm taking the heat on this from the mayor or the press or anyone else, you're crazier than I thought!"

There was a tiny crackling plastic sound as I gripped my phone savagely in rage. I literally could not believe the bullshit I was hearing. A cop had just been killed, and already Starkie's primary concern was how inconvenient it was for his ambitious career?

"That's funny. I have a message for you, too, Starkie. Go—" I managed to get in before I heard his click.

"Who was that?" Doyle said as he came up the stairs carrying a cardboard tray of coffee.

"Nobody in particular," I said, putting my phone carefully away as I motioned to Doyle to follow me down the stairs.

A hundred different emotions and thoughts swirled through me as I descended. I was revolted, of course, and sad and angry and keyed up, but mostly I was disappointed in myself.

Starkie was right about one thing. I'd majorly screwed up. I should never have allowed Naomi to go off and start an investigation on her own. I should have forced a partner on her.

No one had been watching her back, and that was definitely on me.

As I made the ground floor, I looked down at my vibrating phone and saw that Chief Starkie was trying to contact me again. Instead of answering, I turned off my phone as I motioned to Doyle to follow me toward the super's ground-floor apartment.

"What are we doing, Mike? I thought the DT wanted us to wait to be questioned?"

"Change of plans, Doyle," I said as I knocked on the super's door.

"Oh, that poor girl," said Meg Hambrecht as she answered, in jeans and a sweatshirt now. "I remember the day she moved in, how concerned she was about her movers hogging the elevator. Not wanting to inconvenience everybody. She seemed so together. Now something like this. It's just—"

"Thanks, Ms. Hambrecht," I said, interrupting, "but I noticed you have a security camera by the buzzer. We'd like to look at the footage."

She shook her head rapidly.

"I'm sorry, but they're installing a new system, and the building management fired the contractor in the middle of it. The whole thing has been out for a while now, three, four weeks. There is no footage."

"Thanks for your time," I said. "The other detectives are finishing up upstairs. They'll probably be contacting you in a bit."

"Mike, c'mon. What's up?" said Doyle as we left the building.

"I'll tell you what's up, Doyle," I said. "I worked homicide for five years. It's more politically expedient for the department that her death be seen as a suicide. That's why we have to investigate this on our own."

"What about protocol?"

"Protocol and politics and especially Chief Starkie be damned, Doyle. Naomi was part of our team. She was one of us. If we don't catch the people that did this to her, no one will."

Chapter 31

WE RUSHED BACK TO the Harlem office, and for the next half hour, Doyle and I tossed Naomi's cubicle, looking for any notes she might have started on the cannibalism case.

It wasn't looking too good. There weren't any notebooks. The only paper in the place was a ream of copy paper for her printer. Everything we needed to know seemed to be on her password-protected computer.

"Hey, you know, Lopez knows computers," Doyle said as we stood there staring at the Toshiba's screen. "He, like, went to school and stuff before he got called for the cops. You didn't hear it from me, but he even fixes them on the side."

"You tell me this now?" I said. "Go get him."

Lopez arrived along with Noah Robertson and Brooklyn Kale, who we'd informed on the way over. The gang looked pretty torn up about Naomi.

"We need you to do all you can, Arturo," I said. "For Naomi."

Lopez sat down in front of the computer and took a deep breath and began clicking away. After a second, he snapped a finger.

"Hey, we know Naomi had a Yahoo e-mail account through AT&T. The phone company will have her password on file. Somebody call them so we can at least look at her e-mails."

Noah Robertson was doing just that when Lopez cried out.

"Forget it. I got it! Open sesame. I'm in!"

"Arty, my man," Doyle said, giving Lopez an enthusiastic high five.

"What was it?" I said.

"Chast was a Red Sox fan," Lopez said, rapidly clicking more keys and the mouse. "Used to drive me nuts. I mean, go join the Boston cops, why don'tcha? I remembered making fun of her at a softball game for wearing a Dustin Pedroia jersey, asking her if it was his actual jersey since the guy is such a shrimp. So I tried *DUSTIN* plus her birthday and wham-o. Easy beans."

Lopez brought up a Word file entitled *Current Case.*

"Here it is, I think," he said. "Looks like a cut-and-pasted note from her iPhone. She probably e-mailed it to herself. It looks like notes from an interview dated yesterday."

Lopez read a little bit more and looked up at me.

"Mike, it looks like she'd already spoken to the complainant yesterday. Hudson Du Maurier the Third."

Doyle looked at me from the other side of Lopez.

"Don't tell me," Doyle said. "It's time we have a talk with Mr. The Third."

Chapter 32

AS DOYLE AND I went to Du Maurier's address, I sent Brooklyn and Noah and Lopez on a scavenger hunt to see if they could find the sometimes sidewalk artist at one of his usual hangouts on the street.

Doyle and I had just parked in front of Du Maurier's building on Lenox when my phone rang. It was Brooklyn Kale.

"We got him," she said.

"Where?"

"Rucker Park."

"Stay there. We're on our way."

We headed north. She didn't have to tell me the address. Rucker Park, at 155th and Frederick Douglass, is probably the most famous public basketball court in the city. Started in the '50s to give city kids something to do in the summer, the league and tournaments associated with the park had been a stepping-stone for such legends as Kareem Abdul-Jabbar and Dr J.

There was quite a crowd when we pulled up, had to be a few hundred people in the aluminum stands. There was also an MC and even boom cameras and lights as two brightly uniformed three-on-three teams went at it. As I pulled behind Brooklyn's double-parked cruiser, the crowd exploded in laughter and Bronx cheers as some lumbering six-five fifteen-year-old blew a slam dunk.

I sat in the back of the cruiser and shook Du Maurier's hand. Du Maurier was a slim, neat, diminutive light-skinned black man in a dusty, threadbare tuxedo. His strange getup struck me as a cross between a magician and Charlie Chaplin's Little Tramp. He nervously clutched a folding easel to his chest with both hands like it was an instrument he was about to play.

"You wanted to talk to me about something?" the seventy-something man said, rocking back and forth as he stared out at the crowd. He didn't give me any eye contact. I wondered if he was maybe autistic.

"If you could be quick about it, please, Officer. That's MTV filming in there. I don't see these kinds of crowds that often."

"That can wait, Mr. Du Maurier. I need your attention. I also need you to be perfectly honest with me. Did an officer speak to you yesterday? A female officer?"

"Yes, she did. A young woman with reddish-blond hair," the street artist said, rocking even harder now as he began to bite a thumbnail.

"Detective Chist, no, Chast was her name," he said, flicking a quick look in my direction. "I told her about what I saw a few nights ago, those men in the abandoned building by the subway."

"Where did she speak to you?"

"At my apartment. Twenty-three forty-one Lenox Avenue, fiveJ."

"There's a problem, Mr. Du Maurier. Officer Chast was found dead this morning. She was murdered."

The old man stopped rocking momentarily as his eyes went huge.

"Murdered?" he said. "What? How? By who?"

"That's what we're trying to find out," I said. "Now, specifically tell me what you talked about."

Du Maurier grabbed at his hair as he stared intensely at the cruiser's floor mat.

"Just how I saw the men sitting around the grill, about the tied-up girl. I gave her the license plate number I took down."

"Do you still have the license plate number?"

He stared at me almost fearfully.

"No. I gave her the paper I had written it on. Holy moly."

He was really tugging at his hair now. I wondered if he was going to rip some out.

"You don't think I had anything to do with her death, do you? Please, I wouldn't hurt anyone. Ask anyone. I can't believe I'm caught up in this. I was just trying to be a good citizen, a good citizen."

"It's OK. Calm down, Mr. Du Maurier," I said, patting the little old man's shoulder as he began to weep. "I just have one more question. This building where you saw the men. What's the exact address again?"

Chapter 33

THE BUILDING ON LENOX was old and crumbling and had a creepy, vaguely Gothic look to it.

Standing on the sidewalk in front of it with Doyle, I saw that instead of a front door, it had an aluminum riot door with a thick laminated steel padlock. On the hood of the rolling gate, there was a sticker with the name of the Realtor, Luminous Properties, along with a phone number. But even after two calls during which I let it ring a long time, no one picked up.

"What do you want to do now?" Doyle said, giving the steel gate a savage, frustrated kick.

"Let's use your head to bash a hole through the gate," I said as I looked up and down the block. "On second thought, let's take a walk."

We walked the two blocks back to Du Maurier's

building. My theory was that Naomi had left the man's apartment and headed straight to the abandoned building. As we walked, I searched for security cameras that might have picked Naomi up. But there was nothing. It was another dead end.

We were heading back to the abandoned building when I suddenly stopped in front of a hardware store. I stared at its plate glass uncertainly. I had an idea. But it was pretty radical even for me.

"What is it?" Doyle said. "Is your Spidey sense tingling?"

Instead of answering him, I went in. Doyle grinned from ear to ear when I came back out of the store two minutes later with a pair of eighteen-inch bolt cutters.

"I think they must have skipped this lesson at the academy," Doyle said as I knelt down at the front door of the abandoned building.

"Yeah, well," I said as the teeth of the cutters finally bit through the thick padlock. "Sometimes, Doyle, you just have to improvise."

It was surprisingly dark inside. I passed the beam of my flashlight over the ruined floors mounded with crumbled plaster and garbage and busted pipes. The heavy smell of burnt wood and rot was almost sweet.

We could hear birds flapping around on the upper floors as we came up a sketchy staircase. There was a loud, hollow rattling sound as Doyle kicked a bottle back down the stairs behind him.

"Sorry," he said sheepishly.

We walked across a dusty third-floor landing through a doorless threshold into a space that had probably been an apartment. A column of sunlight fell through a gaping hole in the structure's roof.

"This must be the room that Du Maurier saw through the hole in the roof," Doyle said as he circled the beam of light, staring up at the hole. "It lines up. I can see the windows of his building."

I looked around at the walls, the floors.

"Anything strike you as strange, Doyle?" I said.

"Just about everything," the rookie said, shrugging. "This place gives me the damn creeps."

"The floors, Doyle. Look at them."

Doyle looked down and then his eyes suddenly brightened.

"You're right. Downstairs, it's a landfill, but up here, the floors are clean. Broom-swept, looks like. Someone cleaned up this joint recently. What the hell do you think happened?"

I looked up at the column of light. As I watched,

a tiny plane high up in the blue of the sky crossed the hole in the ceiling.

"I think Naomi interviewed Du Maurier and then came here and interrupted somebody cleaning up, and it cost her her life."

Chapter 34

AS I WAS COMING back out into the bright street from the shadows of the building, I got a call from Mary Catherine. It took me by surprise. She hardly ever called me at work.

"Mike, finally I caught you," she said quickly.

There was something in her voice. She definitely sounded strange, subdued and yet sort of frantic, which was not like her at all. My adrenaline and blood pressure immediately spiked. What now? I was still as paranoid as hell about everyone's safety since my brush with the Mexican cartels.

"What is it?" I said quickly. "Is it the kids? Is everyone OK?"

"No, no. They're fine, Mike. Everyone's just fine. It's just…It's too complicated to explain over the phone. Any chance you could swing by the apartment?"

Come home? I thought, squinting. She sounded overly polite, like there was someone there with her. We had a visitor or something? I couldn't for the life of me think who it could be. And why the mystery?

"Actually, I'm kind of in the middle of something, Mary Catherine. Can it wait?" I said.

"No. You need to come home now."

"Why?" I said.

"You'll understand when you get here, Mike. Thanks. Bye now," Mary Catherine said, and hung up.

Five minutes later, I weaved through the crosstown traffic on 145th, racking my brain as to what Mary Catherine's call could possibly be about. Was it one of the kids? They were in trouble? Had Sister Sheilah, the principal of Holy Name, finally decided to make a house call? I couldn't figure it out, and not knowing was really driving me crazy.

Speaking of crazy, I was at 123rd and Amsterdam when I caught a nasty snarl of traffic caused by an almost-jackknifed eighteen-wheeler trying to back up in the middle of the avenue.

I drummed my fingers on the wheel, waiting patiently for an authority figure to arrive and resolve the bizarre traffic situation.

For about one point three seconds.

I threw the cruiser into park and got out and threaded my way forward through the maze of honking taxis and work vans. I really, *really* needed to get home to see what was going on.

"Sir!" I yelled as I got to the rumbling semi's driver-side door. "What are you doing?"

"This move is called backin' up to make a furniture delivery," the young, thin, bearded trucker said with a southern accent.

"See, there's your problem right there," I said. "This is New York City, sir. Backing up eighteen-wheelers is strictly forbidden. You need to go around the block and try it again."

"On one of these narrow side streets?" he said in dismay. "Hell, I ain't got a shoehorn for this rig. Thanks for the advice, but you need to get out of my way and let me work, friend."

"It's not advice, friend," I said, showing him my shield.

There was a cacophony of happy horn honks and applause from the backed-up traffic as the rumbling truck finally pulled away. A big Sikh taxi driver with a handlebar mustache and an orange turban leaned out of his yellow Honda Odyssey and gave me a fist bump as I walked back to my cop car.

I shook my head in wonder as I got rolling again.

I put a cartel head out of business, I get demoted. But I get a truck to move and suddenly I'm Derek Jeter?

Only in New York, I thought.

Chapter 35

ALL THE KIDS WERE in the living room when I finally burst through the apartment door. Besides Chrissy and Shawna down on their bellies by the coffee table playing Sorry!, everyone was looking shocked and subdued. Which didn't make sense, especially the subdued part.

"Guys, what is it? What's wrong?" I said.

"Mary Catherine won't tell us," Eddie said somberly.

Juliana took a break from nervously biting a thumbnail to point at the kitchen.

"They're waiting in there, Dad," she said.

They? I thought, rushing down the hall toward the kitchen.

Inside, I found two men sitting at the island as Mary Catherine poured them coffee. One was a handsome blond, blue-eyed guy in his late twenties who kind of looked like a taller, thinner version of the actor Ryan Gosling. The other one, older, balding, middle-aged, and round, wearing silver-framed eyeglasses, reminded me of Karl Rove or maybe Benjamin Franklin.

At first when I saw their dark business suits, I pegged them as cops, feds maybe, and almost passed out because what were the feds doing in my kitchen? But then I noticed how incredibly well tailored their suits were and I freaked out even more because I couldn't think who the hell they were.

"I'm Bennett. Mike Bennett," I finally spat out. "What is this? Who are you people? What's going on here?"

The two guys looked at each other; the younger blond guy blushed a little and looked down, seemingly embarrassed. Besides the actor resemblance, there was something about the guy that seemed vaguely familiar. Then the older gentleman cleared his throat as he stood and offered his hand.

"Mr. Bennett, how do you do? My name is Peter Pendleton," he said with a cultured southern accent as I halfheartedly shook his hand.

"Sorry for the intrusion," Pendleton said, smiling affably. He laid a pudgy manicured hand on the blond guy's shoulder. "Allow me to introduce my client, Robert Bieth."

"Your client?" I said, dazed.

"Yes, Mr. Bennett. I'm Mr. Bieth's lawyer," the southern gentleman said, maintaining his friendly grin. "I know this must be a bit of a surprise, but we came here today to talk to you about your daughter. About Chrissy."

"What!" I said, on the verge of passing out. "Chrissy? Why? Who are you?"

The lawyer opened his mouth. But before he could get out another word, the young blond guy suddenly stood up. There was emotion in his face now, I noticed. Instead of embarrassment, it seemed like a kind of sadness.

"Chrissy's my daughter, Mr. Bennett," he said. "I'm her father. Her real father. I came here to see my daughter."

Chapter 36

HAVING BEEN A COP in some very crazy situations before, I'm not usually the type to get that fazed by surprises. But, boy, was this one mother of an exception. I suddenly felt dizzy, like all the blood in my body was draining out of my head.

"Chrissy's father?" I said as I placed both of my hands on the cool granite of the kitchen island to keep myself upright. I stared down at the pattern in the rock, which suddenly seemed like it was moving.

"Yes, I'm her father," Bieth said, his pale-blue eyes wet now. "You think *you're* shocked? I just found out myself."

"That's enough, Robert," the lawyer, Pendleton, said quickly. "It's true, Mr. Bennett. Mr. Bieth just found out that he is Chrissy's birth father, and he has every right to see her. You can understand that, right? I believe we saw her when we came in. Could you bring her in here, please?"

I finally looked up at the pushy lawyer and his client. Then I gathered myself together and held up a hand.

"Wait," I said. "Wait one second. You come in here with all these claims and suddenly you want to see my daughter? I don't think so. I don't know you folks from a hole in the wall. That's not going to happen. And who the hell do you people think you are, showing up on my doorstep without even the courtesy of a phone call?

"You know what? Never mind. I'm going to ask you to leave. The both of you. Now."

The lawyer sighed. Bieth stood there red-faced with his mouth open, looking stunned now and quite confused. Like being told off and thrown out was a brand-new life experience for him.

"Let's go, Robert," the lawyer mumbled as he lifted the posh leather briefcase between his feet.

"He's right, Robert. Listen to your lawyer. He seems really smart," I said, crossing the kitchen and throwing open the apartment's back door.

"My apologies for the intrusion," the slick lawyer drawled as he ushered his client out the door.

Bullshit, I thought, staring at the back of the probably thousand-dollar-an-hour mouthpiece's curly gray head. I looked at his fancy briefcase, wondering what was in it. Why did I have the funny feeling that Pendleton had quite the knack for intrusion, for showing up and barging in on people with his honey drawl and his pricy briefcase and Savile Row suit to bowl them over and get them signing on the dotted line before they knew what was going on?

Out on the back landing, Pendleton rang for the freight elevator, then turned and smiled amiably again. Bieth, behind him, already had a phone out, his angry red face aimed down at the screen. He seemed overly sensitive even for today's often childish young adults. In fact, he looked like an upset overgrown baby with an electronic pacifier.

Still, I glanced at the side of Bieth's face again, at the shape of his eyes and chin, his complexion. And began panicking inside some more. Because he did look like Chrissy.

Where is this crazy thing going? I wondered.

The lawyer sighed again. Even the man's sighs seemed pleasant and civilized. I wondered if he billed extra for them.

"I just thought we'd come by on the outside

chance that you might be able to talk reasonably about the situation," Pendleton said as the freight elevator finally arrived. "But doing it the hard way, believe me, is fine, too, Mr. Bennett. You have yourself a good day, now."

My reply to the civilized gent's measured statement unfortunately wasn't as pleasant.

I slammed the back door in his face hard enough to knock the kids' pictures off the fridge.

Chapter 37

“DAD, DAD! WHAT’S UP? Who were those guys?” Eddie said, butting up against me in the hall as I headed out of the kitchen.

I could see that the rest of the kids in the living room were all sitting up straight—eyes wide, still as statues—like patients in a doctor’s waiting room about to get a painful shot. I wondered how much they had heard.

“Nobody,” I mumbled at Eddie as I gently lifted the short thirteen-year-old and moved him out of my path.

“Nobody?!” Juliana said at my back as she stood up from the couch. “Don’t lie to us, Dad. We know something’s up. Those men weren’t nobody.”

“Don’t you ‘Dad’ me,” I said, wheeling around

and stabbing a finger at my eldest daughter's surprised face.

I knew the anger that I was expressing was really just the sense of free-falling fear that I'd felt in the kitchen, growing now with each second. And yet I couldn't stop it. I was pretty much off my rocker at that point with dread and powerlessness and confusion.

"What? You guys don't have homework anymore?" I yelled at my wide-eyed children. "Get out of this living room and into your own rooms with your noses in your schoolbooks, now, every last one of you. And heaven help you if I hear a single sound!"

The kids stared at me in dead silence, then instantly scattered. Had they ever seen me so crazed? Even I knew I was being a jerk, and yet I couldn't stop myself from melting down.

"Oh, Daddy, what's wrong?" Chrissy said, suddenly next to me with tears in her eyes. "Why is everyone so upset? Why are you upset? Are you OK?"

I stared at her, at her pale-blue eyes. I swallowed, my face hot, fighting back tears. *Chrissy's father?* I thought. *Out of nowhere. How can this be happening?*

"Daddy just has a headache, kiddo," I lied as I knelt down and gave her a hug. "But he's going to get some aspirin and get better, OK? Now go find your sisters."

I felt a hand on my shoulder as I stood. It was Mary Catherine. She looked crestfallen.

"Mike, I'm so sorry about this. I was doing laundry when Joseph called from the lobby and told Bridget there were two men here to go over a case with you. She let them in, thinking they were police officers working with you. But when I came back up from the basement and they started talking about Chrissy and what adoption agency you had used, that's when I called you."

She balled her hands into fists as she stared down at the floor.

"I was an idiot. I should have thrown them out right then and there, but I wasn't sure what to do."

"It's not your fault, Mary Catherine," I said, placing a hand at the back of her neck. "That slick lawyer was definitely playing games, coming here out of the blue."

"Do you think it's true?" Mary Catherine whispered to me frantically. "Was that young man Chrissy's father?"

"I'm not sure what's going on, Mary Catherine," I said as I gave her neck a squeeze and turned. "But I'm going to get to the bottom of it right now."

Chapter 38

I WENT INTO MY bedroom and closed the door. I walked over to the small closet that I'd converted into a home office. I paused and took a breath before I opened the bottom file drawer in the desk.

And almost found myself crying again.

I looked at the neat rows of folders and paper, the color-coded cellophane tabs, scanning my dead wife's nunlike script. In addition to being the world's greatest wife and mother, Maeve had managed all our home office stuff with an iron fist, somehow never missing a trick with the credit-card bills, the kids' education stuff, all of our dental and medical records.

I let my fingers do the walking until I got to Chrissy's adoption folder and pulled it out.

Everything came back to me as I slid on a pair

of reading glasses and went through it. Chrissy's birth mother's name was Barbara Anjou, and she was a runaway from a physically and sexually abusive home in rural Pennsylvania. At the age of fourteen, she had come to New York to change her life but instead was almost immediately sucked into the world of drug addiction and prostitution.

When she found out she was pregnant at the age of eighteen, she appealed to a Catholic charity in the rough Hunts Point section of the Bronx that protected battered women. Sister Christina, the nun who ran the shelter, was a friend of the family through Seamus, and when she heard that the only thing Chrissy's mom wanted for her daughter was to be placed with the largest, most loving family possible, she gave my wife and me a call.

I'll never forget how happy the short, spunky, pregnant blond teenager seemed when she interviewed us for the first time at a Dunkin' Donuts on East Tremont Avenue. She teared up as she beamed from ear to ear, knowing that her daughter was going to have what she herself had been denied: a loving mother and father and more protective big brothers and sisters than she could count.

When we asked Barbara if she wanted an open adoption, she was vehemently against it, saying it would be better if Chrissy never knew who she was. And when we asked about the father, she said she had no idea who the father was.

Wait a second, I thought as I took off the glasses and thumbed at my eyes. That had bothered our family lawyer, Gun "Gunny" Chung, at the time, I remembered. That there was no father on the contract had really rubbed him the wrong way.

I put down the file and took out my cell phone. This was one call I really didn't want to make.

After seven rings, Chung's secretary finally picked up and told me he was in a meeting and would call me back.

Gunny, a summa cum laude graduate of Fordham Law, was a sharp-as-a-tack former federal prosecutor who did a lot of pro bono work for the New York Catholic Charities, which was where he had met and befriended Seamus. Gunny was a middle-aged, professorial Korean American gentleman who favored tweed jackets and bow ties and was just incredible with kids. My guys absolutely adored him.

Good old Gunny would figure this out for me, I thought after I hung up. Right? I certainly hoped so.

I leaned back in my creaky old office chair and

stared up at the bedroom ceiling, worrying about everything. I was still in the same position when the secretary called back.

"Mr. Chung is in the middle of a civil case, Mr. Bennett. He said he'll get back to you maybe late tomorrow or the next day. Sorry."

"Yep," I said, sitting up. "Me too."

Chapter 39

I WOKE THAT NIGHT well before dawn, at around five a.m.

At first I took a crack at falling back asleep, tried to do some deep, peaceful breathing, even got up and splashed a little cold water on the back of my neck. But after five minutes of watching the occasional headlight sweep across the ceiling of my darkened bedroom, I sat up, knowing more sleep just wasn't going to happen. Not for me. Not now. Not a chance.

I cringed as I glanced at Chrissy's adoption file still open on my desk. I was even more wrecked with worry than the moment I'd finally put my mind-blown head down on the pillow the night before. I thought about Chrissy still sleeping peacefully on the other side of the apartment, how she was always smiling and bright-eyed and spunky and open.

Then I thought of her being taken away from her sisters and brothers, of having to say good-bye to her in some courtroom, and I closed my eyes and shook my head.

As I sat there continuing to rip myself up inside with stress and worry, my little dark night of the soul was interrupted by a sound. It was a kind of whining coming from outside my door. I stood and followed it until I came to the hall bathroom. I wasn't the only one up and worrying this early, I saw as I knelt down.

It was the adorable border collie puppy I'd brought home. The cute little dummy was curled up and crying on a bunch of balled-up newspaper by the baby gate we'd put up to fence him in at night. We still hadn't decided on a name. His whines subsided as I began petting him, his fuzzy little spotted tail slapping happily against the newspaper.

"See, it's OK," I said to him. "Everything is going to be OK. I think."

When I came back into my room, holding the puppy in the crook of my arm like a baby, there was a soft flicker of light on my nightstand, followed by a chiming sound. I lifted my phone and opened the text Jimmy Doyle had just sent me.

hey boss. just spoke to du maurier the third. some new info. we may have a lead.

"What lead?" I said a moment later, after Doyle picked up his phone.

"Sorry to bother you so early," he said. "I didn't think you'd be awake."

"Neither did I," I said as the puppy started licking and then nipping at the inside of my elbow. "What's up?"

"Du Maurier called me all frantic about an hour ago. Said he's been speaking to some people on the street about the whole cannibalism thing," he said.

"And?"

"Apparently, there's a homeless guy who lives in one of the Amtrak tunnels on the West Side who said he saw the same thing as Du Maurier. A bunch of well-dressed men having a dinner party alongside the Hudson River with a tied-up girl."

"When was this?"

"About two months ago."

I thought about that. The unbidden image of Naomi slumped at her desk flashed in my mind.

"Mike, you there?" Doyle said.

"Do you have the witness's name?"

"Yeah, and a map he drew me."

"Let's do it, Doyle," I said. "We need to find this homeless guy."

"When?" Doyle said.

"Ain't no time like the present," I said, glancing at Chrissy's file again.

Chapter 40

TWO HOURS AND SEVERAL phone calls later, Doyle and I were shivering as we waited out at Broadway and 125th Street near the railroad tracks for a liaison from the Amtrak police to help us look around for our witness.

We were finishing up a couple of Green Mountain French vanillas from the BP gas station we were parked beside when a big green pickup pulled up behind our cruiser. A lanky, goateed Amtrak police officer in an olive-drab tactical uniform hopped out of the Dodge and introduced himself as Sergeant Mark Avila. Then he dropped the covered truck's tailgate and introduced his partner, a Belgian shepherd K-9 named Radar.

"My boss said this involves a murder

investigation?" Avila said as he knelt and attached a leash to Radar's harness.

I nodded grimly.

"We got a lead on a potential witness who's supposed to live in something called the Freedom Tunnel. Do you know where that is?"

Avila nodded back even more grimly.

"All too well, unfortunately. We get calls there all the time," he said.

"Where is it?" Doyle wanted to know. "I've been working in Harlem awhile, and I've never even heard of it."

Avila pointed west toward the Hudson.

"The Freedom Tunnel is what they call the Amtrak train tunnel that runs under Riverside Park from Seventy-Second to a Hundred and Twenty-Fifth," he said. "It was built in the thirties but was abandoned. That's when the homeless started moving in. People talk about the mole people under Grand Central a lot, but up until the 1990s, the Freedom Tunnel was teeming with people. It was like an underground shantytown."

"What happened in the nineties?" Doyle asked.

"They reactivated the track for the Amtrak Empire Corridor line up to Albany and kicked everybody out. Well, almost everybody. We still get reports from the drivers that they're seeing people. There must be a dozen or so of the diehard mole people still left.

"Every once in a while, we find one of them alongside the tracks hit by the train or OD'd or murdered. We can't even ID them, let alone figure out who killed them. It's like another world. Just nuts. What's this witness's name?"

Doyle trash-canned his coffee cup and took out his notes.

"They call him, um, Hamster," he said.

Avila rubbed his chin with a thumb. The shepherd, Radar, looked up at him earnestly as he snapped his fingers.

"Yeah, I know him," Avila said. "He's one of the good ones. Nutty but clean. He sells books or something on the street during the day, then comes back home into his little hobbit hole, an abandoned toolshed that he squats in near the north entrance. Guy's a trip. Has framed pictures on the walls, a La-Z-Boy, bookshelves, even a cat."

"A cat?" I said.

"Yep," Avila said. "All the comforts of home sweet home, only in a train tunnel. Like I said, nuts."

Chapter 41

WE GOT BACK INTO the Crown Vic and followed Avila's truck west underneath the West Side Highway until we were butt-up against a rusty chain-link fence. Two things were on its opposite side: train tracks and the massive clay-colored Hudson River.

We got out of our vehicle and followed the train cop and dog through litter-strewn weeds about a hundred feet along the fence until we found a hole. Hopping down through the gap, Doyle and I exchanged a skeptical glance after we viewed the opening of the train tunnel.

It was pitch black, about thirty feet wide, and completely covered in graffiti. And oh, yeah, it had train tracks sticking out of it. In a word, spooky. In another one, dangerous.

"Yo, Mark," Doyle called ahead to the Amtrak cop. "You sure this is the way? Because I think I saw this movie, dude, and it didn't end well."

"Don't tell me you're afraid of the dark," the Amtrak cop said back with a wink before he disappeared into the dark tunnel's mouth.

The tunnel was no less creepy inside, a dark and seemingly endless cave lined at intervals with piles of garbage and random objects, a tattered camp chair, a broken shovel, a toy shopping cart. Dust motes swirled in the shafts of dim light that fell down from grates high above in the twenty-foot concrete-and-steel-beam ceiling. We hugged the wall as a rumbling Amtrak diesel suddenly rolled in from the north toward Penn Station in a clatter of steel and short, amazingly loud horn blasts.

"Why do they call this hole the Freedom Tunnel?" Doyle asked Avila as the train's red devil-eye taillights disappeared around the long, dark curve ahead of us.

The train cop paused to kick a discarded sneaker out of his way.

"They named it after some graffiti artist named Freedom, I think," he said. "See the way the light from the grates hits the wall, kind of like an art gallery? He would do all these elaborate pieces there. One was a portrait of the Unabomber, if memory serves me right."

"I've always wanted one of those," Doyle said as the dog, Radar, stopped in its tracks.

The black-and-brown shepherd's sharp ears perked up, and then it suddenly swung around to the left, jumping and straining on Avila's leash as it started barking like mad.

Through the string of barks came a scraping sound in the dimness and some movement up on a cement shelf on the left-hand wall that I hadn't noticed before.

"Get down from there now! Move, move!" Doyle yelled, gun already out and trained.

Chapter 42

AVILA SWUNG HIS FLASHLIGHT and spotlit a bearded man standing on the ledge with his hands up.

"Move!" Doyle yelled again, but before the guy even had a chance to comply, Doyle did it for him. He leaped up and seized him by his lapel with his free hand and hauled him hard facedown into the gravel and cuffed him.

"What the hell, man?" the guy said, sitting up and spitting gravel as he squinted into Avila's bright flashlight.

He was a little middle-aged man. Despite his wild gray hair and *Duck Dynasty* beard, I noticed that his jeans and jean jacket and even his construction boots were newish and surprisingly clean.

"What the hell?" the mole man repeated. "What

was I doing? I wasn't doing anything. I was taking a piss. You're roughing me up and arresting me for taking a damn piss?"

Avila nudged me and nodded to indicate that the guy was Mr. Hamster in the flesh.

"Take the cuffs off him, Doyle," I said.

"What? Why?" the young cop said, still shaken from being startled.

"Just humor me, OK?" I said.

"Sorry about that," I said as I helped the man back to his feet. "You're Hamster, right? They call you Hamster?"

"Some people call me that, assholes mostly," the guy said as he haughtily brushed himself off. "But I actually have a real name like you and every other human being on this planet, if you can possibly believe it."

There was a self-assured, forthright, almost snotty tone in his voice. I thought he sounded well educated.

"What's your real name?" I tried cheerfully.

"What business would that be of yours?" he shot back.

"Is it Gollum?" Doyle mumbled from behind me.

I shot a look at Doyle.

"I'm Detective Bennett and that's Detective Doyle. We heard that two months ago you saw a dinner along the river around here, a bunch of men with a tied-up girl," I said.

The haughtiness suddenly fell from Hamster's face. He looked at us fearfully for a long second. Then he turned and looked down into the dark distance of the tunnel. After a few seconds, he began to slowly and methodically crack his knuckles one after the other, loud snaps in the dead silence of the tunnel.

"I've been down here half my life, and I never saw anything like that," he said after a while.

"What did you see?" I said.

"They ate her," he said quietly as he shuddered and looked at me sadly. "They cut her and cooked her and ate her up."

Chapter 43

WE CONVINCED HAMSTER TO walk back out into the daylight and take a ride with us to show us where he had seen the men.

"So, tell me, um, Hamster," Doyle said as we rolled east toward Broadway in the Crown Vic. "You seem like a pretty informed person. Why the, uh, um, living underground thing?"

"You read the, uh, um, paper?" Hamster replied as he stared out the window.

"Not today's," Doyle said.

"How about in general?" Hamster said.

"Yes, I read the paper. Online mostly these days. Why?" Doyle said, looking back at him.

"You ever think with all that's going on today in this sick-and-getting-sicker society that the better question might be why do you live *above*ground?" he said.

Without further ado, Hamster directed us forty blocks downtown, to Seventy-Second, at the other end of the Freedom Tunnel. We rolled over a curb onto a Riverside Park path and down under the steel arches of the raised West Side Highway to a green space along the Hudson.

I couldn't believe what I was seeing as I waited for Avila and Radar to park beside us. Down here under the highway, they'd managed to tuck in a brand-new, elaborate park with basketball courts and baseball fields and a bike path. I'd lived and worked in New York my whole life—actually lived only about twenty blocks away—and had never even heard of this place, or the Freedom Tunnel, for that matter. This city never failed to surprise.

Hamster got out of the car, his big eyes blinking through the tangled gray mop of his hair as he looked around. We listened to the cooing of pigeons nesting in the crevices of the raised roadbed above as we waited.

"This way," he finally said.

We followed him across the baseball field and the bike path and stood right beside the lapping shore of the Hudson. Above some anchored white sailboats bobbing on the dark, choppy water, rose-gold sunlight glinted off a glass high-rise on the New Jersey shore. It was quite pleasant and peaceful along the shore with the wind blowing.

"There!" Hamster yelled, pointing north a couple of hundred feet to a fenced gap in the pale curve of the stone riprap that edged the shore.

We walked over along the path and then made a left over the jagged rocks toward the rusted fence. Behind it, between the rocks, was the concrete base of an old pump house. With one edge of it open to the water, it looked like a little dock.

A perfect place to party, hidden from the path, with a water view, I thought. And a well-used one, judging by the broken beer bottles and used condoms and trash and burn marks that covered the area.

"This is where they were," Hamster said. "It was the middle of the night, and they had a grill with them, and they sat there on folding chairs like it was a picnic."

"A grill?" Doyle said.

"A charcoal grill, swear to God," Hamster said.

"Could you identify these people if you saw them again?" I said.

"No, it was too dark, and I was too far away to

see faces. Just what they did. I thought they were going to rape her at first, but this was way worse."

And you didn't call the cops why? I thought but didn't say.

"Detective, I think they found a body around here," Avila said, looking around. "About two months ago. Badly burned, in a suitcase, of all things."

"Did you guys find it?" I said to Avila.

"No, you did, I think. NYPD. They mentioned it at dispatch."

Doyle and I looked at each other.

"Midtown South, probably?" Doyle said.

"Probably," I said.

"I need to get out of here," Hamster finally said, cracking his knuckles again as he started climbing back up the rocks toward the bike path. "You can arrest me if you want, but I need to get the hell away from here now."

Chapter 44

THE NEXT DAY WAS Naomi's wake.

Mary Catherine and I had been scrambling on such short notice to set it up. Not only did it turn out that Naomi's only family, her stepmother, Monica McKeon-Chast, lived in South Florida, but the poor sixty-something had stage-four bladder cancer. I'd offered to somehow transport the body down to the feisty retired RN, but she wouldn't hear of it.

Naomi's life was being a cop, she had told me in one of our several phone conversations. "She'd never forgive me if she wasn't buried in New York City."

I didn't have the heart to tell Monica how completely crappy the department was being to Naomi. My request for an honor guard, standard operating procedure for an in-the-line-of-duty death, had been flatly denied. The department, aka Starkie, was still treating the whole thing as a suicide.

Which was a complete disgrace. But then again, so was Starkie.

Mary Catherine and I arrived early at Riverside Funeral Home on Amsterdam Avenue, carrying two large flower arrangements. Needing all the help we could get, we'd also brought along Jane and Juliana, whom I'd taken out of school for the day. The girls had been up late arranging a collage of pictures of Naomi that we had gathered from her apartment. Naomi with her college volleyball team, at the beach, at barroom birthday parties, her police academy photo. The girls had scanned them all onto a laptop and set it all to music, and it had come out amazing. They had really stepped up in trying to give poor Naomi a loving memorial. I couldn't have been prouder of them.

We met director John Harrison in the somber, tasteful space's carpeted hall, and he led us into the wood-paneled room where Naomi's closed coffin had already been set up. After we placed the flowers behind it, I walked around with Mary Catherine and crossed myself as we knelt.

"I'm going to find the people who did this to

you, Naomi," I whispered into the steeple of my fingers after my prayers.

I was setting up the In Loving Memory cards by the sign-in book when Arturo texted me that he had just picked up Naomi's stepmother, Monica, from LaGuardia.

What? She isn't due for at least another hour!

I looked at my watch and stared at the rows of still-empty seats and went into full-blown panic mode.

Where the heck is everybody?

This situation was depressing enough. No way could we have this dying woman see her dead stepdaughter's coffin in an empty room.

Mary Catherine and I started calling people, everyone, anyone. I called up the Harlem crew, Miriam Schwartz, several old partners. Since this was a three-alarm Catholic emergency, I got the Holy Name principal, Sister Sheilah, on the phone and told her the situation and hung up and called Seamus.

"Father, listen," I said when he picked up. "I need help. I need a bagpiper yesterday. Riverside Funeral Home, Amsterdam Avenue."

"Done. I know just the man," Seamus said without missing a beat.

I could have kissed Brooklyn when she arrived ten minutes later with Robertson and seven other cops from the Twenty-Eighth Precinct, all of them in dress uniform. Right behind her was Doyle in a suit and tie with his pretty blond wife, Erin, and three couldn't-be-cuter miniature Doyles in little suits.

I went out the funeral home's open doors when I heard a shriek of metal, just in time to see Sister Sheilah getting off the Holy Name school bus with Eddie's entire seventh-grade class. Behind the bus stopped a taxi, and out popped Seamus and Rory Murphy, one of Seamus's drinking buddies, carrying an accordion.

"An accordion?" I whispered to Seamus as I spotted Arturo and Naomi's stepmother turning the corner. "I said a bagpiper, old man! A bagpiper!"

"Ya gave me fifteen holy minutes' notice!" Seamus cried as Rory started up "Amazing Grace" right there on the sidewalk. "You're lucky it's not that Times Square Naked Cowboy fella in his skivvies!"

Chapter 45

AFTER THE BURIAL THE next day, we had a little gathering at a place I loved called Emmett O'Lunney's Irish Pub, near Times Square on Fiftieth between Eighth and Broadway. We almost knocked down the proprietor, Emmett, an old Bennett family friend, carrying a case of wine past the spacious restaurant's wood-paneled foyer.

"Mike Bennett?!" ever-friendly Emmett said with a wide smile and a wink. "Where have you been hiding yourself? I was going to put out an APB on you. I haven't seen you in what? A year? You're not cheating on me with another bar, are you? No, wait, you're on the wagon?"

"Emmett. What kind of Irishman do you take me for? No and heck no," I said. "It's a . . . well . . . a long story. Suffice it to say, I'm back now, and I'll be more than glad to help you get rid of a little Guinness back inventory."

Emmett's dark-haired beauty of a wife, Debbie, was behind the bar pouring me a perfect pint when my phone rang. It was a call I'd been dreading. It was my family lawyer, Gunny Chung, calling me back.

"Mike, haven't heard from you in too long," Gunny said in his calm, kind voice as I went outside to take his call. "How is everyone? How's Seamus and the kids? Have you driven off that saintly young lady, Mary Catherine, yet?"

"Not a chance, Gunny. Forgive me for getting right to the point, but I have a problem. It has to do with Chrissy's adoption. I had a visit at the apartment last Wednesday from two men, a young guy and his lawyer. The young guy claims to be Chrissy's father."

"Hmmm," Gunny said after a long pause. "What did they want?"

"The man said he wanted to see Chrissy," I said. "He said he had just found out that he was the father and that he had a right to see her."

"What did you say?" Gunny asked.

"What do you think?" I said. "I said I don't know you from Adam and get the hell out of my house. I mean, these people are off base here, right? I went through Chrissy's file. All the *t*'s are crossed and the *i*'s are dotted on the adoption contract. We're good, right?"

"Let me ask you something," Gunny said after another thoughtful pause. "Do you think the guy could have been her biological father?"

"Well, actually, yeah," I said. "He's blond and he does look like her. Does it matter? This guy doesn't have a claim for custody here, does he? I mean, coming here after all this time, for heaven's sake?"

"Well," Gunny said. "Probably not, probably not."

"Probably? What do you mean, Gunny? Help me here. Please, I'm going nuts."

"Adoption disputes by birth parents after the fact are usually thrown out, Mike," he said. "But there have been a few very special instances in which the birth parents have won custody. Do you remember the Baby Jessica and Baby Richard cases from the nineties?"

"No," I said. "Refresh my memory."

"Well, in both cases, custody motions were filed by biological fathers who claimed they had never been made aware of the adoption. That's why back when you and Maeve adopted Chrissy, I wasn't pleased that we never received information about Chrissy's birth father. Getting the birth father to sign away his rights is the first thing that needs to get done—so that a situation just like this can never come up."

I closed my eyes.

"So you're saying, worst-case scenario, this guy might have a claim?"

"Unlikely, but I won't lie, Mike. It's possible."

"How did the Baby Jessica and Baby Richard cases turn out?"

"In each case, the birth father won, Mike," he said quietly. "The children were taken away from the adoptive families."

Chapter 46

AMONG A CLATTER OF plates and some amped-up Irish music, Alberto Witherspoon sat in the restaurant part of O'Lunney's among the Times Square tourists, watching the cops at the bar.

When he'd heard the joint's name from their contact, he'd thought it would be some Hell's Kitchen old man bar, but it was actually very nice, clean lines and bright, shining wood and jazzy sconces and chandeliers. And the food was terrific. Even though it was well past noon, he'd ordered the all-day Traditional Irish Breakfast of bangers, rashers, baked beans, eggs, grilled tomato, and black and white puddings. He poured some HP Sauce, this bottled brown Irish ketchup stuff that was on the table, all over his black pudding and took a bite.

Amazing. Just what the doctor ordered. He must have been Irish in another life.

It was too bad he wasn't there to give a Yelp review.

Overall, it looked good for them, he thought. He'd already been to the cop's burial. It had been a pitiful turnout, really. No family to speak of and only a few cops. Definitely not the tear-jerking lines of cops you'd see if they thought the female cop had been shot in the line of duty. He'd thought maybe more NYPD would show up at the after-gathering, but again, pathetic. Naomi Chast had been one big fat zero as a human being.

Which was ironic, considering the struggle the little bitch had put up when he jumped her with the chloroform in the Lenox Avenue house. She'd bitten him in the hand and kneed him pretty good in the family jewels. When she'd finally gone out, he had taken her gun and waited for her partner, cursing himself for not locking the gate from the inside while he cleaned up. But after another couple of minutes, he'd realized there was no partner, no backup.

The suicide idea had been the boss's call after Alberto had read him the personnel file they had gotten from their guy in the mayor's office. The copette was half a wing nut, apparently, already unstable. All it took when he finally got her back to her apartment at 3 a.m. that morning was to forcibly sit her tight little ass down at her desk, hand in hand with her service weapon, and give her a little push.

He was going over that memory again and again, sipping the last of his Irish coffee, when his Galaxy smartphone jingled.

And? was the text from the boss.

Alberto looked back over at the bar, at five measly cops gathered together to mourn the loss of Naomi Chast. Two of them were watching last night's Yankees game while another one looked like he was playing Angry Birds on his phone. They looked bored.

Long live the memory of Naomi Chast. Or maybe not.

We're good to go, Alberto leisurely texted back.

A guy bumped into him in the joint's front vestibule as he was leaving, brown-haired white guy, tall, decent shoulders, forty or so.

"Jeez, sorry, buddy. Didn't see you there," the guy said affably, patting him on the shoulder.

It was one of Naomi's cop buddies from the burial, Alberto realized. He reminded Alberto of an armored-car guard he had smoked in San Francisco in the early '90s. The same deep, almost royal-blue eyes and Dudley Do-Right look on his pale, chiseled face. Alberto hated cops. It would be a pleasure to send this one to the great beyond, too.

Part Three

BACK ON THE BEAT

Chapter 47

A MESSAGE TO CALL Chief of Detectives Ray Starkie was on my cluttered desk when I came in on Monday morning. I decided to answer it. Reluctantly.

"Bennett here," I said.

"I want you in my office today at ten," Starkie said, none too happy sounding. "You got it? Ten a.m. My office. This is not a request."

"What's this about?" I said. "Am I going to need a union rep? What the hell is it about?"

"Ten a.m."

I decided to take Doyle downtown with me. If I was going to be ambushed or reprimanded by Starkie on some trumped-up garbage, I figured at least I'd have a witness along.

But there was a surprise waiting for me when I got off the elevator on Headquarters' dreaded tenth floor. A good one, for a change. I smiled. *Every dog really does have its day, after all,* I thought as I came down the corridor.

Beside Starkie's office door, in a conference room, I spotted Starkie with a small crowd of people sitting at a table. I was smiling because of some of the friendly faces I'd spotted in the crowd. One of them was my old boss, Miriam Schwartz, who gave me a wink. And another one was the police commissioner, Ricky Filkins.

I really was overjoyed to see Filkins. We went way back. The short, pugnacious, legendary cop had been my first precinct commander when I was a rookie in the early '90s. The ex-marine lieutenant and Vietnam vet was a cop's cop, tough and demanding but fair. He, too, had a huge family—seven kids. We'd tipped back more than a few together in Upper East Side bars on St. Paddy's Days over the years.

I'm usually not one for kissing butt and taking advantage of the whole friends-in-high-places thing, but in this case, with Starkie gunning to make my work life a living hell, I quickly decided to make an exception.

I walked around the table and greeted the commissioner warmly.

"Well, look what the cat dragged in," the square-jawed, flattopped Filkins said, smiling widely as he gripped my hand like a vise. "Heard you did good things out in California, Mike. Making the department look good even in exile, huh?"

"Ah, you're making me blush, boss," I said. "It was nothing. I mean, somebody had to show the feds what to do, right?"

"Who's this?" Filkins said, gesturing behind me to Doyle, who looked like I'd just transported him to the top of Mount Olympus.

"This is my partner from the ombudsman squad, Jimmy Doyle."

"The ombudsman squad. Yeah, I heard about your new assignment," Filkins said, glancing across the glossy table at Starkie, who had taken the opportunity to thumb at an imaginary spot on his tie.

"You must be an impressive young investigator, son," Filkins said as Doyle shook his hand. "I know Mike Bennett, and I know he doesn't truck with any dead weight."

"I, uh, try, sir," Doyle managed to spit out.

"Well, sit, gentlemen, please," Filkins said, offering us the seats on his right. "Unfortunately, Mike, we're going to be reassigning you again," the commissioner said after we were settled. "That's the reason I had Chief Starkie call you in. Something's come up, a real pain in my ass that I need you on."

Miriam cleared her throat.

"You're going to be loaned back to Major Crimes, Mike. Starting now," she said.

"Major Crimes?" I said, taking the opportunity to turn and look at Starkie.

There have been many times in my life when I've been overcome with the irresistibly joyful urge to give somebody the finger. But getting to watch Starkie sit meekly in his seat like a neutered dog as I sat there smiling at him was an even more exquisite pleasure.

"Miriam will fill you in on the deets. We need you ramped up to speed pronto, Mike. What do you say? You want your old desk back?"

"You know me, Commissioner," I said as I smiled again at Starkie. "I'm always here to do whatever the department needs me to do."

Chapter 48

AFTER THAT UNEXPECTEDLY awesome departmental meeting, I shook the commish's hand one last time and quickly headed with Doyle and Miriam Schwartz out of Starkie's office for the Major Crimes Division's new digs down on the fifth floor.

"Miriam, I love you," I said as I briefly embraced my loyal lady boss in the elevator. "I'm not kidding. Call your husband, Daniel, and tell him you're sorry but your thirty years plus together just isn't going to cut it. You've found another man."

"Yeah, well, you *should* love me, Mike," the stylish, affable, silver-haired sixty-year-old said, smiling, as she stiff-armed me away. "Favors don't come cheap when that shark Starkie is involved, believe me."

"You've been working behind the scenes, haggling on my behalf the whole time, haven't you?" I said. "And here I thought all rabbis had to be men."

"Can the blarney charm cease forthwith before I change my mind, would you please, Mike?" she said with a laugh. "This is going to cost you more than words, words, words. I want dinner, and not potluck back at that Upper West Side shoe you live in with all those kids, either. I'm thinking you need to help me brush up on my French after what I just pulled. You know, words like *Per Se* or *Jean-Georges?*"

Major Crimes' office space was brand-new. Fresh white paint on the walls, glass-partitioned offices. In all the cubicles were new computers and sleek blond-wood desks and even those futuristic ergonomic chairs. I couldn't wait to park my butt in one and get to work.

We went into Miriam's glass fishbowl office and I sat on a leather couch next to Doyle. The full-length window by my elbow had a spectacularly dramatic view of the low neon sprawl of Chinatown. I smiled down at the familiar vista as Miriam lifted a fat file off a conference table in the corner and came back.

"Catch," she said as she dropped it in my lap.

There were photos in the folder. The first one showed the inside of a small store. By its front door was a horseshoe of glass-and-wood display cases, each and every one of them smashed to smithereens. Shattered bits of glass carpeted the floor next to an overturned advertising sign that had sparkling diamond earrings over a caption that said, *How Badly Do You Want to Play Golf This Weekend?*

"I see," I said, sitting up. "So this is about that jewelry heist out in Brooklyn?"

"Did you see that act of deduction, Officer Doyle?" Miriam said. "Observe closely, young man, and maybe one day you, too, will make detective first grade."

Chapter 49

"YES, MIKE, IT'S ABOUT the jewelry heist," Miriam continued, "except you got the noun form wrong. It's not jewelry store heist singular. It's jewelry store heists plural."

"How many have there been?" I said, shuffling through the photos.

"Four, we think. But it could be as many as seven. We looked at the usual suspects, Mob crews and high-end-robbery guys who might have gotten out of prison recently, but no go. These guys are new, and they're fast. They got in and out in about three minutes. We got there in five, and there wasn't the slightest trace of them."

"But what's the major problem?" I said, showing her the shot of the trashed store. "I mean, this is bad and all, but this store isn't exactly

Tiffany's, is it? Aren't these people just a bunch of smash-and-grabbers?"

"We think smashing the cases was a front. What we left out of the paper was that in the back of the store at the time of the robbery was the owner's brother-in-law, a clerk from a ritzy Madison Avenue designer-jewelry shop who'd stopped in to get some pieces reset. The thieves put a gun to his head and walked out with a briefcase with almost a million in diamonds and black pearls."

"Not bad for three minutes' work," Doyle said.

"If you can get it," I said.

"Oh, they get it, Mike. And they're damn good, too. In the last six months, they hit two places out in Jersey and one in Greenwich, Connecticut."

"How do you know they're the same people?"

"The same way you know it's Mozart playing on the radio," she said. "The excellence in execution. These guys are real craftsmen. In Connecticut, they bypassed alarms and actually busted a safe after they defeated motion and light detectors and a fifty-thousand-dollar glass security door. And we have no leads. The commissioner is under enormous pressure with the upcoming Midtown diamond show. Merchants are coming in from all over the world, France, Russia, Antwerp."

"Not exactly the best time to have a crew of mysterious, highly professional jewel thieves picking up steam, is it?" Doyle said.

"No, it isn't," Miriam agreed.

"And I'm supposed to catch them, huh?" I said, piecing through the evidence. "Mike Bennett to the rescue?"

"In two weeks or head back to the ombudsman office."

"For real?" I said.

She nodded.

"That's the deal I cut for you. It's not the best, Mike, but even a rabbi like me can only do so much. What did you do to Starkie, anyway? That guy really freaking hates you."

"Long story," I said.

"And how ironic. Here we are without any time," Miriam said. "So what's it going to be, Mike? Are you going to catch these guys for me or what?"

I flipped through the file some more. Then I put it down and stood and stared out the window at Chinatown for a moment, the swirl of traffic, the bright Chinese signs beside the gray tenement fire escapes.

"After all you've done for me, Miriam?" I finally said, grinning at her. "It's the least I could do. After all, diamonds are a girl's BFF, right?"

Chapter 50

YOUNG DOYLE WAS uncharacteristically demure and silent and looking none too happy as I drove him back uptown toward Harlem later that afternoon.

"Come on, Doyle, just say it," I said as I weaved around a cackling, shirtless homeless guy doing jumping jacks in the middle of the intersection of Spring Street and the Bowery.

"Say what?" he said.

"How pissed you are that I'm abandoning the ombudsman squad ship."

"Well," Doyle mumbled from where he was scrunched up against the door, "you said it, not me."

"Come on, Doyle, you heard what Miriam said. A new senior supervising detective will be reporting for ombudsman duty first thing tomorrow morning."

"Oh, a new one? Great. The fifth one this month. That's just dandy," Doyle said. "Pardon me for not partaking in your hopeful optimism there, Mike. You were the only one to ever even attempt to lift a finger to get the unit to do something useful. And here I was getting psyched because we were actually doing some investigating. What an idiot."

I did feel pretty bad for the kid. He was a good, talented, hardworking cop. I remembered what it was like trying to make the leap from patrol, how difficult it was to find a challenging investigative gig.

"Come on," I tried. "Never say never. They could send somebody good."

"Yeah, right," Doyle said. "Believe me, tomorrow morning some ass-covering lifer is going to get in there and go into that office, close the blinds, and bust out a pillow. It's going to be nothing other than Harlem situation back to normal, straight back to all screwed up."

My phone rang. It was a number I didn't recognize, and I was going to let it go until I realized with a cold jolt that I did recognize it.

It was the number of Holly Jacobs, the lovely

Harlem woman who was being stalked by her psychopathic boyfriend.

I fumbled Accept and stuck the phone up to my ear.

"Holly? I'm here. It's Mike Bennett. Are you there? What's up?" I said.

There was silence on the line. I checked to see that the connection was still good and was putting the phone back to my ear when she spoke, her tense, terrified voice barely higher than a whisper.

"He's here," she said. "In the hall right outside my apartment's front door. Help me, please. God help me. I don't want to die."

I gunned it north up to Holly's apartment. I slalomed through the logjam of Midtown midday traffic with the siren blazing while Doyle worked the phone, calling the other members of the ombudsman unit and the local precinct.

We got to 116th and Morningside Park in what had to be a record-breaking twenty minutes. Two precinct cars and an unmarked were already double-parked out in front of Holly's building.

Please, God, let this lady be OK, I thought as I screeched up beside them and hurried in with Doyle.

"Hey! What is this? What the hell is this?" some

officious silver-haired Hispanic guy in the middle of the lobby, holding a little yelping black dog, wanted to know. "I'm the super. Who the hell are you people?"

I didn't have time to explain, so I just juked around him and took the stairs two at a time. When I reached the top landing and heard the radio chatter and saw a bunch of uniformed cops and Arturo Lopez and Brooklyn Kale standing in the hall out in front of Holly's apartment, my heart sank. I thought, *That's it. I'm too late. She's dead.*

But I was wrong.

Thank goodness.

Holly came out of her apartment a second later with a bulging garment bag and a set of keys. They jangled in her shaking hand as she attempted to lock her apartment door.

"Holly," I said gently, taking her keys and locking the door for her. "Thank God you're OK. What happened?"

"I'd just come home and was putting on some pasta when I heard something at the front door, like some rattling and clicks at the lock."

"There's some scrapes near the keyhole," Arturo said, nodding. "Someone was definitely messing with it."

"Then I saw the knob turn," Holly said, "and I knew it was Roger. That's when I ran into the bedroom and called you. I can't take this anymore. I'm going to my sister's in Maryland for a few days—maybe longer, who knows? My nerves are shot."

"You see anyone?" I said to Arturo and Brooklyn.

"We just missed him," Brooklyn said. "We were the first ones here, and when we were coming up the stairs, we heard running footsteps and then the alarm on the roof door went off. I went up there and looked around, but all the roofs on this entire block are connected, with plenty of fire escapes to get down to the street."

"See, he's still out there," Holly said. "I need to get out of here before this man kills me."

"We're going to find him, Holly, OK?" I said. "We're getting closer. We just missed him this time."

"And he just missed me, too. I need to get to the train station. Please, someone help me catch my train."

Chapter 51

BACK DOWNSTAIRS ON THE sidewalk, we watched Holly drive off in a cruiser with a couple of uniforms for Penn Station. I was glad to see her go. She was smart to get out of town for a while. This nut, Roger, who was stalking her wasn't just slippery, I thought, scanning the benches and trees of Morningside Park across the street. He truly seemed quite determined to do her some harm.

"So, Mike, you want to tell them the big news or shall I?" Doyle said glumly.

"What news?" said Arturo.

"Well, it seems like the powers that be are transferring me to a different squad," I said sheepishly.

"What?" said Arturo in dismay. "But you just got here! And we're actually starting to make this team work for once, really starting to help the people in this community."

"Where are you going?" Brooklyn said.

"Back down to One Police Plaza. My old squad. Major Crimes," I said.

"They want him on that diamond heist that happened out in Brooklyn," Doyle said.

"Oh, I see," Brooklyn said. "The real powers that be in the city, i.e., the rich and fabulous, need the department's top DT to watch their family jewels. Meanwhile, the Hollys of the world are off fending for themselves, running for their lives."

As with Doyle, I couldn't blame Arturo and Brooklyn for being pissed. In the brief time I'd spent with these misfit young cops, we'd already developed some pretty special chemistry, become a pretty effective, tight-knit team.

"And what about Chast's murder?" Arturo said. "You said we're the ones who need to find her killer, that she was one of ours. You think some new guy coming in is going to let us continue her investigation?"

"Well, being back to Major Crimes is actually good news on that front," I argued. "I'll be able to facilitate any new information or leads between you guys and the Major Crimes Division detectives who caught the case."

They didn't seem like they were buying it. They stood there staring at me, sour and upset. I stared back, not knowing what to say. Though I wanted my desk back at Major Crimes more than anything, in the end my Catholic guilt got the best of me. What else was new?

"Fine, you win. OK. Let me make a phone call," I said as I headed for my cruiser.

"To who?" Brooklyn said.

"Don't worry about it," I said. "Just keep your eyes peeled for Roger Dodger, you pains-in-my-butt."

Miriam answered the phone as I sat down behind the wheel.

"Hey, Miriam. It's Mike. Quick question. Is there any way you can delay the new ombudsman unit supervisor, say, a week?"

"Why? What's up?"

"I still have a couple of cases outstanding up here that I'd like to get a crack at closing before I leave."

"Does this mean you want off the diamond heist?"

"Hell, no," I said. "I'll do both."

"Both?" she said. "Aren't you biting off a heck of a lot here? I don't have to tell you how hot this diamond case is. You're going to be busier than a one-armed wallpaper hanger."

I'll be busy, all right, I thought. I didn't even mention the personal stuff going on with my daughter Chrissy.

"I got this, Miriam. Trust me. I won't let you down, I promise," I said.

"Well, if that's what you want, Mike," Miriam finally said. "It's your blood pressure."

Chapter 52

THE REST OF THE afternoon we spent scouring southwest Harlem for Roger. We hit several parks, showed his picture around to a few soup kitchens and food banks. But we came up empty again. It was quickly becoming a bad theme.

When I finally opened my apartment door, I would have loved to tuck in the little guys, but it was almost ten o'clock, and they were all fast asleep. I stood for a moment in the hallway outside the darkened girls' room anyway, staring at Chrissy sleeping in her bottom bunk, which was plastered with stickers of rainbows and hearts and bunnies. Chrissy and her bunnies. There was a poster on the wall above her with a baby bunny on its back sticking out of a teacup.

I hadn't heard anything further from the guy

claiming to be her father or from his fussy lawyer. I wondered if that was a good thing. Maybe I'd catch a much-needed break and they would just go away. Fat chance, but who knew? I was about due for a miracle after the last couple of crazy hectic days.

As I softly closed the girls' door, I could see Mary Catherine down the hall, filling the dishwasher, then bending to the Herculean task of charging our family's impressive array of electronic devices and phones. The Energizer Bunny had nothing on MC, the way she was always busy keeping everything together—the apartment, the kids, not to mention yours truly.

I remembered it then. A promise that I needed to keep. As Mary Catherine opened a cabinet and started lining up lunch bags on the counter, I stood in the hall and took out my wallet and my cell phone.

"La Grenouille," said a butter-smooth French-laced voice in my ear a moment later.

I'm about as far from a gourmet as most cops get, but even I knew that La Grenouille was one of the last great classic French restaurants in NYC. Kissinger ate there. The megafinancier Henry Kravis. Under normal circumstances, I wouldn't have dreamt of attempting to get a reservation on short notice.

But being an NYPD detective is a weird job that sometimes comes in pretty handy.

"Hello, may I please speak to Claude Pétain?" I said, reading the name off the tattered business card I'd pulled from the back of my wallet.

"Speaking. May I help you?"

"I don't know if you remember me, Claude, but I'm Detective Mike Bennett. I worked a case at your restaurant about a year ago when one of your elderly waiters passed away."

"Oh, yes. Old Paul Tristan. I remember," he said. "When we suggested that he might think about retiring, the old Basque said that the restaurant was his life and that we would have to carry him out. And wouldn't you know, he got his wish in the middle of lunch service.

"I do remember you, Detective, as well as your extreme discretion at removing the body so as not to alarm our patrons. It was well appreciated. It still is. What can I do for you? Is there some kind of problem?"

"No, not exactly. I'm in a bind with a lady friend to whom I promised a very special night out, and I was wondering if I might appeal to you for some assistance. There wouldn't be any way for me to score a reservation there, say, this Friday? I know it's very short notice."

"I see," Claude said neutrally. "Let me check. One moment, please."

I sweated it out as I waited a full minute, then two. La Grenouille on short notice? It was a stupid idea. Who did I think I was? Donald Trump?

Finally, Claude got back on the line.

"How does nine-thirty work, Detective?"

Magnifique, I thought as I looked down the hall, imagining Mary Catherine in a little black dress.

"That would be terrific, Claude," I said quickly. "I really can't thank you enough."

Chapter 53

THE BRAKES ON THE massive, dusty twenty-six-ton Mack dump truck whined like a starving mutt as it swung off West Street onto Battery Place.

It was fifteen minutes past noon and down here at the southern tip of Manhattan, office workers in search of lunch were spilling out of the megalithic glass-and-limestone financial buildings onto the narrow, slotlike streets like a body bleeding out.

Looking out at the crowds through his dark shades, the dump truck driver thought how nice it would be to park and while away the lunch hour trying to pick up one of the tight-skirted money honeys clopping past at the light. Even dressed like Bob the Builder, with a quick flash of his dimples and his born pickup artist's silver tongue, he knew it wouldn't take an hour before he would have some stupid, starry-eyed young working gal giving up her name, her phone number, her heart.

A horn blast behind him redirected his attention to the now-green light. He shifted his mean machine into first and let off the clutch and made another rumbling left onto Greenwich Street.

Rolling off Greenwich at Trinity Place along the left-hand side of the congested street, he began to see construction vehicles, flatbeds packed with rebar and big dump trucks like the one he was driving. The construction vehicles were for the One World Trade Center site, the so-called Freedom Tower, which was being built to replace the Twin Towers knocked down on 9/11.

The area was chock-full of American history, the driver knew. Of course 9/11, duh. But there was Trinity Church on the right, where George Washington went to church after his inauguration, and Zuccotti Park a couple of blocks ahead, where those Occupy Wall Street zeros gathered to defecate on a cop car.

The do-or-die part came as he was crossing Rector Street. Come hell or high holy water, he needed to park this monster somewhere between Rector and Thames in the next five minutes. He was running out of block and was thinking, schedule or not, he had no option but to go all the way around again, when a mail truck suddenly pulled out.

Immediately, he hit the screeching brakes and swung left, almost smushing a moped messenger against a Lincoln Town Car. But at the last possible second, he made it. He drove the bad-boy oversize Tonka toy into the parking spot and up over the curb and down and stopped with a mighty clanking thump.

He leaned out the driver's window and glanced forward at a navy-blue awning with gold lettering on the sidewalk fifteen feet ahead.

It couldn't have been a more perfect setup. He'd nailed it. In another minute, it would all be going down.

Chapter 54

HE TURNED TO THE man in the passenger seat beside him. Like him, the man was wearing a traffic vest over faded green coveralls and had on dark wraparound sunglasses under a bright-yellow hard hat.

"Not bad, huh, Slick? I love it when a goddamn plan comes together," the driver said.

"Amen," Slick said without looking up from his phone.

Honcho didn't have to look at its screen to know that Slick was playing the vintage computer game Minesweeper. It had been an unquenchable obsession of his math-loving nutball of a friend ever since college. Slick played it faster and better than anyone Honcho'd ever seen, adding numbers and planting flags and uncovering tiles faster than a teenage girl texting her BFF, turning calculated guessing into some kind of fricking art form.

Glancing at him now, Honcho felt like reaching out and palming his buddy's forehead to see if it was heating up like the back of an overworked computer server. But what was really funny was the brainiac didn't look or act like a nerd. In fact, the six-foot-one, dark, handsome stud got almost as much tail as Honcho himself when he was in the mood. Almost.

Honcho scanned the sidewalk. Suits, some hard hats, a fat guy in chef's whites curbing a stack of greasy cardboard boxes out in front of an Irish pub. Geeks, geeks, and more geeks. Excellent. All quiet on the southern Manhattan front. At least so far.

Honcho lifted his radio.

"Beast? You around? Come in, Beast. Where are you, baby?"

Before he could even lower the Motorola, the passenger door popped open and an XXL son of a bitch dressed exactly like Honcho and Slick shoved his bulky mass inside.

"You rang?" Beast said with a goofy gap-toothed grin as he clapped Honcho a nuclear-bomb high five that stung his palm even through the thick canvas of his work glove.

Honcho smiled, as he always did upon meeting his perpetually fired-up, massive friend. And why wouldn't he? He had once seen his steroid-addicted buddy lift a thirty-pound sledgehammer off the ground by the end of its handle like it was a Wiffle ball bat. To sum up: Beast was good to have around.

Beast was as retardedly strong as Slick was nerdily smart and as Honcho himself was, well, Honcho. Even after all this time, they were still the goddamn dream team. They had been working their way up to this, circling and closing like sharks around a particularly fat and juicy seal. Now they were here—Manhattan. New York, New York, aka the promised land. The boys were most definitely back in town.

"Everything's ready?" Honcho said to Beast as Slick retreated into the cab's rear and slid on the backpack.

"We're good to go, man. What are we waiting for?" Beast said, bouncing in his seat like the muscled-up three-hundred-pound four-year-old that he was.

"No problems, you're positive?" Honcho said again.

"I look unsure to you?" Beast said, glaring at him now over the top of his Wayfarers. "I mean, I could screw something up on purpose just to make you feel better if you want, Honcho."

"Hit it!" Slick said. "What are we waiting for? It's time."

Honcho closed his eyes, drinking in the anticipation until he was about to pass out.

Then he hit the bulky plastic switch duct-taped to the Mack truck's dashboard and threw open the door.

Chapter 55

BILLOWING BLACK SMOKE WAS already pouring out from underneath the hood of the dump truck by the time the three men hit the sidewalk. In a dozen quick steps, they were under the navy-blue awning, knocking on the thick glass of the door.

"Help, please! My rig's burning and my buddy's in there! Oh, man, help! Anyone, please! He's dying!" Honcho yelled at the security guard on the other side of the glass-and-wrought-iron door.

Honcho had his hands on the side of his head, his face a perfect mask of agonized concern. Sometimes when he was in the groove, even Slick and Beast, who damn well knew better, found themselves believing the bullshit Honcho was slinging.

The guard was a big, mean-looking old white guy with a silver flattop, a crackerjack Clint Eastwood type. His name was Terence Francis Burns, Honcho knew from his research. The sixty-two-year-old hard-ass was an ex-marine and ex-NYPD cop who still ran five miles a day.

"Dude, help, please! He's dying in there! Oh, shit! It's on fire now! Buddy, GET OUT!" Honcho yelled, hopping around and waving his arms frantically at the truck as the smoke billowed at his back.

You had to hand it to the cynical old bad-ass, Honcho thought as he watched the guard trying to check out the situation using the security cameras on the outside of the building beside the awning.

That was when Slick, waiting a little ways off in the street with Beast, initiated phase two. He hit the clacker that set off the half stick of dynamite in the back of the dump truck.

Honcho knew it was going to be loud. *But good golly, Miss Molly!* he thought, biting his lip to keep from laughing. It sounded like freaking artillery!

Finally, Terry F. Burns, who had been in Nam during Tet and at the base of the burning, swaying Twin Towers on 9/11 saving people, leaped to his feet and pulled open the door.

“What for the love of Pete is going on out here?” the guard said, sticking his head out.

When he turned wide-eyed toward the blazing truck, Beast hit him hard in the back of the neck with the electric stun gun.

The geezer went down per the plan. What wasn’t part of the plan was the way he went *straight* down, tangling his power-forward-long arms and legs around the now-closing big, heavy door and blocking the threshold.

The lanky old bastard couldn’t even fall without being a pain in the ass, could he? Honcho thought, kicking at the dope as he wrestled to keep the Fort Knox-style door open.

Improvise! Honcho commanded himself.

He took out his big SIG SAUER 9-millimeter as he hopped over the guard like a malevolent Jack Be Nimble and put three—*blamblamblam!*—into the high-end jewelry store’s coffered ceiling.

“Down, down, down!” he yelled, pointing the gun in the faces of the three shock-struck clerks at the end of the plush mahogany-paneled retail space.

Beast finally got the door unblocked, and quick as spit, Slick went from the front to the back of the golden-lit store, popping one after another of the floor cases.

Instead of using a sledgehammer like on their last job, he used their latest toy, a compressed-air-powered captive-bolt pistol, the same cattle-killing device the security-glass industry used in its testing labs.

It worked like a charm. In twenty seconds, the five display cases were shattered to bits, and he and Beast and Slick were scooping and bagging and scooping and bagging, not individual diamonds but whole huge black-velvet display boards dripping with them.

Forty seconds from entering, they were out the door. They went north up Trinity, walking, not running, not turning around, taking it easy, trying not to draw attention to themselves. They completely ignored the flame-engulfed dump truck parked to the store's south. It was stolen, after all.

Up the block on both sides of the street, people were standing on the sidewalks, emptying out of the stores and buildings to see what was going on. The looky-loos looked even more perplexed when the jewelry store alarm finally went off.

Honcho wasn't worried about it. They would just think it was a fire alarm. Keeping calm, never breaking his easy stride, Honcho led his dream team to the alley at the near corner and turned west.

The hair on his arms stood on end as he heard a fire truck's cranking siren blat in the distance behind him. As always, the mayhem he had just caused made him feel suddenly high, suddenly holy. Like a tightrope walker over the Grand Canyon. Like a barefoot guru over a bed of hot coals.

Now for the fun part, Honcho thought, hardly feeling the sidewalk under the soles of his boots as he walked shoulder to shoulder with his boys down the dusty old alley.

Now for the part where they disappeared.

Chapter 56

BRUNO SANTANELLA FINE JEWELERS was on Trinity Place in the downtown Financial District a block west of Broadway.

It was exactly five to one when I shrieked up to the crime scene tape and joined the squad cars sealing off the street half a block away.

It had taken me less than ten minutes to fire over here from nearby One Police Plaza after I'd gotten the call. But one glance out the window at the slowly milling police personnel and gathered crowds was enough to tell that I was too late. I was looking at a cold trail.

I showed my shield to a First Precinct sergeant by the tape and parked my Crown Vic alongside the brownstone wall of Trinity Church's famous graveyard, where Alexander Hamilton was buried.

As I tucked a fresh notebook into my jacket pocket and clipped my shield to my lapel, I did a double take at the completely scorched dump truck peeking out from between two fire trucks half a block north.

So the garbled first reports were true, I thought with a groan. There had been a burning truck and maybe even some sort of explosion. When I turned, I saw a Channel 2 camera van pull up at the perimeter behind me. I shook my head. I'd wanted a Major Crime, and it sure as hell looked like I'd just gotten one.

Not only that, but I knew that Santanella's was an up-and-comer in the high-end New York City jewelry biz. It was run by Bruno Santanella, an Italian immigrant and onetime Hollywood hairdresser who now glittered up all the beautiful people at premieres and awards shows and Cannes with gems instead of gel.

I'd been on the job long enough to know that glitzy big-money people could be a big pain in the ass. I had a feeling I'd be earning my pay today and then some.

Across Trinity, past a trio of firemen smoking cigarettes, I found NYPD bomb tech Al Litvak, waist deep in the charred ruin of the dump truck's still-smoking front end. When he emerged, his pale mustached face and Tyvek suit and arms to the elbow were smeared with black soot.

"What do we got, Al?" I said.

"It's looking like some kind of accelerant in the engine compartment," he said. "It was set off by a rinky-dink electric switch wired into the cab. From a model railroad, if I had to guess. Pretty sloppy, actually."

"Wasn't there a bomb?" I said.

"Nah, not really," Al said, bumming a cigarette off one of the firemen and blowing a smoke ring into the cab window of the ravaged truck. "I saw a little blackening in the back of the hop loader there, but it was some half-assed firework or something. Maybe a couple of M-80s. It was just a noisemaker."

"So the whole thing wasn't meant to hurt anyone? Just a head fake?" I said.

"Exactly," Al said. "A lot of sound and fury signifying jack squat."

I left Al by the truck and stood on the sidewalk, scanning the street. There was a security camera on the building wall beside the jewelry store's blue awning, so at least we had that. After a second, I walked up to a fit thirtysomething First Precinct detective I didn't know who was standing under the awning talking into a cell phone as he scratched on a clipboard.

"Here's what we got so far," Detective Mike Williams told me after he pocketed his phone. "The truck parks. The truck starts smoking. Three white guys in green coveralls and hard hats and sunglasses get out of it and ask the jewelry store guard for help. There's some kind of a bang, and when the guard opens the door, he's hit with a stun gun. The three rush in, bust three shots into the ceiling, then smash a bunch of floor cases, scoop the ice, and are out in maybe a minute."

"You think it was that fast?" I said.

Williams nodded vigorously.

"Three cars and half a dozen foot patrol uniforms on Homeland Security duty two blocks over on Wall Street were here in three minutes from the time the alarm went off. They secured the perimeter in a heartbeat and scoured the area but didn't see hide nor hair of anybody matching the description. We're still on the hunt, but it ain't looking too hot."

"How's the guard?" I said.

"They zapped him pretty good, roughed him up a little, plus he's an older guy, but he's an ex-cop. A pretty tough old bird. He'll be OK. EMTs just took him to the Tribeca Medical Center for observation."

"CSU here yet?" I said.

Williams shook his shaved head.

"Of course not. You know CSU. They were five minutes away about ten minutes ago," he said.

"Did you grab the security footage on that camera yet?" I said.

"Tried to, but the owner and his wife showed, and they're irate and not what you'd call cooperative. They're inside there now, yelling at their staff, if you want to say hello."

Chapter 57

DETECTIVE WILLIAMS WAS RIGHT on the money. Bruno Santanella and his wife, Ellie, were *both* behind the counter, berating the staff in heated Italian, when I walked through the propped-open door.

Santanella was a tall, middle-aged man with a deep tan and a lot of plastic surgery, wearing a gray chalk-stripe designer suit that was a tad tight around his potbelly. His petite brunette doe-eyed wife, Ellie, was a foot shorter and easily two decades younger. She wore a leather jacket over a cream designer dress and a sparkling diamond bracelet that was as thick as a sweat band on her right wrist.

"Where are my diamonds?" Bruno Santanella said in a thick Italian accent as his orange-tan face went an unhealthy looking beet-red. "Tell me you've recovered them!"

"Not yet," I said. "I know how shook up you guys must be. I'm Detective Bennett. The first thing I'm going to need from you is the footage from that security camera. And a detailed list of everything that's missing."

"Do you think I care what your name is?" Santanella said, suddenly clutching at the sides of his neatly coiffed gray head. "What do you need the footage for? I've already told five of you there were three men, two large men and a smaller man. They were wearing green coveralls and yellow hard hats. They distracted my guard and came in here and let off a gun into the ceiling. Then they smashed all my display cases."

He waved his hands around helplessly like he was swatting at flies.

"Can't you see here what they've done?" he said. "Look what they've done to my beautiful store!"

I nodded as I looked over his shoulder at the wide-eyed male clerks behind the counter.

"Is everyone OK back there?" I said. "They didn't lay hands on anyone, did they?"

"You don't need to talk to them," petite Ellie Santanella said, barking at me even more rabidly than her husband. "Why are you even in here? You need to get out and find the damn thieves. Can't you understand how serious this is? You think this is . . . what? Shoplifting at Walmart? These animals made off with over three million dollars of our finest diamond jewelry!"

"I can leave if you want, Mrs. Santanella. It's completely up to you," I said, laying my card on one of the few unsmashed glass cases. "If you have any questions, please don't hesitate to call."

"Wait! Where are you going? That's it?" Santanella cried as if he'd just been knifed. "Now you're leaving? What about my diamonds?"

I let out a breath. I'm usually pretty tolerant with citizens, especially still-emotionally-sore victims of crimes. But this wasn't getting anywhere. The couple seemed much more interested in yelling at everyone and being ridiculously dramatic than anything else. But then I suddenly thought of a way I might be able to get them to be more constructive.

"OK, let's try this again, Mr. Santanella," I said. "Tell me, did the thieves hit the safe in the back?"

"Are you stupid?" the lovely razor-tongued Mrs. Santanella said, pointing at all the shattered glass. "Are you blind? They just took what was in the cases."

"Even so, I really think we should check the safe," I said, nodding patiently. "You never know with thieves of this caliber. They could have tampered with the safe without you knowing. While I'm here, why don't we all just go to the back, open the safe, and take a detailed inventory just to be sure?"

I stood there and watched as the couple exchanged a worried look.

Of course they were worried. I'd been on jewelry heist cases before and knew that diamonds were a pretty funny business. Dealers often kept on hand what were known as black diamonds, aka black-market diamonds that were bought and sold off the books to avoid taxes. No way did Santanella want me looking in his safe, let alone taking any inventory.

"That's OK—Detective Bennett, is it?" Santanella said, suddenly less dramatic and much more reasonable. "I'm sorry for being so rude. I let my emotions get the better of me sometimes."

"Happens to the best of us," I said.

"Don't worry about the safe," he continued. "I already checked it. It's, eh, fine. Very secure. Nothing missing. Is there anything else besides the security footage and jewelry list that you will need for your investigation?"

"That's all for now, Mr. Santanella," I said as I turned for the door. "Thanks for being so cooperative."

Chapter 58

BACK OUTSIDE ON THE street, a burly Asian patrol sergeant hurried up and told me Detective Williams was looking for me. He quickly led me north up Trinity and then turned left onto an extremely narrow street called Emeric J. Harvey Place.

In the middle of the alleylike street, we stopped before a brick warehouse that looked old enough to have rented a storage locker to Alexander Hamilton.

"He's waiting for you up top," the First Precinct sergeant said, thumbing at the building's old-fashioned tilting fire escape, which had been lowered to the sidewalk.

I pulled on a pair of rubber gloves before I climbed up the rickety ladder and the zigzagging cast-iron stairs to the seven-story warehouse's roof.

Off the roof's terracotta rim, there was a clear view of the new World Trade Center's busy construction site. Too bad I wasn't there to sightsee. Across the tar paper and around the base of a rocketlike wooden water tank, I found Williams standing in the open doorway of the interior stairs.

There was a pile of clothing, green coveralls and traffic vests and yellow hard hats, piled at his feet.

"Security guard just called it in," Williams said. "They must have come up here, lost the outfits, and then went down through the interior of the building and out the front door looking like anyone at all."

"Tell me there's a building security camera?" I said, toeing one of the helmets.

Williams shook his head.

"Disabled since yesterday. Looks like they had a good escape route already worked out. I hate to admit it, but these guys are good."

Back down on the street, there was now another cluster of newsies on the north end of Trinity Place setting up cameras on tripods behind the crime scene tape. A quick-thinking female talking head from NBC turned and knifed a microphone at my face as Williams and I passed.

"Detective, does this robbery look like it's related to the string of heists in Brooklyn and Connecticut?" she said.

"Too early to tell," I said.

"Do you have any leads so far?"

"No comment," I said as I passed by, and almost kicked myself when I realized that with my luck, they would probably edit out the word *comment*.

The only good news was the sight of the newly arrived CSU van in front of the store. Inside, Manhattan South Evidence Collection Unit detective Stacy Bergen was on her hands and knees on the carpet examining the cases and shattered glass fragments with a burning white high-intensity light.

"Anything, Stacy?" I said.

"No blood so far," Bergen said. "Which is surprising, because some of the holes in these cases are very jagged. I'm not holding my breath for getting any prints. They had to have been wearing thick work gloves."

I was just about to tell her about the find on the roof when my phone rang. It was my buddy Arturo Lopez from the Harlem squad.

"Mike?" Lopez said, out of breath. "Did you hear about Holly Jacobs? EMTs are rushing her over to the Harlem Hospital Center as we speak."

"What!" I cried.

Out of the corner of my eye, I saw Ellie Santanella emerge from the rear of the store and make a beeline for me.

"Here's what we lost," the haughty young woman said, thrusting a paper-filled folder at me. "Here's what those bastards stole from us."

"One moment, please, Mrs. Santanella," I said, and watched her face go crimson as I ignored the folder and showed her my palm.

"Arturo, I'm here. What happened to Holly?" I said frantically.

"They found her at her apartment. She was shot, Mike. Multiple times. That son of a bitch finally did it. He got her."

"Wait! Where do you think you're going?" was the last thing I heard as I ran out of the store and into the street for my car.

Chapter 59

BY THE GRACE OF GOD, I just barely dodged bowling over a smiling family clutching Mylar and a bundled blue blanket on the corner of 136th and Lenox by the Harlem Hospital Center. I didn't even have time for an apology as I sprinted past on the sidewalk for the red emergency room awning.

Inside, Brooklyn Kale was at the other end of the crowded waiting room, standing by the nurses' station. She looked down and shook her head somberly as I rushed up.

"She still had some vitals when they brought her in, Mike, but by the time they got her on the table, it was too late. Robertson and Lopez just called down. They were up there trying to see if she would give them a deathbed identification, but she never got even one word out."

Off the hospital elevator on four, we spotted Lopez and Robertson by a room at the end of the corridor. Inside the room, under the huge lighting apparatus and between gray metal cabinets and computer and IV carts, was a gurney covered in a white sheet.

I immediately starting sweating heavily as I entered the bright room and stood over the stretcher. It wasn't just from running, I knew, but because trauma operating rooms are kept at eighty-five degrees to stabilize the plummeting body and blood temperatures of gunshot victims.

Swiping sweat, I finally pulled the sheet and stared down at Holly Jacobs.

There was blood everywhere. Red streams of it from her mouth and nostrils, red pools of it in the folds of the warming blanket she lay on. In addition to the multiple wounds in her head and neck and chest, there were through-and-through wounds in both arms. I let out an angry breath as I looked at the carnage of her left hand, where her ring finger had been blown off completely.

Someone had unloaded a nine-millimeter into her, maybe a whole fifteen-shot magazine at very close range. Looking at the blood in her stylish hair and the sadness and terror in her purple-eye-shadowed brown eyes, I suddenly pictured Holly down on her knees thrusting up her hands to protect herself.

Because there had been no one else there to protect her, I thought, still angry as I wiped at the sweat now dripping off my nose. She'd come to us to save her, had begged for help, and we'd completely let her down.

"What the hell happened? I thought she was supposed to go away," I said when I got back out into the hallway.

"We think it was her cat," Lopez said, shaking his head. "She was so nervous when she left, she must have forgotten about it. We think she probably came back to grab the cat, and he was waiting for her. Ambushed her right outside her building's front door."

A moment later, I heard the sound of muffled weeping. When I turned around, I saw that it was coming from Noah Robertson, who now had his arms wrapped around a shocked-looking Brooklyn Kale.

Brooklyn quickly unclenched the still-crying Noah and turned to me for help.

I felt bad for Noah. The poor young guy was really upset. This must have been the first murder victim he'd ever seen. At least, the first one he'd ever seen this brutally up close and personal.

"Hey, Noah," I said, steering him down the hallway a little as he continued to break down. "You're obviously a very compassionate person, which is good. Caring about people is what we do for a living.

"But if you want to do this job, if you really want to be a detective, you need to put some armor on. It won't help victims or their families to see us emotionally compromised, understand? We're the ones they rely on. The ones who need to be tough."

I glanced through the operating room doorway back at poor Holly, dead on the gurney, as Noah tried to gather himself.

Or am I maybe too tough? I wondered.

Chapter 60

LEAVING ALL OUR TROUBLES behind—well, at least for the current nanosecond—that Friday night, Mary Catherine and I found ourselves outside a flower-and-vine-bedecked little town house a stone's throw east down Fifty-Second Street off Fifth Avenue.

Surrounded on all sides by towering office buildings, the whimsical little structure looked like a fairy-tale house conjured into the middle of Midtown Manhattan by some wizard's magic spell.

Some *French* wizard's magic spell.

"Welcome to La Grenouille," I whispered to Mary Catherine in a terrible French accent as we stepped under the famous restaurant's white awning from the taxi.

We stood there for a moment, peeking in

through the plate glass at the heady swirl of waiters and well-dressed people inside.

"You ready for this?" I said to Mary Catherine, who had her blond hair up and her makeup on and was looking stunningly, amazingly, redundantly hot.

"No," she said with her delicious-looking scarlet lips as she fussed with her pearl choker.

"Then that makes two of us. Geronimo!" I said as I tightly hooked her elbow and pulled open the door.

The maître d' at the stand inside was pretty much exactly what you'd expect from the fanciest and most famous classic French restaurant in New York City. He was tall and handsome and dressed to the nines like a French Cary Grant.

"Good evening," he said in a deep, smooth Gallic-accented voice. "May I have your name?"

"Bennett," I said, lowering my own voice a little for the intimidating occasion. "Detective Michael Bennett."

He unstiffened an iota and smiled brightly as he came out from behind the podium and firmly shook my hand.

"Oh, yes. Welcome, Detective. Claude mentioned you would be arriving. I am Michel, at your service. *Bonsoir,* Madame, and welcome to La Grenouille."

"Thank you," said a blown-away Mary Catherine as the *très debonair* son of a bitch actually kissed her hand with a little bow.

"We are delighted to have you," he said a tad too smoothly for my liking as he batted his dark eyelashes at her. "Would you allow me to take your coat, Madame?"

As I was about to tell Mr. Handsome Frenchy to get his googly eyes and dirty mitts off my dame, he unwrapped Mary Catherine and my jaw dropped.

She'd been buttoned up in a raincoat when we met in the lobby of our building, so I hadn't had a chance to see what she'd chosen to wear underneath. Now I could see that it was more like what she'd chosen *not* to wear.

Instead of the little black dress I was expecting, she was in a little red dress. A very little red strapless one that showed off a lot of back and even more leg.

Even the unflappable maitre d' looked a little flapped.

"Yes," he said, finally recovering. "Welcome to La Grenouille. This way, *s'il vous plaît*"

Chapter 61

LIKE I SAID, I'M not exactly what you'd call a gourmet, but even I thought entering La Grenouille's famous and fancy dining room was dazzling, like stepping into a vivid French Impressionist painting.

There were gold damask wallpaper, bloodred banquettes, waiters in white berets performing tableside service from shining copper carts, waiters in white dinner jackets bearing bright-silver buckets of champagne.

And the flowers!

They were everywhere. Yellow firework bursts of chrysanthemums in huge vases, soaring whimsical constellations of late-summer flowers and grasses arching toward the high ceiling.

The patrons at the tables were pretty impressive

as well. They seemed to fall into two categories, filthy-rich-looking older men with eye-candy models or skeletal grande-dame socialites holding court under thick layers of diamonds and pearls and Chanel.

A lot of the eyes in the room, both male and female, shifted discreetly toward us as Michel sat us side by side at a rear banquette. And by toward us, I of course mean toward Mary Catherine.

She snuggled in next to me on the soft red banquette as Michel assured us that our table captain was on his way.

"Our table *captain?*" I whispered to Mary Catherine as I adjusted my tie. "I hope he doesn't throw us overboard."

That was when I turned and took in Mary Catherine's thoroughly bedazzled face.

"So what do you think so far?" I said, smiling. "I mean, if you want, we could still head home. I thought I saw a can of tuna fish behind the Cheerios in the back of the pantry."

Mary Catherine gripped my hand like a vise.

"This is..." she said, her eyes wet as she stared at the magical room around us, "...wonderful, Michael. Just wonderful."

I did a little double take. I didn't think she'd

ever called me Michael before. And definitely not like that.

"You deserve wonderful, Mary Catherine," I whispered in her ear. "And remember, this is just the first part of my little town-painting. I made us another reservation at the—"

Her hand flew to my mouth before I could get the word *Plaza* out. Her fingertips were warm on my lips, her shiny red nails scratchy on my cheek.

"I know, Michael," she whispered.

The bold look she gave me next made my mouth dry as it pinned me deep into the velvet at my back. She moved a red fingernail to her own lips and held my gaze as a white-jacketed waiter approached under the canopy of flowers.

"Some things, Michael, are better left unsaid."

Chapter 62

TWO AND A HALF surreal hours later, in a glamorous fog, we finished dessert.

"I finally found it," Mary Catherine said, gently placing her fork on her plate, now empty of Grand Marnier soufflé.

"What's that, *mon amie?*" I said, feeling very little pain after the multiple courses paired with wine.

"The best thing I ever ate," she said, sounding a little tipsy herself.

"But you said that was the lobster-and-tarragon ravioli," I reminded her.

"That was then," she said with a wink. "This is now. How about you? What would you want if you could have anything in the world right now?"

Cocking my head, I lifted my dessert wine and

began to swirl it as I gave it some thought.

"For you to call me Michael again," I suddenly said truthfully before draining my glass.

She glared at me.

"Maybe I will. Maybe I won't. *Michael*," she said, suddenly standing.

"Hey, where are you headed?" I said.

"*I* am going to the powder room," she announced with a giggle. "What are *you* going to do?"

"*I* am going to sit here and watch *you* go to the powder room," I said.

As I, and every other man there, watched Mary Catherine cross the room, I was interrupted by the waiter, who discreetly brought the bill. The bill itself was not discreet. With wine and the tips, in fact, it was pretty staggering.

But I smiled as I dropped my Amex card on top of it. You get what you pay for, and what I'd just paid for was truly a New York, New York, once-in-a-lifetime sort of night.

Now for the good part, I thought as I caught up with Mary Catherine by the door.

After we got Mary Catherine's coat and said *au revoir* to La Grenouille, we saw that it was raining cats and dogs outside and that more than half the restaurant's hoity-toity patrons were huddled under the narrow awning waiting for taxis and town cars and limos.

Breathing in Chanel No. 5 and shoe polish as we waited with the movers and shakers, I looked across the street at the diamond-filled windows of Cartier. Then I quickly looked away. Because I was off tonight.

I'd even gone and done the unthinkable in this modern and insane 24/7 wired-up world we lived in. I'd turned off my cell phone. The city, both uptown and downtown, would have to take care of itself. At least for one measly night.

"Your cab, *Monsieur et Madame*," suddenly called the house manager as he scored us a taxi.

I hooked elbows with Mary Catherine, and we jogged into the rain for our cab.

Chapter 63

MARY CATHERINE AND I both laughed as we fell into the back of the taxi.

"Excuse me, nice young people, but where to?" said the middle-aged little cabbie with an Indian accent.

"The Plaza Hotel. On the double!" Mary Catherine yelled out before I could open my mouth.

I stared at her, my mouth gaping as the cab pulled out. "Oh, that's how we're going to play it, are we?" I said as I began to tickle her. "What happened to all that 'things better left unsaid' stuff?"

"That was then," she said, laughing, and then she did it. Mary Catherine leaned in and gave me what I'd wanted more than anything since the night started.

A nice long taste of her red lips.

"This is now, Michael," she said, pulling me closer.

We kissed slowly as the lights of the city swept through the windows and the rain pounded hard on the cab's roof. We came up for air as we stopped before a dripping red traffic light.

"Sorry," Mary Catherine said to the cabbie.

"No, please. Perfectly fine, in fact," the cabbie said, looking at us in the rearview. "I like to see people in love. And I know the real thing when I see it."

I watched Mary Catherine reapply her lipstick as there was a hum. But it wasn't my phone, for a change—it was Mary Catherine's.

"Hello?" she said.

I watched her listen. After a second, her expression changed as she sat up straight.

"What is it?" I said.

"It's Brian," Mary Catherine said. "Something's wrong. It's Seamus."

I grabbed the phone.

"Brian, what is it?"

"He's not talking, Dad," Brian managed to say through his bawling. "I just came out to say good night, and Gramps is on the couch and all he does is just stare at me."

"Is he breathing?"

"Yes, a little, I think."

"We're on our way, Bri. Hang in there. I'll call the paramedics and call you back."

I turned toward the cabbie. "Change of plans," I yelled as I dialed 911. "Ninety-Fifth and West End Avenue. Please hurry."

Chapter 64

FIVE MINUTES LATER, BRIAN called and told us the EMTs were taking Seamus to the emergency room, so instead of going home, we redirected the cabbie to St. Luke's Hospital on Amsterdam Avenue.

Another day, another hospital, I thought as we pulled up outside. My stomach churned as I considered the worst. That the inevitable had finally happened to my grandfather. That Seamus was already dead.

Please, God, let me be wrong, I prayed as we came through the revolving doors into the waiting room. *We still need him more than you do.*

They let us upstairs to six, where Seamus had just been admitted.

But surprisingly, when we entered his room, instead of being laid out on a gurney, he was sitting up in bed with his arms crossed and one of his patented scowls on his face.

"Seamus!" I said, beating Mary Catherine to him by a half step to hug him. "You're OK! Jeez, you scared the heck out of us! What happened?"

"He had a stroke," said a short, handsome young doctor as he stepped into the room.

"See, here on the MRI where it's gray?" Dr. Jacob Freeman said as he held a readout up to the light. "Regions in both the parietal lobe and the gustatory area have damage from blood loss."

"Oh my goodness, Seamus! You've had a stroke?" Mary Catherine said.

"Of course I had a stroke," Seamus said. "So what? Don't go measurin' me for a pine box just yet. I feel fine. Whaddya think? This many years on this old rock, the plumbin's *not* goin' to get the occasional clog? Where's me clothes? What is it that Eddie always says? Time to blow this clambake!"

"A stroke is very serious, Mr. Bennett," the doctor said, shaking his head. "I'm sorry, but you can't leave now. You need to stay overnight for observation, and we still have more tests to run."

"Tests," Seamus said, rolling his eyes. "You seem like a nice little fella, but I'm in no mood to hear any more of your medical school mumbo jumbo. I made a call and my personal physician is on his way. If he says I'm good to go, I'm good to go, agreed?"

"Is he always this way?" the doctor whispered to me. "Your grandfather seems quite disoriented."

"Actually," I said, smiling sheepishly at Dr. Freeman, "this is normal, believe it or not."

Chapter 65

"PARDON ME! COMING THROUGH!" said a bellowing Irish voice from the hall a moment later.

It was time to roll *my* eyes when I saw the skinny old man who walked in. It was no doctor, but Jimmy "Dowdy" Dowd, one of Seamus's drinking and poker buddies. Actually, I think he had been a doctor, but, like, in the 1970s. He was well into his eighties now. How the heck was he still practicing medicine?

"If you would all step back and give us a little room. Thank you, thank you," Dowdy said as he rummaged in the big old-fashioned black leather doctor bag he'd brought and put on a huge '60s-era black stethoscope.

Dowd started out the examination by getting Seamus to stand. The second Seamus was upright,

Dowd started snapping the bony fingers of both hands loudly and rapidly in Seamus's face.

"What in the world are you doing?" said Dr. Freeman as Seamus jumped back.

"Testing his reflexes. Getting him to look alive," Dowd said.

"Easier said than done with you for a physician, James Dowd," Seamus said, clutching his chest. "Where'd ya learn your bedside manner? The enhanced interrogation team at the CIA?"

"Enough of your squawking," Dowd said, giving Seamus the peace sign. "How many fingers would I be holding up?"

"That'd be two last time I checked," Seamus said. "Though I'm surprised it isn't one, considering how badly I took you at the end of our last poker game. All in on pocket threes? What were you thinking?"

"Ah, he's obviously fine," Dowd said to me. "Strong as a stubborn donkey and still about as charming, which I don't have to tell you fine long-suffering people about. I'm sure I don't see any brain damage. Well, any more than usual, that is."

"This is highly unusual," Dr. Freeman said almost to himself.

Dowd turned to him.

"Enough of that now, Doctor, please. His physical coordination is fine, right? He's thinking fairly straight. His tongue's as sharp as ever. Therefore, I hereby deem this man fit to go home, and that's where he's goin' to go. Now, be a good lad and fetch a wheelchair, would you? And bring back the paperwork while you're at it."

Freeman opened his mouth, then quickly closed it before leaving.

"OK, now that he's gone, time for a little medicine," Dowdy said, producing a pint of Jameson's and a couple of little steel cups from his bag of tricks.

I shook my head and then shared a laugh with Mary Catherine as the two tough, nutty old men shared a stiff belt of the good stuff. Obviously, I would have felt better if Seamus had stayed for some more tests, but I knew it would be fruitless to try to persuade him. He did look OK. Plus the fact that he was back to his old Emerald Isle vaudeville routine was definitely positive.

When I turned on my phone to tell Brian the good news and that we were on our way home, I saw that I had several new texts. Three of them were from Starkie.

The gist of his messages was that he'd recently

been fielding complaints about me from the jewelry store owners, Bruno Santanella and his wife, Ellie. The Santanellas were claiming that I'd left the crime scene at their store even faster than the thieves. Which was completely unfair. I'd stayed at least five minutes. The thieves had been out in, like, two.

Starkie concluded that he wasn't real happy with the investigation so far. Or with me, for that matter.

Fair enough, I thought, filing the aggravating criticism in the memory hole with a tiny flick of the Delete button.

I'd been running the length of the city like a beheaded chicken since I'd gotten back to New York, and now the one special night I'd finally planned with Mary Catherine had gone belly-up.

I honestly couldn't say I was real happy these days with things myself.

Chapter 66

THE RESTAURANT HONCHO SAT in forty-five minutes past noon was on Prince Street in the very center of SoHo.

The modern French bistro was called 82 Clichy, after the address of Le Moulin Rouge in Paris, and like that famous cabaret, it was over-the-top posh, with black satin wallpaper and pale-plum-colored leather banquettes and an antique mirror the size of a billboard over its massive gleaming zinc bar.

Though decadent bordello was definitely Honcho's style, especially in the tailored black seventeen-hundred-dollar Prada suit he was now decked out in, he wasn't there to soak in the atmosphere. Sitting by a window open to the sidewalk, he kept glancing at the street through the zoom lens of his Nikon between bites of his scallop ceviche. As he pretended to snap pictures of the area's charming Venice-like cast-iron loft buildings like some geeky tourist, he kept keen watch on an establishment two blocks west on the southwest corner of Wooster.

Through the camera's magnifying lens, he could easily read the gold-leaf sign on its door: WOOSTER FINE DIAMONDS.

He turned from the window when he finally heard the loud clopping. The tall, curvy platinum blonde who stomped up to his table wore a seemingly painted-on black sleeveless turtleneck Givenchy dress with big black Dior shades and too-high Louboutins. With the not-so-demure diamonds at her ears and throat and the flashy Barbour and Kate Spade shopping bags clutched in her hands, she looked like a high-end stripper who'd bagged a billionaire.

Which was precisely the look Honcho had been shooting for when he hired the mobbed-up Ukrainian looker for this latest job.

"You're late," Honcho said, dropping a hundred on the table and quickly leading Iliana back out into the street by her elbow.

"You told me to shop!" Iliana shrieked in her

heavy accent, waving the bags as they crossed the Belgian-block street.

"For over an hour!?" Honcho said as they headed west. "I told you we were on a schedule. Anyway, you know what to do, right? Want me to go over anything?"

"Do I look like an amateur to you?" Iliana said, ripping her elbow out of his hand. "I was picking pockets before you had peach fuzz on your nuts, so you worry about your part. And you better have my money in cash right after, like you said, or I'll *have* your nuts."

"What a sweet-talker you are, Iliana. Look lively now," Honcho said as they made a beeline up Prince Street toward the jewelry store.

Chapter 67

THE TALLER OF THE two armed security guards opened the jewelry store door as Honcho and Iliana stopped in front of it.

From casing the joint over the last three months, Honcho knew that the dark-haired, heavyset white guard with the throwback macho-man mustache was named Gary Tenero and that he was easygoing and probably a pushover. It was Tenero's intense Hispanic partner, Eric Galarza, who was shaved bald and chiseled like an MMA fighter and on the NYPD hiring list to become a cop, who had Honcho much more worried.

Spotting Galarza through the window, stationed in the center of the store, Honcho was racked with a sudden and strong bad feeling. Before his eyes came a prophetic vision of himself down on his hands and knees leaking blood on the luxe retailer's expensive carpet.

Should I abort? Honcho thought.

But then Iliana was clicking up the jewelry store's cast-iron steps and everything was going down.

"Are you effing kidding me?" Honcho said, starting the script.

He put on a pretty convincing Russian accent for the benefit of the guard. Honcho was acting Russian and had chosen the Ukrainian Iliana because of the sudden influx of megarich Russians and Europeans into the super-wealthy SoHo shopping area.

"How many times do I have to tell you?" Honcho complained loudly at Iliana's back. "I am not going into one more store. I am already late."

"It will just take a minute. Come on," Iliana barked.

"I don't have a minute, you idiot," Honcho said, going into his pocket and slapping a knot of hundreds into her hand as the wide-eyed white guard watched. "Pick out whatever, OK? I need to be in a cab. If I keep my boss waiting any longer, he'll cut my dick off. I'll call you later."

"No, you must come," lliana said as she stamped

a Louboutin. “How can I pick out my engagement ring by myself?”

“But isn’t it bad luck?” Honcho said.

“No, that’s just the dress, you moron. C’mon,” she said, pulling him inside.

Honcho avoided the gaze of the intense guard as a vampire-pale redheaded female clerk stepped up to them. She reminded Honcho of the curvy carrottop from *Mad Men,* only instead of being plus-size, she had cheekbones you could chop lines of coke with.

“Hello, I’m Rebecca. May I help you?” the clerk said.

“We want to see some diamonds,” Iliana said.

“Well, you’ve come to the right place,” the clerk was beginning to say, when suddenly all hell broke loose by the front door behind them.

“FBI!” someone screamed. “FBI! You with the blonde! Hands up now if you don’t want to die!”

Honcho stiffened and began turning around slowly. He caught a glimpse of two men wearing navy Windbreakers and bulletproof vests with badges around their necks. They were standing in the jewelry store’s open doorway, guns drawn.

“Hands!” one of the FBI agents said. “Don’t move! Don’t you move!”

Honcho ignored him and dropped down on his knees, digging into the Kate Spade bag for his Beretta. The gunshot that followed was deafening in the tight interior of the store. Honcho fell facedown on the carpet.

Over the next thirty seconds, it was hard to tell who was screaming more loudly, Iliana or the redheaded clerk.

“Oh, man. I think you got him,” Honcho heard as the intense guard, Galarza, was suddenly kneeling over him.

“You wish!” Honcho said, rolling over and pressing the Beretta to the guy’s chin.

As Honcho stood, the two “FBI agents,” Beast and Slick, already had the door closed and their guns trained on Tenero and the other male clerk.

Iliana took her own piece out of the bag and placed it between the redheaded clerk’s wide green eyes.

“Keys to the front, now!” Iliana screamed as Slick slipped the bolt closed on the door.

Chapter 68

I WAS HEADED TO the squad room when I heard it. I was stopped at a red light on Broadway and Great Jones Street in the Village when the cruiser's radio suddenly blew up with about fifteen staccato calls.

I listened intently. Someone had just pulled the silent alarm at Wooster Fine Diamonds on Prince and Wooster!

"That's five blocks away!" I yelled at myself as I hit the siren and peeled out through the intersection and then pinned it south down Broadway.

"We are on foot pursuit. Caucasian male running east on Prince. No, scratch that. North on Mott! North on Mott!" said the radio as I ran another red light.

I shrieked through the next red light at

Houston, almost running over a muscular bike messenger in the intersection before flooring it east to Mott Street. Just as I arrived, a lean white guy with a bulging backpack shot gazellelike straight across all four lanes of Houston and continued north on Elizabeth.

I raced up and shrieked left onto Elizabeth straight after him, staring at his blue backpack as he ran along the sidewalk on the west side of the street.

And almost slammed head-on into the back of a parallel-parking moving van!

I added my horn to the shrieking siren to move the van, but to no avail.

“Screw it,” I said, popping the door and leaving the cruiser stopped dead in the middle of the street as I took off on foot.

My new wing tips were starting to cut the hell out of my feet when the guy reached the end of Elizabeth and went left onto Bleecker. When I got to the corner, I could see that the suspect was all the way west near the corner of Lafayette, where Con Ed had a manhole open.

It was out of sheer exhaustion and frustration that I hollered to the work crew: “NYPD! Stop that guy! Stop that guy!”

So I was a little surprised when that was exactly what they did. A burly black hard hat in blue Con Ed coveralls bobbed out from under the orange traffic tape like a boxer into a ring and clotheslined the runner as he was trying to get past.

The guy went off his feet, knocking the corner trash can over like a bowling pin before landing flat on his back in the gutter on Lafayette. He was still moaning when I landed on him and flipped him over and slapped on the cuffs.

As I knelt on his head, I zipped open his backpack, expecting gems. But it wasn't gems. Not even close. I couldn't believe it as about three pounds of rancid-smelling marijuana in little plastic bags spilled out onto the sidewalk.

"Where are they?" I yelled.

"Where's who?" the red-faced suspect said.

"Not who. The diamonds! Where'd you put the diamonds?"

"What diamonds, man?" the suspect said, opening his eyes wide. "I just got weed. Just weed. When I saw the cop running, I got scared. I'm really sorry. It isn't even my weed. I'll tell you whose it is, OK? I'm just a college kid. I go to NYU, man. Please, I don't want to go to jail."

"This ain't him," I said as a precinct car

screeched to the curb. "Just a spooked dealer. Did you see anybody else?"

"No," the sarge said, punching the steering wheel. "It doesn't make sense. The clerk inside said they'd been gone less than thirty seconds when we rolled up. When we came out of the store, we saw this fool on the corner of Greene just take off. I thought it had to be him."

Thirty seconds, I thought, staring out at the newly arriving cruisers and gathering crowd on the sidewalk.

I kicked at the pile of weed bags that had spilled out of the backpack. I didn't stop until I'd knocked every one down into the corner sewer. I was so frustrated I would have tried to kick the dealer himself down there, too, if I'd thought he would fit.

How could we have missed them by thirty seconds?

Chapter 69

I WAS EXPECTING TO see shattered glass everywhere when I arrived at Wooster Fine Diamonds, so I was shocked to find all the jewelry cases still intact.

I quickly figured out why. This latest hit had been a takeover robbery instead of a mad-dash smash-and-grab.

Their plan had been quite elaborate. A woman and a man had come in acting like a rich couple a moment before two more males entered acting like federal agents there to arrest them. After they'd gotten the drop on the guards and buttoned down the staff, they took their time, almost ten minutes, as they unlocked cases and selected the best diamonds. They'd also been cool-headed enough to take the surveillance video this time.

The three males matched the descriptions of the three from downtown. And now there was a woman, apparently. I couldn't have been more pissed.

I had to admit these crooks were good. They had flair and must have been well dressed to blend in with the ritzy area.

Takeover robberies could go south in a breath and become a bloodbath, I knew. I really wanted to catch these people.

If there was any silver lining, the fact that they had struck again so quickly impressed me as amateurish. They seemed too eager. I knew that some thieves get off on the adrenaline high, and like any junkie, they start to make mistakes to get it.

I was still puzzling over how they'd gotten away so quickly when who should come in the door but my boss's boss, Chief of Department Peter Vonroden.

"Thanks for showing up, Bennett," the short, fiftysomething former competitive body builder said as he scowled at the crime scene. "Think you might stick around a bit this time? You being the new lead detective and all."

If I had to guess, I would have said that Vonroden probably wasn't very pleased that I had been hand-selected by the commissioner to come back to Major Crimes. Vonroden was known to be a tough political infighter, not to mention very good friends with my old nemesis, Chief Starkie.

What really sucked, though, was that I was nowhere on this case. Which had been on the front page of the *Post* and the *Daily News* this morning.

So instead of banging heads, I wisely ignored his taunts. Or at least tried to.

"These guys are switching their script now, Chief," I said. "Instead of a smash-and-grab, this was a takeover. Got the drop on the guards, locked the front door. They took their time."

"I hear they were Russians," Vonroden said. "Or Serbians?"

Vonroden was referring to a theory that was being batted about that the infamous Serbian Pink Panther gang that had targeted over a hundred fifty stores throughout the world, including dramatic heists in Tokyo, Dubai, Paris, and London, had come to town.

"They had some kind of accent," I said. "One of the clerks lives in Brighton Beach. Swears they sounded Russian, but who knows? We can't really verify. This crew has a flair for the dramatic. It might be possible they were just putting on another show."

"Looks like some real Ringling Brothers and Barnum and Bailey Greatest Show on Earth shit so far, from where I'm sitting," Vonroden said. "But for some strange reason, I don't feel that entertained. Not even by the clown sideshow you keep putting on."

Tell me what you really think, Chief, I thought, biting my tongue.

He leaned in to whisper to me. I didn't think it would be sweet nothings. I was right.

"Got a call last night from a friend of mine, Bennett. He was asking my help about trying to get you off this case and out of Major Crimes Division, but you know what?"

"What's that?" I said, playing along since I had no other choice.

"It looks like you're doing a far better job of getting booted off this case than I ever could," Vonroden said.

As the chief left, I got a call from Detective Siobhan Barton, one of the responding Fifth Precinct detectives I'd sent to canvass the neighborhood. She was calling from the Kate Spade's around the corner, one of the stores whose bag the female thief had been seen holding.

"Hey, good news, Mike," the rookie detective

said. "We got a lead, I think. Clerk in here says a woman came in and bought some sandals about an hour before the robbery. She paid in cash, but they have a camera, and I got a pretty good shot of her."

"Was anybody else with her?" I said.

"No, but it's the woman. She fits the description exactly. Same platinum-blond hair, same black dress."

"Excellent," I said.

"That's not all," Detective Barton said. "It's just like the jewelry store staff said. She had a Russian accent."

Chapter 70

ABOUT AN HOUR LATER, with the processing of the SoHo crime scene wrapping up, I made some phone calls and got into my cruiser and headed east and then north up the FDR for the not-so-trendy Boogie Down Bronx.

Just over the Harlem River at Macombs Dam Bridge, I pulled over onto Jerome Avenue in front of Yankee Stadium's Gate 2 and parked. I made another phone call. About ten minutes later, one of the stadium's maintenance doors opened and out came a guy in a security guard uniform. He was a short, potbellied middle-aged man with a huge bald head and an even huger grin on his face.

"Mike, I am so glad you called me," said my old buddy, Yaakov Chazam, as he happily climbed into the cruiser.

Yaakov was quite an interesting character. An immigrant from Moscow, right after the Berlin Wall fell in '89, he'd been a brilliant math professor at NYU before he ditched academia for the life of a professional poker player. We'd come into contact over the murder of a young Wall Street trader I had worked five years before.

As it turned out, the murdered guy had been killed over gambling debts to Russian mobsters accrued in the underground Brooklyn gambling dens that the mobsters controlled and where Yaakov played. Yaakov, who had been a good friend of the young guy, had done the right thing by contacting me and anonymously named enough names to get the loan shark enforcer and his Mob boss put away.

Since then, Yaakov had turned out to be a veritable font of information about the Russian Mob in Brooklyn. I would tap him for info from time to time, as would the FBI and the DEA.

Though squealing about the Russian Mob was highly dangerous for him, Yaakov couldn't help himself because he was an incurable mystery reader, police buff, and lover of all things cop. Which explained his choice of low-paying security guard jobs like the one here at the stadium. He didn't even need a job, with all the money he made playing poker. He just wanted to wear a uniform.

"So, Yaakov, staying out of those poker dens?" I said as I made a U-turn and drove up 161st Street past the iconic Bronx County Courthouse.

"Oh, yeah. Only a little here and there when I'm tight," he said, rolling his eyes sarcastically. "Actually, my new wife, she hates when I go, yet she never objects to going on these monster shopping sprees when I win. Weird, huh? What can I do for you, Mike? You got something juicy for me?"

"I'm trying to identify a woman. Might be from your neck of the woods," I said, turning onto the Grand Concourse and pulling over and taking out my iPhone.

"Oh, pictures!" he said excitedly as I brought up the video I'd gotten from the Kate Spade store. "I love pictures. Is it of a crime scene? Is she dead? Naked, maybe?"

"Sorry, Yaakov," I said as the security footage loaded. "Unfortunately, she's alive and dressed."

"This isn't so bad," he said as he watched the mystery blonde put on shoes. "She has nice legs. What am I supposed to be looking for? If I know her? Seen her around?"

"Exactly," I said.

He peered at the screen.

"No, I don't know her. I don't think so. Though it's pretty impossible to tell with those big sunglasses, and that looks like a wig, right? Though she is Russian Mafia."

"She is?" I said. "How do you know?"

He rewound and hit Pause and pointed.

"See here? The green mark on her left ankle. That's a *nakolki,* a Russian jailhouse tattoo. These Mafia idiot types are gaga about their stupid tattoos. A cat wearing a hat like that one is Mafia from way back. What is she? A hooker?"

"We think she was involved with a robbery. A diamond heist today in SoHo around noon."

"There was another diamond heist today? Like the other one downtown that was in the paper? That's the case you're working? That's so cool!"

"Let me ask you, Yaakov. Do Serbians and Russians get along?"

"Actually, they do a little. They trace a common ancestry. At least, a lot of Serbians say so. Why?"

"There's a group of Serbian crooks in Europe called the Pink Panther gang. They travel around the world knocking over jewelry stores. Japan, Paris, London. Do you think if Serbians came here they'd work with a woman from the Russian Mob?"

Yaakov shook his head.

"No, I don't think so. Why go to all the trouble to come to the States and then use some woman you might not trust so much? Last time I checked, Serbian thugs had their own bitches to do shit for them. Why not bring one along with you?"

"Good point," I said as I finally thumbed off my phone.

I tried to piece things together. I was having some trouble. So it wasn't Serbians?

"Stolen diamonds, mysterious blondes," Yaakov said, staring at my phone. "This is like Hitchcock, only for real, man. What a freaking awesome country this is!"

Chapter 71

INSTEAD OF ANOTHER round of La Grenouille's prix fixe, that night's dinner consisted of stale vending-machine Oreos washed down with even staler vintage instant coffee. My repast was served cubicle-side in Major Crimes' deserted squad room as I stayed late running down leads on my case's potential new Russian connection.

With a blown-up printout of my mystery woman taped to the shade of the desk lamp beside my computer, I scoured the entire female Russian Mob suspect section of the electronic mug book from the NYPD's Organized Crime Control Bureau. But even after two hours of clicking through the Russian female version of the mad, the bad, and the crooked, there was nothing even resembling a match.

My informant, Yaakov, had been right, I thought as I unsuccessfully tried to blow the cookie crumbs out of my keyboard. With the woman's wig and big glasses, she could have been anyone at all.

My only luck came around eight-thirty when I took a stab in the dark and managed to get Sergeant Eileen Alexander, a sympathetic OCCB detective, on the phone to help me. The Organized Crime Control Bureau detectives were good to have on your side, since they worked with the FBI and had federal security clearances. After much cajoling and some downright begging, I managed to get Eileen to agree to run the photo through the feds' more extensive Russian Mob databases.

"Not exactly a family portrait, huh?" the cop said skeptically after I e-mailed her the security camera still. "This is the best you got?"

C'mon, Eileen, I thought but didn't say, since every Eileen I knew cringed whenever someone brought up that aggravating '80s pop song.

"It's *all* I got, Eileen," I said.

"And I thought I was having a bad day," the detective finally said. "I'll be in touch if I get anything, but waiting by the phone might not be the smartest move for you."

I decided to take her sage advice.

Twenty minutes later, I came over the threshold of my apartment to find Joseph, our faithful new Polish doorman, standing watch.

"Hey, Joseph, you're here late. You change shifts or something?" I said.

"No, Mr. Bennett. Ralph call in sick," he said forlornly. "Last minute, too. I had concert ticket. Bullet For My Valentine at Roseland. Girlfriend is pissed. Hundred fifty bucks gone. Wish day was just over, you know?"

"Joseph, I know all about it," I murmured as I got into the elevator.

By the time I'd unlocked my apartment door, I'd whittled down my wants to two, a cold beer and a hot shower. I'd just decided on both at the same time when I spotted Mary Catherine on her cell phone in the kitchen. Mary Catherine on the phone, red-eyed. Crying?

I immediately panicked. Mary Catherine did a lot of things. She baked brownies, doled out Band-Aids, guided people through the perils of fifth-grade geometry, usually all at the same time. What she didn't do was weep. And yet here she was, doing precisely that.

My first thought, of course, ran to Seamus and his recent stroke.

“Mary Catherine, what is it? Is it Seamus?” I said.

Mary Catherine stared at me perplexed as she continued to listen. Then she nodded and hastily said good-bye and hung up.

“Oh, no, no, no, Mike. Seamus is fine. It was my sister, Claire, on the phone. It’s about my mother. She just had a brain aneurysm about three hours ago. She’s in the ICU at South Tipperary General Hospital in Clonmel. She’s in a coma, Mike. On a ventilator. I can’t believe it. I was just talking to her three days ago.”

“Oh, no, Mary Catherine. I’m so sorry,” I said, embracing her.

“I have to go back to Ireland, Mike. Perhaps for a week or two. But how can I? We’ve barely unpacked and gotten the kids settled here. How can I leave you guys in the lurch?”

“It’s not a concern, Mary Catherine. Your mother needs you. You’ll go. End of story,” I said, wiping a tear from her cheek with my thumb.

Chapter 72

"OK, MIKE. SO JULIANA and Fiona have dental appointments at eleven on Tuesday," Mary Catherine explained as we sped along the Cross Bronx Expressway early the next morning.

"What else?" she said. "Right. Wednesday is the after-school parent-teacher meeting over that scuffle Trent had with that bratty bully, Julio, in his class. And don't forget, the super is going to install the new dishwasher that's coming on Friday, but you have to remind him. He's got a brain like a sieve. I should probably write all this down."

"Mary Catherine," I said when she came up for air. "You did. You printed it out. I got it. I got it under control," I said, patting her knee.

That was a complete lie, of course. I didn't know what on God's green earth I was going to do once she left. But the least I could do for Mary Catherine, after all she'd done for us, was to try to keep her as calm as possible as she went back home to the unenviable task of attending to her terminally ill mother.

"Don't worry, Mary Catherine," Juliana said as she leaned forward and gave Mary Catherine a huge hug from the seat behind her. We know what to do. We won't forget what you taught us. All of us, even the boys, will make you so proud. You'll see."

I looked away, kept my face on the horrible potholed roadway. I, like everyone, had been on the verge of complete emotional devastation after hearing the news that Mary Catherine had to leave. There was definitely something weird about the whole situation that I couldn't put my finger on.

Instead of her leaving for just a week or two, it really felt, for some strange reason, like we'd never see Mary Catherine again. Or was it just the possibility? It was almost scary how much we loved and needed her. Mary Catherine wasn't the only one who was going to have to say good-bye to their mother.

"Holy cow, Dad! Look!" Ricky suddenly cried from the back of the van as there was a thunderous ripping sound and three South Bronx youths shot off an expressway entrance ramp. At first I thought they were on motorcycles, but then I looked again and realized they were on ATV four-wheelers. *Huh?*

"Check it out!" Eddie yelled as they roared around the van. "They're not even wearing helmets!"

"And they're wearing blue bandannas and LA Dodgers jerseys," Ricky said. "I saw this on the Internet, Dad. They're Crips! Actual Bronx gangbangers!"

"On actual ATVs," Eddie cried excitedly. "Quick, Dad! Lend me your phone so I can video this! YouTube, here I come!"

Instead, I slowed down to let the Bronx Inner City Road Warriors get safely ahead before I shared a head shake and a smile with Mary Catherine.

"Mary Catherine, if we can handle getting you through this city to the airport alive, we can handle you being gone for a couple of weeks. Everything's going to be fine," I said.

We did manage to escape from the Bronx and get to JFK about thirty minutes later. I got us a little lost when I instinctively took us to the massive, busy airport's Terminal 4, where I'd been many times before, sending off and receiving Irish relatives hopping the pond on Aer Lingus for weddings and visits and wakes. But Brian looked up on my phone that Aer Lingus had recently moved to JetBlue's Terminal 5.

Everybody had been doing relatively well in the stiff-upper-lip department, but as we finally approached Terminal 5, it started. Everybody, seemingly at once, started weeping. When I stopped the van and turned to my right, I saw why.

There, on the other side of the fence, it was, standing on the tarmac, waiting. The big green-and-white Aer Lingus 747 with the shamrock on its tail that was about to take Mary Catherine away from us.

"Stop crying, please, now, would you? It's not so sad," Mary Catherine said, using both hands in a useless attempt to stop her own tears.

I quickly popped the doors and got out and grabbed the bags as Mary Catherine doled out hugs to the sobbing children. Shawna, who seemed to be taking it the hardest, clung to Mary Catherine so fiercely I didn't think she'd ever let her go.

"It's OK. I'll be back before you know it," Mary Catherine whispered to her between her own sobs.

But Shawna wasn't having any of it. She just kept clinging and silently crying as she shook her head. Smart kid.

I finally got Juliana to take Shawna into the van

and was just about to tell Brian to sit in the front seat until I got back from seeing Mary Catherine off inside, when Mary Catherine put her foot down.

"No, Mike. I got it from here," she said, taking her bags from me.

Then she was kissing me, clutching me almost painfully, sobbing wetly against my neck.

"I..." she said.

A plane took off from somewhere with a terrific vacuumlike whoosh as we clinched on the sidewalk. Around us, car and trunk doors thunked opened and closed. And then it was happening. She was letting me go.

Torn from her, I stood, rooted, on the sun-bleached concrete beside the van, watching her leave. As if as long as I kept my eyes on the bob of her curly blond hair, on the outline of her sweater and jeans, it somehow wouldn't happen.

But it did. She went through the sliding doors. I still stood there and stood there.

Even when the parking enforcement guy walking toward the van to get us moving stopped and turned around when he saw my face.

Part Four

LAST SUPPER

Chapter 73

THAT MONDAY MORNING, AFTER somehow getting my still-devastated kids off to school, I put my high-profile jewel-heist case on the back burner for the moment. Instead, I trekked up to Harlem to head the Ombudsman Outreach Squad morning briefing.

As we went over all the current open cases as well as some new ones, I could see that good things were happening here in terms of the group dynamic. Doyle and Brooklyn Kale seemed to be getting along much better now, Noah Robertson had toned down the sartorial splendor, and good ol' Arturo Lopez actually seemed to have lost a few.

Like every great squad, they were acting much more like a team now, depending on one another, developing their own unique culture. Best of all, instead of being laid back like on the first day I'd gotten here, everybody seemed to be stepping up and taking personal ownership of the squad's mission to truly help people. How do you like that? Progress at last.

Suddenly, Ariel Tyson, the squad's affable clerk, burst through the open doors, not looking so affable. In fact, her eyes were wide and looking pretty panicked behind her red-framed eyeglasses.

"Detective Bennett, I just got a call from dispatch. The Twenty-Eighth Precinct squad supervisor just spotted Holly Jacobs's murder suspect. They pursued him and apparently now he's holed himself up in a construction site on a Hundred and Twenty-Seventh between Madison and Fifth."

The entire squad cleared out and headed over. Three blue-and-whites were there already. Half a dozen worried-looking uniforms were outside their cars, standing in front of a row of scaffolding-clad town houses on the north side of 127th Street neighboring St. Andrew's Episcopal Church.

The house the cops were focused on was in horrendous shape. Bricked-up windows and crumbling stairs and an NYC subway system of cracks webbed over the whole narrow length of its brownstone facade. It was leaning a little to the left like it was going to collapse. Even the fantasy sales brochure mockup of what the run-down block was going to look like on the huge LUMINOUS PROPERTIES sign attached to the scaffolding was faded and covered in graffiti.

"What do you got?" I said to Gomez, the wiseacre cop Doyle and I had dealt with at the gang-related shooting scene a couple of weeks before.

"An alert security guard at the dollar store on Lenox ID'd your guy from those flyers we handed out and called us the second he walked in," Gomez said. "He took off as soon as he saw us. Guy is faster than a Kenyan.

"I thought we had him penned in between Fifth and Madison, but then he squeezes himself into the leaning tower of Harlem here. Went through the tiny gap between those padlocked doors like a rat or something, the skinny bastard. I got another car around back covering the back alley. He hasn't come out. He's holed himself up. ESU is five minutes out."

I turned as Doyle went to my car and returned with the bolt cutters from the trunk.

"ESU?" Doyle scoffed as he stepped up the stairs. He gave me a wink as he snipped neatly through the chain.

"Haven't you ever heard of improvising, Gomez?" he said.

Under the cavelike shade of the scaffolding, I watched Doyle borrow a flashlight from one of the patrolmen and take out his gun. His usually glib expression was tauter as he stood by the brownstone's now-unlocked plywood doors, his brows knitted in concentration. Then I watched Arturo take out his gun as well, along with Brooklyn and Noah.

My squad was stepping up, all right, I thought, walking to the front of the line and taking the flashlight from Doyle.

The plywood door swung in silently when I toed it. The narrow building was even rougher inside, if that was possible. There was no sign of the decorative wainscoting or pocket doors that charming brownstones are generally known for. There was nothing but rubble and squatters' garbage and the almost unbearable smell of a backed-up sewer.

"And I thought Detroit was bad," Brooklyn said, covering her nose with a hand.

Within a minute of carefully stepping inside, we heard a scuffing sound from up the stairs directly opposite the front door. I ran the flashlight over the staircase. Some of the steps were missing, as well as the banister. I kept the light's beam trained on the top, where Roger was holed up somewhere, probably waiting for us.

I was just about to tell Doyle that we should wait for ESU after all when he started up the stairs.

That was when the odd creaking sound came. A split second later, something huge and square fell from above and exploded onto the staircase a foot in front of Doyle's nose. It went through the stairs with a crunching, thunderous metal bang. The staircase ripped apart like a bomb had hit it, sending plaster chunks and dusty wood shrapnel flying all over everyone.

Through the dust and my fluttering heart, I watched Doyle teetering on the edge of the gaping hole that had been the staircase.

I was on the bottom step when he lost his balance and fell forward and disappeared.

Chapter 74

LUCKILY, WE FOUND DOYLE after a minute of screaming for him. Disoriented and bleeding and extremely pissed off but thankfully very much alive, he stumbled up from the rear stairs of the basement he'd fallen into. He'd been banged up pretty good in the fall. His face was scratched and his right arm had been sliced open almost from his wrist to his elbow. He was also covered in sewage, which wasn't doing any wonders to soothe his Irish temper.

"What the hell happened?" Doyle said as we quickly led him out of the death-trap hovel and back outside.

It was a stove that had been airmailed, we found out later. Since he was out of anvils, I guess Roger had pulled a Wile E. Coyote from the structure's third floor with a vintage Royal Rose oven that he had pushed through a gaping hole in the floor. Another step and Doyle would have been instantly killed by two hundred pounds of falling rusted steel.

I immediately instructed Brooklyn to take Doyle to the hospital for some stitches, not to mention a tetanus shot.

The unkindest cut of all came when ESU finally arrived. The SWAT cops cleared the house twenty minutes later with no sign of Roger. They speculated that he might have escaped over the rooftops and scurried down into the alley at the back of the church. We'd missed him. *Again.*

I brooded in my car for a bit, feeling sorry for myself, then looked out my window at the deplorable disgrace of a building. Staring at the LUMINOUS PROPERTIES sign, I took out my smartphone. The more I researched, the angrier I got. Twenty minutes later, I left my squad mates at the scene for my morning's first I'm-mad-as-hell-and-not-going-to-take-it-anymore moment.

I pointed my Crown Vic south below Ninety-Sixth Street until I shrieked up in front of a pagoda-like glass office building on Lexington near Grand Central Terminal. Still covered in dust from the near-death experience in Harlem, I got quite a few looks from the well-heeled office workers inside.

Luminous Properties was on two. The receptionist was a too-thin, harshly beautiful brunette, her big dark eyes rimmed with garish makeup. She reminded me very much of some of the Russian hookers from the Mob database I'd been searching, so I was a little surprised when she said, "Uh, yeah?" with an accent straight out of Staten Island.

I took out my shield and showed her who I was and then told her why I was there. Five minutes later, I quickly left and took a spin west and then north over to Fifty-Seventh and Seventh, to the site of a luxury condo that was going up beside Carnegie Hall.

The cofounder of Luminous Properties, Maximilian Schlack, looked very much like his glossy photo in the *New York Magazine* Power 100 Real Estate Edition, so I was able to spot him straightaway as I got off the rickety construction elevator on the site's unfinished thirty-second floor.

The tan, buff thirty-three-year-old was standing at the orange-safety-netted north edge of the windy, still-open floor. He was with a group of other guys in expensive suits and hard hats, listening intently to a tall, curly-haired exec as he gestured with his hands at the money-green sea of Central Park.

I'd decided to introduce myself to ol' Max when he suddenly moved off from the group a little ways to type a text. I snuck up behind him and tapped him on the shoulder. The look he gave me over his phone was equal parts annoyance and disdain. As if I were a new waiter who'd just tried to clear the cheese course he was still enjoying.

He didn't seem to like it so much as I stood there silently staring at him.

"And you are? Silent Bob, one of the new contractors? I give up. Try to spit it out, OK? I'm busy," he said.

His haughty expression switched off instantly, his hazel eyes flashing with a sudden panicked guilt, when I reached into my pocket and showed him my shield.

"Guilty conscience, Max?" I said.

Chapter 75

"NYPD? WHAT IS THIS about?" Max Schlack said, quickly leading me away from the group and back down the freshly Sheetrocked corridor for the elevator.

"This is about a dump you own on a Hundred Twenty-Seventh Street," I said.

He stared at me. We were about the same height. When he took off his hard hat, I saw that his deep, rich tan continued to his cleanly shaved head. He was one of those white guys who actually look good bald. It suited him. He was also broad in the shoulders. I remembered the article saying he had played rugby at Yale. A real stud.

"I own a lot of properties. Who are you, again?"

"Oh, it's yours," I said, ignoring him. "I looked it up. Twenty-Seven East One Hundred Twenty-Seventh Street is owned by Luminous Properties.

You own Luminous Properties, ergo you own the dump on a Hundred Twenty-Seventh. ”

He was also the owner of the building we thought Naomi had been abducted from. But I didn't say that.

"It—like almost the rest of the block—was purchased three years ago. Since then, you've been fined thirty-six times for various building and fire code violations. I didn't make the Power One Hundred list this year, but even to me, that seems like an excessive number."

"And you're telling me this because?" the tall, tan GQ-ish guy said, glancing at his BlackBerry again.

I reached out and placed my hand over his device's screen.

"Because I was just there chasing a suspect into your hazard zone, and my partner almost got greased when the floor collapsed. My partner is in the hospital right now. Do I have your attention now, moron?"

"OK, OK. I think I know what you're talking about. A Hundred Twenty-Seventh Street is in rough shape. That's why we're developing it. Why was your partner on my property, again?"

"Bullshit you're developing it," I said. "You

slapped up some scaffolding about a year ago on the outside, but inside you haven't touched a thing. Just like with so many buildings you own. You buy them and then let them fester. Make the block as horrendous and unlivable as possible to drive down the values and drive everybody out, especially the rent control people.

"Then you rush in with your buddy—Gabe Chayefsky, is it?—and his private hedge fund equity money and scoop up the whole block at cut-rate prices. Too bad *New York Magazine* doesn't do a Scumbag 100 edition or you would have made the cover."

"You read too many blogs, Officer," Max said, smiling easily, guilt erased now. His teeth were even and very white in his tan, exfoliated face.

"That's idle speculation," he continued. "Listen, I am aware there are some problems, and it's true, we have been fined. But we've paid those fines, and we're working in good faith to get square with all of it. You can ask Judy Quincy at the Department of City Planning or Alan Dawes's office.

"You know Alan, the speaker of the City Council? Maybe not. I do, though. Perhaps your boss's boss's boss might. Anyway, all of our properties are secured. The criminal must have entered illegally.

How am I to blame for that? I'm the victim of trespassing here, as far as I can tell."

I stood there staring at him. I wasn't getting through to this guy, and I knew I wasn't going to. The fact that Doyle wasn't dead was a miracle, but this guy could not care less. It made me mad.

After a moment, I glanced at the edge of the construction site's open floor.

"You look like a smart guy, Max. Ivy League, am I right? Objects fall at nine point eight meters per second squared, right?" I said. "We're what? Thirty-two floors up? That's three hundred and twenty feet. In a mere ten seconds, you could be in Carnegie Hall. Imagine that, Max. And it wouldn't even take any practice at all."

"What?" he said, outraged.

"Clean 'em up. That's what I'm here to tell you. Clean them the hell up or sell them. I don't give a shit."

"Or what?" he said, smiling again, almost amused.

"Or your next *New York Magazine* photo shoot is going to go overtime when they have to try to figure out how to shoot around your badly broken nose."

"Are you kidding me? This is unreal. You really are threatening me, aren't you?"

I leaned in until we were almost chest to chest. "Look in my eyes. What do you think?"

"This is outrageous. You can't do this. Who the hell are you?"

"My name is the Ghost of Your Ass-Kicking Yet to Come, Schlack. If you don't get your company's shit together," I said, turning and walking back toward the elevator.

A horn sounded far below down between the metal grates as I pressed the elevator button. When I looked up, Schlack was suddenly beside me, his sneering, haughty look back. It seemed to be his natural resting expression.

"What are your name and badge number? I want them now," Schlack said, squinting at me.

"Oh, my badge number. Sure," I said, reaching into my pocket. I wrapped my fist around my shield and then held my closed fist up in front of his face.

"You'll have to guess, Max. I'll even give you a hint. The first number is a six. You know, the same percentage scumbags like you make in commission when you flip a slum house."

Even I could hardly believe where I was taking this, how angry I was, how much I wanted to start trading punches with this guy. I usually didn't go around threatening to kick people's asses or throw them off buildings. Even punks like this one.

Was it all the stress I'd been under since coming back home? All my cases? The fact that Mary Catherine had left? Was I projecting all my troubles onto Max here, I wondered?

I couldn't decide. Or care. Instead, I stood there and waited, staring at him.

"Guess you didn't want it that bad, huh?" I said as the elevator finally arrived. "You didn't even guess."

Chapter 76

AFTER MY FAIRLY UNHINGED and completely fruitless freakout near Carnegie Hall, I drove back up to Harlem to check in with Robertson. He thought he might have found something connected to Naomi's murder and he wanted to show me in person.

As I came through the squad office door, I watched as Noah immediately spun around in his cubicle. He knocked over one of the precarious stacks of printouts covering his desk as he frantically waved me over.

"I think I've found a lead on the cannibal angle, Mike," he said as he brought up a website on his computer. "It's beyond bizarre, but I really think this might be the break we've been waiting for."

Noah clicked through some pages and then showed me what looked like a classified ad.

PECCATUM KITCHEN PRESENTS

CANDLELIGHT AND DARKNESS

FINE WINE AND FABULOUS TABOOS

YOU KNOW WHO YOU ARE WE KNOW WHO YOU ARE

DINNER—MONDAY NIGHT 11ISH

WHERE—SOMEWHERE IN NYC (BELOW 96TH) TO BE ANNOUNCED FOR OBVIOUS REASONS

COST—$2000 PER COUPLE

RESERVATIONS AND REFERENCES A MUSTY MUST—AS ALWAYS

"This is from Craigslist," Noah explained. "It's a screen shot. I found it about an hour ago when I called you. It stayed on for five minutes, then disappeared. I just lucked on it."

"Well, let's see. *Peccatum* means 'sin' in Latin, I know," I said offhandedly as I read it over again.

"How did you know that?" Noah said, surprised. "I had to look it up."

"Freshman Latin at Regis High," I said. "This ad sure sounds pretty weird, but how does this relate to Naomi's murder? Do you think this is some sort of cannibal dinner or something?"

Noah nodded as he restacked the papers that had fallen. Beside the printouts, I noticed a copy of *Grimm's Fairy Tales* open to a picture of Hansel and Gretel sitting in a cage while the witch stirred the pot.

"For the last week or so, I've been really delving into cannibalism research," Noah said. "Especially the cannibalism subculture on the web. For obvious reasons, I concentrated my searches on Deepnet sites."

"Which sites?" I said.

"Deepnet. It's Internet stuff that doesn't register on surface search sites like Google. A bunch of underground sites use this thing called the Tor network, which is basically a bunch of connected random volunteer servers that pass data back and forth in an elaborate routing system with multiple levels of encryption to maintain secrecy."

"Sounds like the seedy underbelly of the Internet," I said.

"Exactly," Noah said. "It's unregulated and filled with open communication about black-market commerce and hacking and criminal activity. It contains a lot of really, really sick and spooky stuff."

"So it's true that cannibalism is an actual subculture now?" I said.

"Shockingly, yes," Noah said, blinking at me. "I found four sites that had open forums about it. Dozens of people on threads going on and on about killing and eating people. Most of it seemed like sick fantasy stuff, except for this one site that seems to be based in the NYC area.

"These creeps who were exchanging Hannibal Lecter-style recipes kept giving references to the initials *PK*. 'When is PK going to happen again?' and 'Have you heard about the next PK?' One of the weirdos said he had heard something was going to be posted on Craigslist soon, so I kept an eye out.

"And then an hour ago, voilà! I was trolling through the bowels of Craigslist NYC and found this. PK must be Peccatum Kitchen. Has to be. And it's happening tonight."

"Great job, Robertson. This does seem like a lead," I said, smiling. "Especially the two grand for dinner part. Both witnesses described what definitely seems like some sort of bizarre upscale underground supper club. How do you contact for reservations?"

"That cell number there in the upper left-hand corner," Noah said, tapping the screen. "I already had the phone company trace it, Mike. No luck on a name. It's a temp cell phone bought with cash from a Radio Shack in Times Square."

"We definitely need to check this thing out," I said. "Sign us up. Two of us will go to the dinner undercover, and the rest of the team will be backup."

"Where are we going to come up with the two grand?" Noah said.

"The squad has about eighteen hundred dollars in the petty cash account, and we'll pass around the hat for the rest," I said. "Everyone wants to bring justice to Naomi and her family."

"And references?" Noah said.

I stared at a photograph of Noah and what looked like his twin sister pinned to his cubicle wall as I thought about it.

"Get the phone company to give you every number that calls that cell number," I finally said. "Then back-trace for a name to use as a reference."

"Brilliant," Noah said excitedly. "So that's it? Just like that, we're going to go undercover?"

"Bon appétit," I said grimly, nodding at the screen.

Chapter 77

"WOW, MIKE. NICE SUIT. You scrub up pretty fine. I could almost eat you up. Metaphorically speaking, of course," Brooklyn Kale said, laughing, as we walked down a cruddy section of West Twenty-Seventh Street that night around ten-thirty.

"Sorry," said my young, attractive, black-cocktail-dress-wearing, six-foot-three "date" as we continued to walk east near the border of the Koreatown and Chelsea neighborhoods. "I'm just nervous. I'll shut up now."

Noah had done it. He'd tracked down a recommendation and scored an invite for tonight's freakish underground dinner. Brooklyn and I had drawn the short straws to attend the event, while Arturo and Doyle and Robertson were parked around the corner of Seventh Avenue in an unmarked car in case we needed backup.

The street was mostly dingy office buildings and Korean wholesale stores and nail salons, but the address on the invite turned out to be a beautiful two-story Spanish mission-style town house with a terracotta roof and a tall black wrought-iron fence that looked like it was from the early 1900s.

The short old woman who answered the arched wood-and-iron front door looked like she was from the early 1900s as well. She wore a faded old green housedress with a brown paisley head scarf and looked easily eighty.

Looking at the witchlike woman, I suddenly remembered the *Grimm's Fairy Tales* on Robertson's desk. I also suddenly wondered how good this undercover idea really was. I definitely didn't want Brooklyn and me to end up like Hansel and Gretel.

"What do you want?" the woman said with some kind of Eastern European accent.

"We're here for the dinner," I said, handing her the invite.

Or are we the dinner? I thought.

The old lady assessed the paper and then both of us carefully with her little black eyes.

“Money,” she said, holding out her hand.

As the cash-filled envelope touched her palm, she opened the door fully and smiled, showing hard little brown-and-yellow teeth that reminded me sickeningly of corn kernels.

This probably wasn’t going to be the last time I felt nauseous before this night was through, I thought as I took a breath and followed Brooklyn through the door.

Chapter 78

THE HAUNTED-GINGERBREAD-COTTAGE feeling continued as we were led through the house's interior, past unlit and dusty empty rooms. The stove in the kitchen looked an awful lot like the falling one that had almost killed Doyle that morning.

Nothing was cooking on it, I noticed, which was weird. Wasn't this supposed to be a dinner?

We suddenly heard classical music when the spooky old lady opened the set of French doors at the back of the kitchen. Through the doorway off a back deck was a wide-open courtyard with a huge garden and trees strung with garlands of soft white lights.

A pristine white tent stood in the garden's center, and beneath it about twenty people were standing around, chatting casually with drinks in their hands as if they were at a fancy wedding reception. There were several Japanese men and women, I noticed straight off the bat, and several gay male couples.

Was one of them Naomi's killer? I wondered. Were all of them?

No one seemed to notice us except for a black-clad waiter who stepped up and took our drink orders. After five minutes, two strikingly tall platinum-blond women in matching silver sequin dresses came over to us. In their high heels, they were both six and a half feet tall or more. They were both shapely, nice-looking ladies, but from the width and squareness of their shoulders and jaws, you could tell they were transgender.

Brooklyn shot a now-there's-something-you-don't-see every-day look at me as they clomped up to us.

They introduced themselves as Lucy and Barbara.

"Don't I know you?" Lucy said to me between sips of her whiskey sour. "San Diego two years ago? You were at Christian Gazenove's birthday with that snotty fashion photographer. The one that ended up in the hospital?"

"Wasn't me. Sorry," I said, shaking my head slowly at whatever the hell it was she had just said.

"Hey, brown sugar. You hungry? You look hungry," Barbara said to Brooklyn with an irritating little smirk.

"Excuse me! If everyone would—Excuse me!" called a voice from behind us before Brooklyn could reply.

We all turned toward a man now standing on the deck. He was a pudgy but neat and pleasant-looking sixty-something dude in a beautifully tailored dove-gray suit. He didn't look like a cannibal. With the white goatee he was sporting, I thought he looked very much like that nice old guy who sang "Frosty the Snowman" in that vintage children's Christmas special.

"Thank you," the genteel holly-jolly fat man said with a smile. "To those who have been here before, welcome back, and to our first-timers, how do you do? My name is Dale Roanoke, and I have the pleasure of being your culinary guide this evening. Any questions about any of tonight's courses, do not hesitate to ask me. Now, without further ado, if you would follow me, culinary adventurers. Our chariot awaits."

Chapter 79

OUR CHARIOT, NOW PARKED out front on Twenty-Seventh, turned out to be an antique London double-decker bus transformed into a beautiful two-level polished-brass-railed bar on wheels.

I'd seen a picture of it once in a *Vanity Fair* article about fancy parties out in the Hamptons. Cannibals were moving up in the world, apparently.

We decided to chill at the back of the bar on the top deck. The bus made a left on Sixth Avenue and then another quick left and then went all the way to the West Side Highway. At first, I got nervous that we were losing our backup until I spotted Arturo and the boys off the back of the bus following two cars back.

About fifteen minutes later, the bus pulled into

the parking lot of a marina on the Hudson near Battery Park. It stopped alongside a dock where a hundred-foot white yacht was tied.

"As you see, our ship has come in," came the voice of the Frosty the Snowman guy over the bus's speaker.

"Mike, what about backup? Are we actually going to get on the boat?" Brooklyn said as the bus began to empty.

"You still have your Glock in your clutch?" I said.

"Of course," she said.

"Well, I have mine on my ankle. That's our new backup," I said.

We got on the rumbling boat and were led into a dining room. The vessel was OK, I guess, but much more Circle Line than *QE2*. Definitely less upscale than the bus. It also had a sour cafeteria-like smell to it. It was sort of chintzy, actually.

A jazz quartet in the corner of the room started up as more waiters hustled out for even more drink orders. *Why all the drinking?* I wondered. Could one only consume human flesh while pie-eyed or something?

A waiter brought us two more Amstel Lights as a perfectly normal-looking couple of fine young cannibals stepped up and introduced themselves.

"Hi, I'm Steve," said the guy with a Texas accent. "This is Gail, my baby. We just got married three weeks ago."

Handsome and drunk in a suit with an undone tie, Steve looked like a Wall Street guy after a long day. Tall, brunette Gail baby was also good-looking and very drunk. She hummed to herself loudly as she took out her phone and started texting. Real charming couple.

"It's my first time. Is it like they say?" Steve said to me. "Does it really taste like chicken?"

"I have no idea," I said truthfully. "It's my first time, too."

"I call the penis," Gail said with a giggle, without looking up.

"Oh my God! Do you think they'll actually serve that?" Steve said in horror. Then he took out his own phone and started typing. Googling about it, perhaps.

I looked at the idiotic young couple in awe. I'd been doing OK up to that point, but as I stood there, I really started to become angry. This couple was actually going to eat another person. Why? So they could write about it on their Facebook wall? For nothing, I realized. For kicks.

How had they and Lucy and Barbara and the rest

of the folks here become such amoral, mixed-up, disgusting, animalistic excuses for human beings? I wondered. I mean, Stone Age savages ate people because they were Stone Age savages. Or in the case of the Donner Party, it was in order to survive. That a modern person, or in this case a busload of modern people, would actually pay two grand to experience what eating another person was like was starting to piss me off like you would not believe.

There was prearranged seating, and Brooklyn and I took our places at a table with half a dozen polite middle-aged Asian cannibals as the boat pulled out. We headed south for the harbor. I could see the Statue of Liberty lit up outside the window off to my right.

It was about five minutes later when the lights dimmed and then a spotlight hit a black curtain beside the jazz quartet. I remembered what the witness to the murder in Harlem had said about a woman being bound like a leg of lamb. If that actually happened, if they actually brought someone out like that, I was going to take out my undercover Glock and start either arresting or shooting people.

Because I was sick of these freaks, just sick to my stomach.

But instead of a bound woman, a line of waiters

suddenly appeared from between the parted curtain, bearing covered silver platters. As one of the platters was set down in front of me, I wondered if I was about to see a head under the silver dome like John the Baptist's.

My head swam as I started sweating. *There better not be,* I thought. Or someone was seriously getting hurt.

There was a drumroll, and then all at once, the waiters pulled up the domes. Underneath on a white plate was a nouvelle-cuisine-looking dish with raspberry-colored sauce over what looked like pork.

As I stared at it, suddenly all of it, the whole night, the old woman, the sway of the boat, and especially the sight of the mystery meat on my plate, hit me like a sledgehammer.

I screeched my chair back just in time to puke my three light beers between my shoes.

Chapter 80

THE ASIAN CULINARY ADVENTURERS at my table started complaining loudly in a language that wasn't English as I sat there bent over, dry heaving.

"Are you OK, Mike?" Brooklyn said at my back.

"Not even a little," I said as I stood, wiping my mouth.

When I turned around, Frosty was at the front of the room holding a microphone.

"The wine for our first course—" he began as I grabbed the tablecloth in front of me and pulled like a magician. But I guess I was no David Blaine, because instead of just pulling out the tablecloth, I sent everybody's dinner sailing. There was an enormous clatter as plates and silver went into laps and across the dance floor.

The jazz quartet honked to a dead-silent stop as

everybody stared at me. I took out my gun and my shield as I stepped forward.

"NYPD! Nobody move!" I said.

"Hands on tables now!" Brooklyn cried as she followed me.

"What in the hell are you doing?" the evil Frosty wanted to know.

I shoved him down into his seat.

"You're under arrest, scumbag," I informed him.

"I know my rights! This is not illegal!" he shrieked, redfaced. "Cannibalism is not illegal!"

What he said was shockingly true. Noah had told me that though there were laws against the desecration of bodies, as of yet cannibalism wasn't technically illegal. Though after tonight, I was definitely going to write my congressman.

"Are you listening to me?" brayed the pudgy sap. "No crime is being committed here. What's the charge?"

"I'll think of something," I said as I lifted him up, no mean feat, and hauled him out the dining room door to the outside deck. The cool, fresh air off the water was wonderful after the humid cafeteria stench of the dining room. I immediately felt a thousand times better.

"You have no idea who you're talking to, do you?" Frosty screamed in a high voice. "Ever hear of PRG Trucking? Maybe not. My family's firm is not *the* biggest trucking company in the country, it's just the third biggest! When my army of lawyers is done suing you and your department, you're going to wish you'd never been born!"

"I already wish it after tonight's festivities, you roly-poly sack of puke. Now, who killed her? Was it you?"

I shoved him against the side of the boat.

"You feel like going for a swim?"

Frosty fell to his knees and started blubbering.

"No, no, no. You're wrong. It's a mistake. The meat we have is from a cadaver, someone who donated their body to science. We bought it off a lab rat at a car company. They use bodies for crash dummies. We're epicurean cannibals, not sexual sadists or serial killers. This is just the final frontier of culinary experimentation. We didn't kill anybody. I swear to you!"

I let out a breath as I watched him blubber. I knew he was telling the truth. Noah had told me all about the different types of cannibalism from his research: sexual cannibalism, aggression cannibalism, spiritual and ritual cannibalism, epicurean cannibalism. It was obvious now that the group here tonight wasn't a pack of budding Jeffrey Dahmers. Sick, amoral assholes who needed a beating and some lessons on how to be human, maybe, but not actual killers.

It looked like we had come upon cannibals in the city, only they were the *wrong* type of cannibals. Super.

I went in and spoke to some of the waiters. When I stepped back out onto the deck, they were behind me, pushing rolling carts with all the "food" on them. One by one, I started Frisbeeing the plates into the harbor. Brooklyn came out and started enthusiastically helping me.

"What are you doing?" Frosty the Jackass wanted to know.

"It's called a burial at sea. This is the remains of a human being. That means something to me because, see, I'm a human being, too. It's called human fellowship. You and the people in that dining room there might want to look into it."

"But you can't do this," he said.

"No?" I said, flinging another plate into the drink. "Now go get the captain to turn this boat around for shore, would you? I'm sorry, but tonight's culinary adventure has come to a close."

Chapter 81

IT WAS AFTER MIDNIGHT when I got home. I was tapped out, all right, officially out of patience and in absolutely no mood for any more nonsense from anyone after the night's fiasco.

The night wasn't a complete waste, thanks to Brooklyn. Though I continued to fume as the boat made its way back to the dock, my partner wisely managed to keep her head. Ingratiating herself with a few of the diners, she managed to get more insight into the cannibal subculture and, better yet, score a few names of some even sketchier culinary adventurers that we might want to look into.

Though we were still in the dark on Naomi's murder, I was quite proud of Brooklyn and the rest of the gang. If nothing else, at least my Harlem crew was really coming along as investigators and as a team.

A funny thing happened as I walked through my front door. I heard singing coming from the kitchen. Though the rest of the apartment was dark, in the lit kitchen doorway I could see Seamus at the sink, singing to himself as he washed dishes.

It was the old Irish tune "The Fields of Athenry," about a poor Irishman who gets sent to a penal colony for stealing food for his family. Seamus had a good singing voice, and it was nice to stand there in the darkened hallway for a few peaceful moments and listen to him sing the sad and yet somehow hopeful old ballad.

I waited until he was finished before I walked in. He gave me a pat on the back and a gentle smile as I grabbed a towel and started drying beside him.

How he could grin or sing after picking up the slack of babysitting and dinner and homework without Mary Catherine was beyond me. Seamus was certainly a wise guy and a prankster, but he was also one of the most selfless and truly faithful people I'd ever known. Plus he loved my kids as much as I did, if that was possible.

In his calming presence, I felt embarrassed by my night's out-of-control emotional outbursts, especially my rough treatment of the heart-attack-candidate suspect, Dale Roanoke. Wrath was a sin

I'd been really wrestling with since coming home from California.

"Anita's not still here, is she, Seamus?" I said.

Anita was Anita Ciardi, the longtime live-in housekeeper at Holy Name's rectory, where Seamus worked. The saintly seventy-year-old and seventy-pound little fireplug had insisted on coming over to help out once she'd heard that Mary Catherine had to go back to Ireland. The Bennetts had more than one guardian angel floating around, apparently.

"Just sent her home after she got the laundry done," he said. "When I came into the kitchen, she was taking out the flour to bake the kids some of her famous Italian cookies, but I told her I'd excommunicate her on the spot if she didn't leave. How about you, Detective? You're looking pretty tired. Any collars tonight?"

"Not a one," I said, thinking of my many still-open cases.

"Well, you made it home in one piece, right?" he said, staring at me with his serene blue eyes as he handed me the dripping spaghetti pot. "You can chalk that in the win column, at least."

"Hey, how about you? You had the doctor today," I said. "The real doctor, not that Dowdy character."

“Passed all the tests with flying colors,” Seamus said. “Like I told that doctor, I’m fit and fine as Rory McIlroy. And to prove my point...”

Still wearing his rubber dish gloves, Seamus dropped down and did twenty push-ups, which nearly gave me a stroke of my own.

“See,” he said, standing. “My own da lived till he was ninety-five. Three heart attacks and cancer didn’t slow him down. Not a step. Well, until he took his last one, I suppose.”

“That’s enough, Father. Good night now,” I said. “It’s late, so call me when you get back to the rectory.”

“Call you?” Seamus said as he snapped off his gloves and went for the door. “How about I just text you instead, you dinosaur?”

When my comical priest grandfather had left, I grabbed a beer and took it into the bedroom. I kicked off my shoes and hopped up on the bed and checked my e-mail on my phone. There was a message from my lawyer, Gunny Chung.

Mike,

Just a quick note. First, I just wanted you to know I have my best people working on this. We are scouring the records for Mr. Bieth, including a thorough background check and examination of all social media sites to get to the bottom of exactly who he is, where he came from, what he wants, and what his motivations are. With that said, I have some bad news. We have a court date with Mr. Bieth and a judge scheduled on the 14th that you and, unfortunately, Chrissy, must attend. I will e-mail you the particulars as we get closer to the date.

All the best,
Gunny

I looked out at the lights of Manhattan and thought of my dear departed wife, Maeve.

"I'm blowing it, right? You agree with me?" I asked her. In my mind, I pictured her in a golden field somewhere, happy and waiting for me. *The fields of Athenry,* I thought.

I finally wiped my tired eyes and finished my beer and laid the bottle carefully on the night table.

Those Irish ballads, I thought with a sigh in the dark as the heavy lids of my eyes finally and joyfully closed.

They'll get you every time.

Chapter 82

I WOKE INSPIRED AT six-thirty the next morning, and by seven-thirty, the dining room table was set for ten and everything was lined up.

There was a platter of bacon and sausage, both Irish and American, no cultural bias here this fine morning. A steaming yellow hill of scrambled eggs. Next came a bowl of peppery golden home fries crisped to my exacting standards. Set beside it was a loaf of white bread, toasted and liberally buttered and fanned niftily around the rim of a plate like a deck of cards. The only thing not made from scratch was the towering stack of pancakes beside the syrup.

No one's perfect.

Well, except for Mary Catherine, of course, but she wasn't here.

"What the...?" said Ricky as he came in, followed by a groggy Eddie and Brian. Ricky looked at the food and then down at his plaid tie.

"Oh, no, is it Sunday?" he said.

"No, son. It's still Tuesday. Thought I'd give you guys a surprise hearty breakfast to kick-start your brains into learning mode. Pull up a chair and a plate and have at it."

I didn't have to tell the boys twice. Or the girls. Pretty soon, ten backpacks were ready and waiting by the front door as my ten little Indians dug in around the table like lumberjacks.

When I'd gotten out of bed, I'd wisely decided to do as MC would occasionally do and drop a surprise Sunday breakfast on everyone in the middle of the week to shake things up. It seemed to be working. There was no fighting and even an occasional giggle as I stood sipping a cup of coffee, watching the gang eat.

Seamus arrived five minutes later, startled and seemingly impressed to see the kids gathered around the dining room table in relative quiet.

"I see you've woken up on the right side of the bed this morning," he said as he poured himself some joe. "I thought I'd have to pry you out of bed with a crowbar with that long face you had on last night, but here you are, running the Bennett Diner."

I winked as we clinked mugs.

"Carpe diem, Padre," I said.

Then something great happened. Something really great and even more unexpected. It was a text on my phone. A suggestion, along with some instructions.

"What is it? What's up?" Seamus said.

"Stay right there," I said, running into my bedroom.

When I came back to the dining room, I was holding my laptop. I cleared away some dishes and laid it on the corner of the table and turned it on.

"What are you doing, Daddy?" Chrissy said, trying to peek.

"It's a surprise," I said. "You can't look. Just wait one sec."

I clicked some more buttons, changing screens.

"Ta-da!" I said as I held up the laptop to show Mary Catherine smiling ear-to-ear on Skype.

"Mary Catherine!" everyone cried at once.

Chairs scraped loudly as the kids rushed over beside me. Chrissy and Shawna jumped into my lap as Seamus practically jumped on my back. A dozen heads bonked together as everyone tried to get a look at our long-lost nanny.

"Now would you look at all the happy faces," Mary Catherine said. "On a Tuesday morning before school, no less. I guess I'm not that missed after all, seeing you so happy."

"Noooo!" Shawna cried. "We miss you! We really, really miss you!"

"I miss you, too, Shawna. Like you wouldn't believe," Mary Catherine said. "I feel like I've been gone a year. How long has it been?"

"Ten years," I said.

"Guess what we named the puppy, Mary Catherine?" Fiona said, holding him up to the screen.

"Tell me," Mary Catherine said, smiling widely.

"Jasper!" the kids cried out together.

"And don't forget that the hamster's name is now Puddles. That suggestion was me own, actually, on account of his reaction each time I pick up the nervous little fella," Seamus said as the little ones giggled.

"I love you all. That includes Jasper and Puddles. I'll be home to you as soon as I can. Bye now," Mary Catherine said as she clicked off the connection.

"Not soon enough, Mary Catherine," I mumbled to the blank gray screen.

Chapter 83

AFTER DROPPING THE KIDS off at school, I drove up on a loud commotion by the Harlem squad's office building on 125th Street.

As I parked behind a donut cart near the corner of Adam Clayton Powell Boulevard, I could see a one-legged homeless guy on the plaza in front of the building. He was putting on some kind of a show. Jumping around energetically like a middle-aged black pogo stick, he was shaking a coin-filled coffee cup while singing the Marvin Gaye classic "Let's Get It On" at the top of his lungs.

Was he harmless? Dangerous? Bath-salted? I wondered as I stepped toward him. Entertaining? Definitely.

"Well, hello there, sir. Tucker Johnson's the name," the man said, jingling the change in his coffee cup like a tambourine as he hopped toward me with a surprising athletic alacrity. "You have a request? What can ol' Tucker sing for you? You like the Platters? I do a real nice 'Twilight Time.'"

I shook my head. I could smell the cheap wine off him from ten feet. Handicapped people are able to accomplish a lot of amazing things that deserve applause. But drinking oneself into oblivion by eight-thirty in the morning isn't one of them.

"I don't mind you hanging out, Tucker. You just can't hang out here making so much noise, bothering the good people of the world trying to go to work. No singing until noon. At least. Also, getting sober first might be nice."

"Ah, man. I ain't hurtin' no one," he said. "I'm just tryin' to spread a little sonic joy out here this morning. Plus this is my work, man. You gonna put an artist outta work?"

"Fine," I said. "How does ten bucks sound to go away?" I reached into my wallet.

"Twenty sounds better," Tucker said, getting surly.

"Twenty what?" I said, staring at him sternly. "Days in jail for disturbing the peace?"

"On second thought, ten'll do just fine," Tucker said, brightening.

The crowd waiting at the donut cart on the corner of 125th gave me a cheer as I escorted Tucker Johnson on his way. I took a modest bow before heading back toward the building. And why not? Not even in the office yet and I'd already solved my first civil disturbance of the day.

But before I got even halfway to the building's front door, my phone rang. It was Arturo.

"Mike, I just picked up the office phone. A cop stationed over at Harlem Hospital said Rachel Wecht just came in, in terrible shape."

I stopped in my tracks. Rachel Wecht was Roger's new punk rock girlfriend, I remembered.

"Apparently, Roger really did a job on her last night," Arturo continued. "They were smoking crack, and he went nuts and threw her out a second-story window face-first. She broke both her arms and cheekbones and knocked out her front teeth. The good news is she spilled the beans on Roger's location. He stays at the Charles H. Gay shelter for men out on Wards Island."

"Come down on the double, Arturo," I cried as I headed back for the car. "I'll meet you in the lot. We can't let this guy get away again."

Chapter 84

A SEEMINGLY ENDLESS CSX freight train was slowly making its way from Queens to the Bronx across the Hell Gate Bridge as we came through the Triborough Bridge toll for the island made up of Randall's and Wards islands.

In the middle of the East River between the Bronx, Manhattan, and Queens, Randall's and Wards was a weird area. It housed the FDNY Fire Academy and a New York State Police facility, but its most infamous institution was the Manhattan Psychiatric Center, a dizzying network of massive tan brick buildings with barred windows that had once been the largest mental asylum in the entire world.

Beside the municipal buildings were open fields that had been converted into recreational facilities, baseball and soccer fields, tennis courts, picnic areas. There was even a driving range.

Our destination, the Charles H. Gay Men's Shelter, was at the bottom of the off-ramp, a large, wide four-story redbrick building behind a black iron fence. It almost looked like a private school until we got closer and saw the broken beer bottles and piles of vomit peppering the curb by its gate. We parked just beyond the M35 bus stop out front, where a white-bearded old Hispanic man lay splayed flat on his back on a bench, sleeping.

We told the security guard inside the door what we wanted, and he buzzed us in to see the facility's day director, Nolan Washington, in his office just off the lobby.

"There must be some mistake," said Washington, a well-dressed XXL black man and former air force medic. "You're looking for a criminal? Here?"

He rolled his eyes as he sat us down on his office sofa with some coffee.

"That's a joke, in case you were wondering," he said, accepting the photo of Roger that Arturo handed him. "We got plenty of people with serious criminal histories here, especially sexual assaults. They commit offenses, go upstate to jail, and then when the jails dump them back out, they come back home to nothing and we get to deal with the mess."

"This place looks pretty empty," I said. "How does the shelter work?"

"We open at eight p.m. and close the doors at the ten p.m. curfew. Everybody has to be out by eight the next morning. They're supposed to look for work, make some attempt to try to become self-sufficient. But they don't. They mostly drink and drug and lie around all day like oversize alley cats until we open the doors back up at eight p.m. It's pretty frustrating."

"So have you seen Roger?" I said, redirecting his attention to the photo.

"Let me grab my glasses," he said, lifting a pair off his desk.

He slipped on bifocals and stared at the sheet thoughtfully.

"Wait a second," he said, his eyes suddenly brightening. "I think we just hired this guy in the kitchen. But his name isn't Roger, it's Simon. Simon Ritt? No, Britt. That's it. Simon Britt."

He blinked up at us.

"He should be here right now."

Chapter 85

WASHINGTON TOOK OFF HIS bifocals as he lifted a phone.

"Hey, Sam, is that new guy, Simon, in?" he said.

He listened.

"Uh-huh. OK. Thanks."

"He's on his morning break," Washington said as he hung up. "They said he just took one of the maintenance carts to go to the snack bar by the driving range."

We rushed back outside with a trailing Washington, who hopped into the backseat. We were coming along the concrete columns of the Triborough about a quarter mile north on one of the island's access roads when Washington pointed forward through the windshield.

"There he is! That's him in the green cart."

Instead of the golf cart I thought he'd be driving, Roger, wearing kitchen whites, was on a green John Deere quadlike off-road vehicle. He turned his head as we were coming alongside him. I smiled as our eyes met.

Then Roger disappeared.

I almost ran him over as he suddenly cut savagely to the left in front of the Chevy, up over a curb under the Triborough Bridge overpass.

I immediately slammed on the brakes and wheeled left, the Chevy's tires throwing dirt and gravel as we bumped up off the road into a construction site under the bridge.

"Aw, c'mon, man," I heard Washington say in the back as he clicked on a seat belt.

When we came back out on the other side of the overpass, we saw Roger. He was back near the shelter, tearing away on the deceptively fast little vehicle across some baseball fields toward the shore of the island, where there was a footbridge back to Manhattan.

I couldn't let him get away. Not again. Arturo and Washington and I almost hit the roof of the Chevy twice as I sailed down and up over the access road's two curbs. The Hispanic man sleeping at the bus stop got a rude awakening as I raced past the shelter into the baseball field at about sixty and climbing.

I'd been on a few car pursuits in NYC in my time, but never an off-road one!

Roger looked surprised when he turned around and saw me right on his quad's bumper. He tried to turn again, but I was waiting for him. He and his vehicle went flying as the right front bumper of the Chevy tapped the rear of the quad, sending it into a fishtail that soon turned into a barrel roll over the diamond's infield dirt.

I screeched to a stop about a millimeter from home plate just in front of the fenced-in backstop, turning to see if Roger was still alive. Of course he was. Off the toppled quad and on foot now, he slipped through a gap beside the backstop and ran for the footbridge about a football field away.

"I got this," Arturo said, already out of the car and up-righting the still-running quad.

I could hardly believe my eyes as my chunky partner pinned it after Roger through the gap in the fence.

Roger was twenty yards from the base of the footbridge when Washington and I, watching through the chain-link, saw a fired-up Arturo leap from behind the wheel of the speeding quad. Like a three-hundred-pound Puerto Rican cannonball, he sailed through the air toward Roger's sprinting back.

It was a direct hit, center mass. Roger and Arturo went facedown in a plume of dust.

When I finally got the car around the fence and screeched up, Arturo had already cuffed him. Still amped on adrenaline, Arturo leaped to his feet, dancing around, arms raised over his head like Rocky.

"How's that for fast, Mike?" Arturo yelled as Roger lay there gasping. "Oh, yeah! Uh-huh! Done! *Finito!* Over!"

"Not bad, Lopez," I said, laughing, as I finally got out of the car and gave him a high five. "Your form could use some work, but I have to hand it to you. You definitely nailed the landing."

Chapter 86

A WINDOW-SHAKING RUMBLE of thunder woke me without preamble that next Monday morning. Sitting up on the edge of the bed, I remembered the meeting I had to be at in a couple of hours.

How could I forget it?

We'd been subpoenaed to appear at a preliminary custody hearing for Chrissy at ten a.m. at the Manhattan Family Court House downtown.

I'd been going crazy on the phone with Gunny Chung all weekend. We'd been working hard on a pretty good game plan to nip this in the bud ever since Bieth had come uninvited to my house. We'd uncovered some very interesting information about Robert Bieth and his relationship to Chrissy's birth mother that definitely threw this whole matter into question.

But now, with the hearing staring me in the face, I wasn't so sure.

I clamped a hand over my stubbled chin as I stared out through the blinds at the rain pouring down from the glum, dirty-gray sky.

Why the hell is this happening?

I was still sitting there frozen with worry a minute or two later when my phone hummed on the nightstand.

Michael God bless you and God bless Chrissy said the text from Mary Catherine. I let out a breath. Despite the fact that my nanny was an ocean away dealing with her own heartbreaking problems, she'd insisted that I keep her in the loop on Chrissy.

What time was it in Tipperary? I wondered. *Noon? And how did Mary Catherine even know I was awake?*

Because she was Mary Catherine, of course. Nothing was hidden from the angels and saints.

The phone gave off its little hum again as I was putting it back down.

Everything will turn out well. I know it will, Mary Catherine had typed.

"I'm glad you're confident, lass," I whispered to the screen in the dark as I stood. "Because I'm not so sure."

Shaved and dressed ten minutes later, I walked into Chrissy's bedroom to find her not only already awake but already ready. Her face was scrubbed, her curly blond hair washed and carefully combed and ponytailed, her nails polished. Wearing her nicest poufy dress and a cardigan and tights, she looked like she was on her way to Easter Sunday Mass.

"Look, Daddy. I'm all ready for our special day," my little girl said.

I'd been very vague to Chrissy about the whole situation from the beginning. Today I had promised her a special lunch, just the two of us, after an appointment I had with some people downtown. I wasn't sure if that was the right thing to do, but I was out of ideas, as well as time. I just couldn't stand scaring her.

I shook my head as I smiled at Juliana and Jane standing behind her. Without being asked, my two eldest daughters had gotten up early and gone way above and beyond.

"You guys are the best sisters in the world, you know that, don't you?" I said to them.

"We had to help, Dad, especially with Mary Catherine gone," Jane said solemnly. "We also know how important it is that everyone know how much we love Chrissy, even if they don't know us."

That was when my dread came back with a vengeance, along with a dull wave of anger and sadness. Because I could see now what this whole ordeal was doing not just to me and not just to Chrissy but to all the kids in my entire fragile family.

This was an adopted kid's worst fear come true, I suddenly realized.

The feeling that no place was secure no matter how much you were loved. That you were always just one knock on the door from being taken away.

Chapter 87

THE OLD TWENTY-STORY stone courthouse building just west of lower Broadway on Worth Street was about as cheerful as a cell block. I'd been doing relatively OK on the ride south, but as our cab pulled up in front of the soulless gray monolith of a building, I didn't think I'd ever felt so hopeless and helpless and alone in my life.

It was so bad that instead of going straight in after getting out of the cab, I actually stood in the rain with Chrissy, racking my brain for a way not to go to this horrendous hearing. The alternative plan I kept coming back to was to go home and pack and pick up everybody from school with the van and just keep on going.

Because if living in New York meant that some flaky stranger could just march into my house and take my daughter away, then maybe it was high time to go find some new place to live. We'd done it before.

As I stood there continuing to stall, Chrissy tugged her hand out of mine and suddenly jumped and splashed with both feet into a huge sidewalk puddle.

"Chrissy, what are you doing? Stop, you'll ruin your shoes!" I cried.

"It's OK, Daddy. I'm making them shinier. See?" she said, kicking and sloshing her feet through the water.

I pulled her out of the puddle and finally caved and reluctantly walked us in through the Family Court building's old brass revolving door. After we went through the always-exciting lobby metal detector procedure, during which Chrissy was actually wanded, we took a dusty elevator car up to seventeen and came down a wide, dingy, dimly lit corridor to a pebbled-glass-paned door.

On the other side of it, I gave my name to a grim, heavyset brunette clerk behind a cluttered desk. I stared at the JUDGE CEYAK sign on the mahogany door behind her. I already knew from reading the subpoena that Ceyak was the name of the man who somehow had been handed complete control over my family and the rest of my daughter Chrissy's life.

"And what's your name, young lady?" the clerk said cheerfully to Chrissy, smiling. "You look so pretty. I love your dress."

The clerk seemed nice enough, but Chrissy wasn't having any of it. In response, she dug in behind my leg and said absolutely nothing. I didn't blame her. Disney World this was obviously not.

As we sat dripping on a wooden bench by the door, I handed Chrissy the Nintendo DS I had smuggled from the house to keep her distracted. Over the chimes of Super Mario collecting coins, I could hear an indistinct voice talking softly into a telephone from behind the dark-wood door. I was just about to text Gunny again, when he opened the door to the hall.

Robert Bieth was right behind him with his own lawyer, Pendleton.

"The judge is ready, gentlemen," the clerk said, standing and opening the door behind her desk.

I reluctantly left Chrissy on the bench and followed my lawyer into the judge's chambers. I was thinking that there would be two tables set up, like in a courtroom, but instead there was a line of padded folding chairs in front of a small writing table.

Behind the table, wearing his robes, was Judge Ceyak. Fiftyish, with gray hair and a scruffy beard, he reminded me of the gravelly-voiced "you're gonna love the way you look" guy from those men's clothing store commercials. I seriously wondered if we were gonna love the way we looked after these proceedings.

"Firstly, Your Honor," Pendleton started in his dulcet, genteel southern tone before everyone was even seated. "I'd like to apologize for being late. Our flight up from Miami was delayed and—"

"Thanks, that's fine," Judge Ceyak said impatiently, cutting him off in much gruffer, less genteel New Yorkese. "Gentlemen, I know you must be as eager to begin as I am, so let's get right to it. Mr. Pendleton, do you have your client's DNA test results, which I requested over the phone?"

"They're right here, Your Honor," Pendleton said, handing over a sheaf of papers from his Cross briefcase.

"And you, Mr. Chung? Do we have the Bennett girl's DNA information?"

"Yes, Your Honor, we do, but first, I'd like to present something else that has recently come to light on this issue that I believe is of even more import," Gunny said, removing a stack of papers from his battered valise.

"Of more import than DNA?" Judge Ceyak said, giving Gunny an annoyed look. "What could be more important than establishing genetic linkage, Mr. Chung? I thought I explained on the phone that this is just a formality to get the ball rolling and that we would have plenty of time to get into everything else as the case proceeds."

"I do remember, Your Honor," Gunny said, still offering him the papers. "But if you would humor me just this once, I promise, you won't be sorry."

I held my breath in the silence that followed. This was really the do-or-die moment for our plan. We needed to bring this legal machine to a screeching halt before its gears could start turning and pull Chrissy and all of us in.

"You have five minutes," Ceyak finally said with a sigh. "This better be good, Chung."

Chapter 88

GUNNY STOOD AND TOOK a Post-it-flagged *Us Weekly* magazine off the top of the stack and folded it open in front of the judge.

"I'd like to direct your attention to this photo from the American Music Awards of last year," he said. "As you see, in the top right-hand corner of the page, Mr. Bieth here is accompanying the celebrity pop singer Amora on the red carpet."

"Magazines? Really?" Pendleton said. "This is silly. That Mr. Bieth is in a relationship with Amora Searson is common knowledge. Mr. Bieth worked for the celebrity singer as a backup dancer. They fell in love. Will we next be shown the *Entertainment Tonight* clip that chronicles their relationship? How does this matter, Judge?"

"Mr. Chung?" the judge said.

"Because of this," Gunny said, peeling a printout from the stack. "This is a copy of a TwitPic and a tweet Amora sent out to her thirteen million followers three months ago. As in the magazine photo, again we see Mr. Bieth and Amora, but this time poolside with Amora's two adopted boys from Rwanda, Alexander and Harry. The accompanying tweeted caption reads, 'Just hanging with my boyzzz livin the good life finally after the tour. Though a pretty little girl would make my life even good-er I think . . .'"

"Which means?" Pendleton said.

Gunny turned toward the judge, who seemed to be losing his patience.

"Mr. Bieth's claim is that he's here for his daughter because he just found out about her existence. How curious it is to see this sudden revelation coinciding with his celebrity love interest's desire to acquire a new human accessory—I mean, excuse me, to adopt a little girl."

"Coincidences happen all the time, Chung," Pendleton said. "The fact of the matter is, my client never knew of this pregnancy, let alone signed off on any adoption. Now trot out the DNA that proves paternity. This poor young man has been put through enough. He wants his daughter back."

Gunny looked at Pendleton for a long beat. Then Gunny looked at me, and we both smiled. My fingers were crossed even tighter now. It was time to reveal our ace in the hole. Or was it the joker?

"Of course he does," Gunny said, reaching into his jacket. "But first, there's just one more thing."

He laid a photograph on the desk in front of the judge.

"This photograph was found on Barbara Anjou's memorial Facebook page, posted after her suicide three months after Chrissy's birth."

Instead of the red carpet or a mansion poolside, this last photo had been taken in what looked like a crummy hospital room. But Bieth was in this one, too. Along with Chrissy's birth mother, who was holding a day-old Chrissy.

"If you want a magnifying glass to read the tag on Chrissy's wrist, Your Honor," Gunny said, taking one from his pocket, "I happen to have one right here.

"This photo proves the fact that Mr. Bieth knew about Chrissy from the very beginning," he said. "He chose not to care about her in the slightest. That is, until now, when custody of Chrissy would provide him an opportunity to stay in the good graces of his wealthy paramour.

"This case hinges on the claim that Mr. Bieth had been kept in the dark. It's obvious that was never the case. We move for you to dismiss this claim right now."

Judge Ceyak looked through the magnifying glass for a long minute, then laid it down on top of the photograph. When he looked up, Pendleton and then Bieth both put their heads down. Pendleton raised his head and opened his mouth for a moment; then he closed his mouth and lowered his head again.

In the silence through the doorway, I could hear the glorious sound of my beautiful daughter humming happily and obliviously as she played her video game.

"I have one question for you, Mr. Pendleton," Ceyak said.

"What's that, Your Honor?" Pendleton said.

"With this rain, you're going to find it difficult to get a taxi back to the airport," Ceyak said. "Would you like the number of a good car service?"

Chapter 89

EARLY THAT FOLLOWING FRIDAY afternoon, I found myself back in the thick of things at work.

After several—at times heated—meetings between me, my boss, Miriam, and the chief of detectives, a proposal of mine had finally been approved concerning the diamond heist case.

With all the panache and boldness that the crew had already displayed, coupled with the fact that each score had been bigger than the one before, it was obvious they weren't done yet. It was my theory that they would strike again in the splashiest way possible sometime during the International Diamond Conference, which had started on Wednesday. Also, considering how quickly the thieves had escaped in each robbery, I knew we needed to be right there on the scene when it happened.

So after much debate and volunteering my Harlem squad guys for the special assignment, a multilocation round-the-clock surveillance detail had finally been approved for Tiffany's and Harry Winston and the Diamond District. Straws were drawn, and for the last three days, Arturo Lopez and I had been having our breakfasts at Tiffany's.

Across from the famous jewelry store on Fifth Avenue at Fifty-Seventh Street, we sat in the back of a graffiti-covered white box truck watching the world go by on the surveillance vehicle's hidden high-def camera. So far there had been no sign of the thieves. Or even Audrey Hepburn.

I was getting concerned. Surveillances, with all the overtime, were quite expensive, and the one thing I didn't need any more of was egg on my face.

"Hey, Mike, check this out," Arturo whispered from the corner where he was working the camera.

"What is it?" I said, rushing over to see that he had the camera trained on two tall, attractive, well-dressed young blond women hurrying across Fifth.

"Man, look at them! Look how tall they are, and they're like superrich and so hot! They're models, right? They have to be."

"I think you're right, Arturo," I said, rolling my eyes. "Why don't you hop out and ask for their numbers? Show them the badge. You know, lay down some of that famous Latin charm on them."

Lopez looked up hopefully. Then he frowned. "Yeah, right. In my dreams. They're wooml."

"Wooml?"

"Way out of my league."

"In that case, how about you keep the damn camera focused on the store where it belongs," I said as I plopped down on the camp chair behind him and cracked open a Red Bull. "I vouched for you on this gig, Arturo. The least you could do is *pretend* you've been below Ninety-Sixth Street before."

I pressed my push-to-talk radio.

"Hey, how are things with you guys?" I called to Brooklyn and Robertson, stationed ten blocks south down Fifth Avenue in the Forty-Seventh Street Diamond District.

"Same as they were when you asked us five minutes ago," Brooklyn radioed back. "So far, so quiet. Not to mention that Robertson just came back with coffee and forgot the diamond necklace I asked him to buy me. Imagine, and I thought we were partners."

"Stay on your toes, Brooklyn. Don't forget these guys used guns last time. Who knows what they have planned now."

"Don't worry, boss," Brooklyn said as I stared into the screen at the waves of people crisscrossing back and forth in front of Tiffany's doors.

"We got everything wired tight."

Chapter 90

HONCHO, IN BAGGY BLUE Rockefeller Center maintenance coveralls, was sweeping some peanut shells and a cracked plastic spork out of the gutter outside the Five Guys across from the NBC studios on Forty-Eighth when he received the one-word text message.

Ready

He pocketed his phone and dropped the broom and dustpan into a wheeled garbage can on the sidewalk and immediately rolled it under the archway of a midblock pedestrian corridor beside Five Guys that cut straight through to Forty-Seventh Street. Thirty seconds later, he stepped out of the tunnel.

And took a breath.

He almost couldn't believe it. Eighteen months of meticulous planning, and now it was actually happening. The final job was actually going down.

He was smack-dab in the center of the bustling Diamond District.

He stood for a moment, soaking in what some called the Wall Street of Diamonds. Lining both sides of the two-and-a-half-football-fields-long block were diamond shop after diamond shop, where stones changed hands to the tune of four hundred million dollars a day. Instead of being glitzy like the two jewelry stores he'd recently robbed, the closely packed stores seemed utilitarian, almost grimy.

Honcho pulled up the sleeve of his coveralls and checked his watch. He swiped a drop of sweat from the back of his neck.

T minus three minutes and counting, he thought, taking another ragged breath. Counting to what, though? That was the question.

He moved north up the sidewalk, pushing the garbage can alongside a Ryder Eurovan, a Brink's armored truck, a UPS truck, and a FedEx truck, then two more huge armored vans. The vans were from none other than Malca-Amit, the premier international diamond-shuttling security firm based in Israel, which transported diamonds between the major diamond hubs of Tel Aviv and Antwerp and Mumbai and New York City.

On the sidewalk beside the trucks were scores of tourists and armored car guards and merchants. Most of the merchants, Orthodox and Hasidic Jews, were the descendants of the Jewish Europeans who had fled Antwerp for the United States after 1940, when Hitler invaded Belgium, Luxembourg, and the Netherlands, Honcho knew. There was little about the block that he didn't know, having cased it for almost the last two years.

Honcho was rolling the can past a kneeling bike messenger chaining his ride to the pedestal of a phoneless phone kiosk when he spotted the sketchy gray work van with tinted windows across the street.

What the hell? he thought, eyeing it.

Honcho slowed and swallowed, his heart pounding, his breath suddenly on hold. There was something wrong.

Chapter 91

HONCHO HAD GOTTEN THE rhythms of the block down pat over the last year, had made sure to note most of the service firms that worked the block. Especially in the last few weeks. That was how fine-tuned his research had been. But he'd never seen this van before.

It took him another second to figure it out. The markings on its door said it was from a Queens glass company. But the rig on the van's side held no panes of glass.

It was cops. *Shit! No doubt about it,* he thought. He had figured there would probably be more heat than usual after his last two jobs, but it had been an abstract thought. Actually seeing the cops right there twenty feet away was blood-chilling. He could practically feel the lens of the surveillance van's camera tracking him as he passed it.

How many undercovers are around me right now? he thought, panicking suddenly. And what if they had gotten a decent look at him from a camera on one of the previous jobs?

He started sweating more then, under his arms, down his legs. Black spots started to dance in his peripheral vision. Everything was riding on this last job. Thousands and thousands of dollars and eighteen months of meticulous planning. But it didn't matter, he finally decided. He couldn't do it. It was useless. His nerve had imploded. The cops were onto them. It was over. It wasn't going to work.

Besides, he already had a couple of million in stones. He needed to just keep rolling, roll right the hell down to the end of the block, drop the garbage bucket on the corner, and walk right down the stairs to the Rockefeller Center subway station. In a matter of hours, he'd be down to Miami, living out the rest of his life, day after day, fishing the blue water during the day and the bars at night, like Hemingway.

It was definitely plan B, but it was a damn sight better than going back to jail. It would be real jail this time, he knew. No thanks. Time to fold them and cut and run.

Screw his friends who were waiting on him and would probably get busted in about a minute and a half's time, he thought. *Sorry, fellas. Every man for himself. Just keep moving. Walk away.*

Honcho was just about to do it, too. Get out, pull the plug, abort the whole heist.

That was when he suddenly noticed the traffic sawhorse on the street. A word was stenciled in black on the orange-and-white-striped board. One word.

TRIUMPH

The silent toll of a bell went off in Honcho's head. He felt an almost holy chill down his spine as his nerve returned stronger than ever. He could see it clearly now. There was no more reason to panic.

"Triumph," Honcho whispered to himself as his watch finally beeped once and the first clattering alarm began to blat.

Chapter 92

I WAS OUT OF MY chair, rolling my stiff neck and doing a standing calf stretch against one of the cold, depressing metal walls in the cramped cube of the surveillance truck, when Arturo, sitting in front of the monitor behind me, let out a whistle.

There was movement on the tiny screen of the laptop connected to the truck's hidden camera. A black Lincoln Town Car with tinted windows was slowing alongside Tiffany's famous stainless-steel front doors. As it came to a stop, Arturo pointed the protein bar he was eating at the top of the screen, where a construction worker, a big thick-necked white guy in a kelly-green hard hat, was jogging across the avenue directly at the store.

Remembering the construction outfits the thieves had used in the first Manhattan heist, I immediately lifted the strap of the shotgun propped in the corner. But before I could even turn for the truck's gate, the hulking hard hat passed by Tiffany's harmlessly down Fifty-Seventh as a couple of white-haired octogenarian ladies-who-lunch types emerged from the Town Car.

False alarm, I thought, relieved, as I laid the long gun carefully back down.

But I thought wrong.

A split second later, a double chirp came from one of the radios on the upended milk crate we were using for a table. The shrill sound of it pinged almost painfully off the metal walls. It was radio #3, the one for Brooklyn's team. It blooped again three more times rapidly as I lifted it. Something was up.

"Mike here. What is it?" I said.

"Mike, we have something here!" she said frantically. "We have alarms going off!"

"Alarms? For which store?"

"All of them, I think!" she said. "We're looking at multiple alarms up and down the block. We're breaking cover from our van. People are looking freaked out in the street. I think you should get over here, Mike. Now!"

My thumb shook slightly as I hovered it over

the heavy police radio's key. I stared at Tiffany's on the monitor again, trying to think fast.

Was this a head fake? I wondered. Was this a ruse to get us over to the Diamond District so the thieves could then hit Tiffany's?

There was no time to figure it out. I put down Brooklyn's radio and lifted the one for Doyle and the two Midtown North Precinct detectives who were stationed inside Tiffany's security room.

"Heads up, Doyle," I said as I pointed for Arturo to get behind the truck's wheel. "We need to get over to the Diamond District. You stay put, but look sharp. You're on your own for the time being."

Chapter 93

WE JUMPED INTO THE truck's cab, and Arturo turned it over with a roar, and we made a suicidal, multiple-horn-inducing left turn through the red light onto Fifth. Ten blocks later, we could hear the incredibly high-pitched clanging of alarms as we got out on the sidewalk by one of the plastic-diamond-topped lampposts that flank Forty-Seventh Street.

The scene on the street was chaos on steroids. To the west down the block, diamond industry workers were pouring onto the sidewalks. On the street, armored car guards had weapons drawn beside their trucks. As if the deafening alarms weren't enough, from somewhere came the strong, acrid stench of smoke and burnt rubber.

A fire? Or was it a bomb? I thought.

The sound of sirens joined in with the alarms a moment later as Midtown North squad cars began arriving on both sides of the block. I stared at faces in the milling crowd, trying to eyeball any of our suspects. Instead, out of the chaotic swirl came Brooklyn and Robertson, running.

"What's up with the smoke?" was the first thing I said.

"We don't know," Robertson said. "All we know is five minutes ago most of the store alarms on the south side of the street just started going off at once."

"We'll have to start checking the stores one by one," I said loudly over the bedlam. "Arturo and I will start on this end. You guys head down the other end and grab some uniforms for backup and start working your way back toward the middle. Take your time and do this by the book, guys. We know these guys are armed and dangerous. There's potential for a hostage situation, OK? Potential for any damn thing, so be careful."

Arturo and I grabbed the first two uniforms we could and told them the plan. The male–female patrol team nodded, pale-faced and wide-eyed. They looked like raw rookies just out of high school, which wasn't making me happy, considering they'd be behind me with drawn firearms. Too bad we didn't have time to complain to the personnel department.

I peered through the bulletproof window of the first luxury jewelry store whose alarm was jangling on the southeast corner of Fifth and Forty-Seventh. I couldn't see much because the inside of the store was obscured by the tiers of diamond rings and necklaces and watches. I hefted my Remington pump and pulled the door open.

"NYPD!" I yelled.

Inside were four baffled-looking female clerks holding their ears as they pointed us to a back room. Inside it, behind a steel desk, a broad-shouldered, slightly bug-eyed middle-aged man was hollering in Yiddish into a cell phone. A chunky revolver held down a clutter of invoices on the blotter in front of him like a paperweight.

"What is this? What's going on?" the balding owner said. "Why are all my alarms going off?"

"We're not sure yet, sir," I said. "Are you OK? Is everybody OK? Did you see anything? Is your safe secure?"

"We're fine. Everything's OK," the owner said, rubbing at his eyes. "I just checked the safe in the basement. It's fine. My alarm is going off for some reason, and the alarm company won't even pick up. What is this? Terrorism? My cousin Moshe up near Sixth said he heard there was an explosion?"

I didn't have time to stay and chat with the man. Or his cousin, for that matter. We immediately cleared out to the sidewalk and were about to go into the jewelry store next door, whose alarm was wailing, when my radio blooped.

"Mike!" Robertson said. "You need to get up here. Sixth Avenue. We're at the bank and it's locked. The front door of the bank is locked!"

"The bank?" Arturo and I said in unison as we stared at each other. Then we took off west through the churning crowd.

Chapter 94

ABOUT A HUNDRED FIFTY feet in from Sixth Avenue, Robertson and Brooklyn were standing with a trio of uniforms by the front door of a branch of the Northwest River Bank.

A lot of banks in New York are the old-fashioned fancy columned granite jobs, but this one was a storefront affair like a dry cleaner or a pharmacy. It was the only bank on the block, I quickly noticed. In fact, it looked like the only establishment on the block that wasn't a diamond store.

I pulled at the glass double doors, and like Robertson had said they wouldn't budge. They were definitely locked.

A Midtown Manhattan bank just up and closes in the middle of a Friday? I thought. *Not likely. In fact, impossible.*

I cupped my eyes and leaned my forehead against the cool glass. Same as in the two stores we'd been to, the bank's alarm was firing on all pistons. Past the ATM foyer through a second set of glass doors, I could see the teller counter beyond the stanchions for the customer line. But there were no tellers at the counter and no customers on line.

I called over a patrol cop, who handed me a tactical knife that had a tungsten carbide glass-breaking tip on the bottom of its handle. It was incredible how thoroughly and easily the door shattered when I leveled the tip perpendicular to the glass and gave it a slight tap. I cleared the glass and crawled in under the push handle, and then repeated the process on the locked glass door on the other side of the ATM foyer.

Inside, in the corner of the bank to the right, ten feet from the door, a dozen or so wide-eyed people were lying bound and gagged in a line on the industrial carpet. There were several male and female tellers, two Hasidic Jews in funeral black, a security guard, even a female traffic cop. All of them with their ankles and wrists and mouths wrapped with heavy-duty duct tape.

Pegging a thin middle-aged man in a dark-gray suit on the far end of the line as the manager, I flicked open the blade of the tactical knife I was still holding as I hurried over, and cut the tape off his wrists.

"Three men," he whispered immediately after he peeled the tape off his lips.

He pointed animatedly at a corridor on the other side of the bank by the tellers' counter.

"They went down that hall for the basement vault maybe ten minutes ago," he said in hushed panic. "Be careful. They have guns. Machine guns, it looked like. I believe they're still down there."

Chapter 95

I HANDED HIM THE knife to free the others as Arturo, Robertson, Brooklyn, and three other cops followed me toward the hall. Beyond an empty office was a stairwell that went down to a half-flight landing and then made a blind turn.

"Mike, this is nuts, man," Arturo whispered, wiping his sweaty hand on his jeans before retightening his grip on his Glock. "We can't handle machine guns, can we? Shouldn't we get ESU for this?"

I put a finger to my lips before I tiptoed down the stairs and waited by the turn in the stairs, listening carefully. The only thing I could hear was the muffled clang of alarms still going off outside, so I shot a quick peek around the corner.

At the bottom of the stairs, a pudgy

thirty-something black bank guard sat gagged and duct-taped like the folks upstairs. As I stared at him from up the half flight of stairs, showing him my shield, I thought he might indicate with his eyes where the still-unseen thieves were in relation to him. But he only stared at me in terror as he tried to say something through the gag of tape.

I finally went down the last flight of stairs over the barrel of the shotgun. Past the neutralized guard was the thick steel door of a huge floor-to-ceiling vault. It was wide open. The vault filled the basement space, and I could tell immediately that it was empty. The thieves were gone.

"Where'd they go?" I said to the guard as Arturo cut his hands free and helped him take the gag off his mouth.

"They got something from the vault and went back up the stairs," the guard said between hyper-ventilating breaths.

"How long ago?" I said.

"Five, maybe six minutes."

I stared at him as I hurriedly thought about that. The manager upstairs would have seen them leave through the front. But he hadn't. He thought they were still down here.

"Brooklyn, Robertson," I said. "They must have gone up the stairs and left out the back of the bank somehow. Get up there and check."

They ran back up the stairs, and I poked my head into the vault and looked down at its floor, thinking I'd see it completely trashed like at the first jewelry store. But it was surprisingly clean. There was nothing on the concrete floor. Everything was as neat as a pin.

Everything except for one small anomaly.

Above and a little to the right of center of the wall of steel triple-key safe-deposit boxes, a small box—little bigger than an apartment house mailbox—stood open. Its stainless-steel door was scratched up and mangled, hanging off one hinge.

I clicked on a small flashlight from my belt and walked over and played its beam over the interior of the empty metal slot.

"What the hell?" Arturo said. "These guys knock over two diamond stores and then they come in here for this one little bank box? Was it a special kind of diamond in there, maybe?"

"Maybe it wasn't diamonds," I said. "Maybe it was never about diamonds at all."

We stood there dumbfounded for another ten seconds, thinking about that.

"OK, I'll say it if you won't," Arturo finally said. "What in the hell could have been in that little box?"

Chapter 96

THE THIEVES HADN'T FLED out the back of the bank, we quickly learned.

They'd exited through the bank's ceiling.

It was Arturo who found the rope ladder in the bank's janitor closet. Though it looked like it was from a child's swing set, it was surprisingly sturdy when I went up it into what looked like a vacant office on the bank building's second floor. My eyes went directly to an open window, outside of which I could see scaffolding extending from the construction site to the east of the bank.

Arturo and I went back down the ladder and sprinted out of the bank and past a middle-aged Hispanic guard into the five-story construction site. I cursed and immediately started running when I saw that the site went all the way through the block to Forty-Sixth Street.

"Hey, you see anybody come through here in the last twenty minutes or so?" I yelled at a thinner, younger, and more bored-looking version of the Forty-Seventh Street guard.

He squinted as he began picking at his teeth with his pinkie.

"Just those three messenger dudes," he said as he wiped his pinky on the lap of his cheap rent-a-cop pants.

"Bike messengers? Where'd they go?" I said.

"They got on their bikes and, like, jetted, you know. I wasn't really watching them. I just check people coming in, man. I figured they must have come in from Roberto's side. Did they have anything to do with those alarms?"

"Where were the bikes?" Arturo said.

"They had them, like, chained to the shed pole there."

"What did they look like?" I said.

"They was, like, three white boys, like ESPN host types."

Three minutes later, Arturo and I were in the dingy, sweltering back security room of a Dressbarn beside the construction site on Forty-Sixth Street, playing back footage from its sidewalk-facing security camera.

The first guy came out from under the construction site's shed with the bike at the 12:13 mark.

He was a medium-size man in black-and-white sport-racing gear on a modern sky-blue multisport bike that had weird, almost cartoonishly thick black tires. The other two were on beat-up silver bikes and were wearing camo shorts and gray hoodies. It was hard to get their facial features under their sunglasses and helmets, but the sizes and general descriptions were a match for our suspects, three thirty-something white guys, two large and one smaller.

I was calling in the descriptions when I screamed at Arturo.

"Wait! Hit the Pause button!"

In the security footage, the biggest and smallest suspects had immediately crossed to the south side of the street without incident, but the third one, the medium-size guy on the blue bike, had to stop at the rear of a UPS truck to wait for a Poland Spring water truck to pass.

I bent closer to the desktop security monitor until my nose was almost touching the screen. Then I turned and fled the cramped room.

"Lopez, come on!" I yelled, scrambling at top speed out the back-room corridor into the bright store, past the bulging racks of clothes.

"What the hell, Mike?"

Instead of answering him, I pushed out through the front doors and back out onto the street.

"Freeze! Police! Don't move!" I yelled at the UPS guy twenty feet to the east, who was rolling an empty hand truck toward the rear of the brown truck in front of the store.

"Mike, what the hell?" Lopez repeated behind me.

"The medium-size guy on the blue bike touched the truck here to balance himself when he was crossing the street," I said, pointing at the UPS truck's gate. "He wasn't wearing gloves. Arturo, we need to get CSI down here yesterday. I think we just got lucky. I think we just got ourselves a print."

Chapter 97

I WAS RIGHT. We did get lucky. Half an hour later, all the planets finally aligned.

The prints that veteran CSU tech officer Gabriela Tremane took were beautiful. From the rear rolling gate of the UPS truck, she had peeled picture-perfect thumb, index, and middle fingerprints and a partial palm of the suspect's right hand. Then, right there on the spot in front of the Dressbarn, she put them into her portable scanner, and before I even had a chance to cross my fingers, she smiled knowingly.

"We have a winner," she said. "He's in the system. Jeremy Rylan. Two Beekman Street, apartment four H, New York, New York."

"If I weren't in such a hurry, I'd go in there and buy you a dress, Gabriela. Make that two," I said as

I hopped into an undercover Chevy that we borrowed from the responding Midtown South detective squad.

"And I'd, uh, help you raise a barn to put it in," Arturo said merrily as he hopped in beside me.

The address was downtown near City Hall on the northern end of the Financial District, at the intersection of Nassau and Beekman. It was a really nice, architecturally interesting building, a nineteenth-century palace of terracotta and brick that made me think of a red velvet wedding cake.

About an hour and twenty minutes had passed from the time of the robbery when we pulled up to the address. That was our advantage. There was no way Rylan would suspect that we could be onto him so fast. Especially after all the success he'd had.

As we were just about to get out of the car, we saw a guy on the sidewalk turn off the corner of Nassau from the north.

It was a guy on a bike.

A fancy sky-blue bike with funky black tires!

Too bad Rylan saw us at the same second. He immediately spun a lightning 180 and whipped to the right down Nassau.

I gunned the engine and roared forward into the intersection in pursuit.

For eight feet.

Nassau, the one-way street he'd turned down, at the moment was a no-way street. The middle of the road had been ripped up and a World War I–style trench was carved into the center of it, where earthmoving equipment stood behind barricades. Our car wouldn't fit, and Rylan was on the left-hand sidewalk racing away.

I ripped the transmission into park and jumped out into the street, hitting the sidewalk at a dead run.

"He's heading south!" I yelled to Arturo as I ran, clutching my radio like a sprinter's baton. "There's not much Manhattan left where he can hide. Coordinate with everyone. We need to box him in!"

On the sidewalk, I immediately almost plowed into a trio of Jamaican construction workers pushing a Sheetrock-filled Dumpster out of a building. As I ran stumbling into the street, alongside the construction barrier I could see that Rylan was already at the next corner, Ann Street, slaloming around pedestrians.

As I watched, Rylan blasted through an old Chinese food delivery guy, sending him flying back into the intersection. Then there was a sickening, bone-crunching crash as the Chinese guy got creamed by *another* bike messenger, a teenage Asian guy coming west on Ann.

As I ran up, I could see that the poor old food delivery guy's nose and mouth were bleeding as he crawled around in the gutter on his hands and knees. On the ground beside him, the teen biker was making a hissing sound as he rocked back and forth, gently cradling what looked like a badly broken wrist.

"I need to borrow this!" I yelled as I jumped on the messenger's fallen bike. "You'll get it back. I think."

Chapter 98

I LOOKED UP TO see Rylan make an abrupt left onto Fulton Street, but when I got there, no blue bike was to be seen down the narrow street or on either sidewalk. Then my eyes fell on the descending stairs to the subway in the left-hand sidewalk, and I jumped off the bike and lifted it as I ran down the stairs.

There was a yell as I hopped the turnstile with the bike and came out onto a train platform. I could see a businesswoman sprawled on her back and just beyond her, Rylan on his sky-blue bike pedaling like mad.

"Move, move!" I yelled to the waiting passengers as I followed Rylan down the platform. At the other end of it was a set of three steps that I had to hop off the bike to mount. At the top, I spotted Rylan pedaling furiously down a long, brand-new pedestrian tunnel with shining white graffiti-free tiled walls.

I watched Rylan go around a bend in the tunnel, and when I finally got around the bend myself, I was just in time to see him leap nimbly off his bike and carry it gracefully through an exit turnstile before taking the stairs two at a time.

Damn, this guy is in good shape, I thought, gasping as my elbow painfully clipped the metal frame of a billboard on the wall.

Finally coming up the exit stairs into daylight, I could see Rylan in the distance, south along traffic-filled lower Broadway. He skidded around a dog walker in the crosswalk, then did an actual wheelie between an old tow truck and a Smart car blocking the box.

"Arturo! Come to Broadway! We're on Broadway heading south!" I yelled into the radio as I split the gap between a flatbed and a Range Rover.

Through my sweat, I was just able to see Rylan shoot around a pedicab and hook a right off Broadway onto Dey Street. Following him a moment later, I slammed the side of a delivery truck with a palm as it almost ran me over. Then I wobbled to my right and scraped the left side of my face against the side of a stopped city bus. A jutting burr or bolt or something on the bus cut my ear, and I added blood to the sweat I was already dripping onto the blurring asphalt.

When I made a lane-shifting, skidding right onto Dey myself, I was just able to see Rylan's sky-blue guided missile make a left onto Church. I knew Church turned into Trinity Place, where the first Manhattan robbery had occurred.

Is that where he's heading? I wondered between my ragged breaths.

It wasn't, I found out a few seconds later. Rylan made a right on Rector, and then as I hit Rector, I saw him make a left onto West Street.

"He's coming south on West Street," I called happily to Arturo as I pedaled like a man possessed. We were near Battery Park now, Manhattan's southernmost tip, and Rylan, for all his phenomenal riding skills, was running out of city.

"Pin it down Broadway, Arturo," I called into the radio over the driving tempo of my bike chain, "and you can cut him off by the Battery! There's nowhere to run!"

But I spoke too soon.

Far ahead, I watched Rylan, racing down West

Street, suddenly veer to the left and do a bunny hop over a low railing. Then he was rocketing down a short embankment onto an entrance ramp under an overpass. As I got closer, I read the sign on the overpass he'd just disappeared into and groaned.

HUGH L. CAREY TUNNEL, it said.

Chapter 99

WHEN I GOT TO the spot where Rylan had jumped the rail, I stopped and lifted the bike over it and jogged down the embankment with it like a civilized madman. A multitude of drivers lay on their horns as I hopped back onto the bike on the entrance ramp's shoulder.

"It's OK," I said to them. "It's all right. I was actually dumb enough to want to be a cop."

After I skittered over an empty Coors Light bottle on the shoulder, almost wiping out, I pawed for the radio in the pocket of my raid jacket to tell Arturo my location. That was when I noticed something. My radio was AWOL. It had fallen out of my pocket during all my running and jumping around.

I screamed in frustration as I stood up on the pedals and started pumping into the dark mouth of the tunnel for the first leg of my Tour de Brooklyn.

The inside of the Hugh L. Carey Tunnel, more commonly called the Brooklyn–Battery Tunnel, was about as charming as you would think. It was humid and dark, the air so thick with exhaust my lungs felt like they were chewing on it. To add some excitement to my recreational afternoon spin, I almost came off the seat as I hit a dip, only a moment later to have an eye-opening seat-to-crotch collision as I hit an unseen metal street plate.

A gust from a massive speeding Verizon reel truck had almost plastered me to the tunnel's dirty tiled wall when a blue light started bubbling behind me. There was the deafening double bloop of a siren, and I turned to see a sight for sore eyes.

"Mike!" Arturo said from our Chevy's driver-side window as I hopped off the still-rolling bike and ran for the car.

I shoved Arturo over to the passenger side and pinned it. *Now, this is more like it,* I thought as we roared at top speed.

"What's up, man? You're bleeding like a stuck pig," Arturo said.

"Thanks for noticing, Lopez," I said as I gunned it on the shoulder, siren blasting.

I weaved around the Verizon truck, and after another thirty seconds, I could see light at the far end of the slightly curving tunnel. What I couldn't see was any sign of Rylan as we came out into daylight by the tollbooths.

Then I did see him out of the corner of my left eye, a speck of light blue as Rylan, running with the bike on his shoulder, hopped over the railing on the opposite side of the Gowanus Expressway.

I hit the switch for the car's megaphone as I turned all the sirens up to eleven. "Go through the tolls! Now! Move, move!" I called to the three cars I was waiting behind.

We jetted through the tolls and hit the first exit ramp we could find, a quarter mile farther south down the Gowanus. I floored through the light at the end of it, and kept it floored until I saw an underpass in the direction where Rylan had bolted.

We roared through, into a quiet residential Brooklyn neighborhood of brownstones and low buildings, screeching to a stop at intersections to look up and down the blocks. We were stopped at the third one, beside a dry cleaner, when we saw Rylan bullet across the road three blocks ahead. We got to the corner just in time to see him disappear under yet another underpass.

"Now he's just starting to piss me off," I said as I raced down the hill.

On the other side of the underpass, the residential neighborhood morphed into an industrial area. There were clusters of windowless industrial hangars behind rusting chain-link on the right, a sole orange Hyundai shipping container in a weed- and rubble-strewn field on the left, and Rylan in the middle of the forlorn street between them, still pedaling madly.

But we were gaining on him now.

Rylan rolled up on the sidewalk to the right and looked back at us once under his left arm the way a jockey would. Then again.

Then he simply disappeared.

There was a guardrail at the foot of the dead-end industrial block, and Rylan hit it head-on at almost thirty miles an hour and went flying up, up, and away over the handlebars and into a stand of high strawberry-blond weeds.

If it weren't for the ABS on the Chevy, we would surely have hit the guardrail as well. Instead, we skidded to a hard, seat-belt-whipping stop against the raised curb, and I was out of the car and over the rail, scrambling and sliding over takeout containers and Preston cans down a weedy, rocky slope toward where Rylan was doing the doggy paddle in a body of brownish water.

I stared around me in wide-eyed wonder at the seagulls wheeling over the recycling center on the opposite shoreline and the 1950s-era Airstream trailer with plastic covering its rear windows jutting from the middle of the water behind Rylan like a half-sunken art deco sub.

Rylan had been flung into the Gowanus Canal, one of the most polluted bodies of water in New York City and probably on the planet. Despite the afternoon's heart-attack-inducing chase, I actually felt sorry for the poor guy. Especially after I was treated to the canal's aroma, which was heavy on the raw sewage, accompanied by strong sulfur notes and a not-so-invigorating waft of burnt plastic.

Rylan, doggy-paddling about thirty feet from where I stood, made a few valiant strokes away, as if he were actually going to try to swim the nearly two-mile-long canal.

"Really, Rylan?" I said, trying to control my gag reflex. "I mean *really?*"

He looked at me again and then lowered his eyes and quickly began swimming back toward me.

Chapter 100

AN HOUR LATER, ARTURO and I were huddled together in a dim closet in the Major Crimes Division squad room watching closed-circuit video of Rylan in interview #2.

The puffy-marshmallow white Tyvek jumpsuit we'd let him change into from his stinking clothes made an annoying crinkling sound as Rylan, arms crossed, rocked back and forth with his head down. With his lean, boyish good looks, he reminded me of an athlete, a closing pitcher angry at himself for having just given up a disastrous home run on the game's last pitch.

"For a guy who claims he doesn't know what the heck is going on, he sure seems pretty darn upset," Arturo said.

Arturo was right.

Rylan had been playing dumb so far, acting relieved when we said we were cops and quickly apologizing for running, claiming he owed some scary guys a gambling debt. He also claimed he didn't know why in the world we were chasing him and since there seemed to be some kind of huge mistake, it would probably be best to have his lawyer sort it out.

In the meantime, we'd had a chance to go over his priors. We learned that instead of being a burglar in his previous life, Rylan had run a small Wall Street investment firm that had been exposed as a Bernie Madoff-like Ponzi scheme. He'd done two years at a white-collar prison and had gotten out almost two years before.

Rylan didn't have a Facebook profile, but I managed to google a *New York Magazine* article about young Wall Street hotshots that described his rising from a tough section of Staten Island to become the captain and quarterback of the Columbia University football team.

I shook my head at Rylan on the screen as he rolled his office chair into the corner and began cursing at himself.

"I don't know how good he was in the pocket uptown at Columbia, Arturo," I said, "but I don't think even Eli Manning could scramble his way out of this bloody mess."

On the other side of the squad room was the office of my boss, Miriam Schwartz, now abuzz with several VIP visitors. The Manhattan DA had shown up along with the chief of detectives. The FBI had even sent over a couple of bank robbery guys. The press didn't know that we had made an arrest, and we wanted it to stay that way. There were still Rylan's accomplices to round up, along with the over four million in gems still missing from all the heists.

Speaking of things that were still missing, the contents of the bank safe-deposit box were still a mystery. The bank had told us that the box was registered to one Aaron Buswell. What was curious was that there was no Aaron Buswell in the New York State driver's license system, and the contact number given was disconnected.

On a brighter note, Brooklyn and Robertson had re-interviewed the young guard at the construction site next to the bank, who broke down and revealed that he had been given five grand to be an accomplice in the heist. Not only had he given Rylan and his partners access to the construction site, he had hidden the clothes they had used in the heist in the guard shack. Fortunately, Brooklyn was able to recover the items. The CSU lab was already in the process of getting DNA off the coveralls to link to Rylan.

Rylan's legal representation showed up twenty minutes later. He was an intense-looking fortyish blond guy in a beautifully cut dark-gray suit. He looked expensive. Very expensive. As I watched him confer with the brass across the squad room, I wondered if Rylan had bought him with the diamond money.

After watching the mouthpiece's chat with my boss, Arturo and I escorted him down the corridor to Rylan. When I opened the interview room door, I apparently surprised Rylan, who leaped to his feet so suddenly that he knocked over his chair. He was sweating, red-faced. He looked extremely distraught.

"Whoa! Calm down, Rylan. Your lawyer is here."

Panic flashed in Rylan's face when he looked at the lawyer behind me.

"No," he said. "Forget it. I changed my mind. I don't want to talk to my lawyer. I, uh, can I talk to you? I want to talk to you, Detective."

"That's not advisable, Mr. Rylan," the lawyer

said quietly. "I'm here to help you. You should speak with me first."

"Screw you!" Rylan said to his lawyer with a sudden explosive anger. "Get the wax out of your ears. I'm not talking to you, so go look for an ambulance to chase!"

Chapter 101

I TOLD ARTURO TO take the lawyer back to the squad room and went in and sat down across from Rylan.

"What the hell is going on, Rylan?" I said. "First you claim you don't know why you're here. Then you want a lawyer. Now you don't? I mean, I'll give your strategy points for originality, but this is getting a little tiresome, don't you think?"

Rylan squinted down at the scuffed linoleum floor. "You've been a cop for what? Fifteen years?"

"Over twenty," I said. "Why?"

He began absently thumbing at the doodles and phone numbers scribbled on the chipped Sheetrock beside the handcuff rail.

"I need to know if you're, like, an old-school decent person, not a corrupt piece of crap out for a buck. Being a cop is a vocation for you?"

"Yes, it is," I said honestly.

Rylan looked at me intensely for a moment with his intelligent brown eyes.

"I'll talk," he said. "To hell with it. I'll talk to you, but you have to help me. Because I don't know which direction it'll be coming from. You don't understand how powerful he is. I'm going to need protection."

"Protection from who?" I said.

He looked at me. His face pale. His hands trembling.

"The billionaire, Gabe Chayefsky. He's the guy who hired me to empty that bank box."

I sat up. Straight.

Chayefsky was the rich hedge fund guy who bankrolled Luminous Properties, one such building being the slum where Doyle had almost gotten creamed.

"It was all about what was in the box from the beginning," Rylan started. "Frickin' Houdini couldn't crack that bank's high-security vault during a burglary, so we had no other choice than to go in during the day. When we tripped the alarms, we only had a few precious minutes, so we had to have you thinking diamonds. That's why we did those other jobs. We had to establish a pattern."

"That was a pretty smart head fake," I said. *It worked, after all.*

"Yeah, I'm so smart, look where I'm sitting," Rylan said, rolling his eyes.

"How does a budding young Gordon Gecko know about knocking over jewelry stores?" I said.

"I'll be straight with you, Detective. Growing up, the closest thing I had to a father was an uncle out in Staten Island who was a nine-to-five real-deal professional thief.

I worked for him a few summers, driving up and down the East Coast hitting places. We had this cherry-picker tree-trimming truck that we would use to get onto roofs and cut into joints. Supermarkets, mostly. Pharmacies. I was his apprentice until he died from cancer, and then my mom made me concentrate on school and getting a scholarship."

"They didn't mention that in the *New York Mag* article," I said.

"Listen, Detective—"

"Call me Mike," I said, hoping Rylan would feel he could tell me anything.

"Well, Mike, my illustrious Bernie Madoff bio is tabloid bullshit. It wasn't like that. I was legit. Well, maybe not legit, but I wasn't doing anything that everyone else wasn't doing.

"Sure, I was down in the books and shuffling investors' money out the door, but it was to buy time. You don't think the big firms do it? Grow up. It's standard operating procedure. Had the feds come in three days later—three days later—the position I had planned would have made everyone whole again plus ten percent.

"But the market was crashing and the feds needed a quick sacrifice to hide the thumb they perpetually have firmly wedged up their ass, and I didn't have the political juice to make it not be me."

I nodded.

"What does that have to do with this bank and Chayefsky?"

"Well, when I got out of prison, I wanted to get my life back, clear my reputation, and get back into the financial industry. I loved being a trader, not just for the Lambos and bimbos, but for the juice. The risk. The daily tightrope walk. The best way I could think to do it was to rejoin the Greenwich Road Rats club I'd started back in oh-six."

"The Road what?"

"So many financial guys are macho ex-NCAA student athletes who've never grown up. Like me. I started out with triathlons. I actually came in fourteenth in the 2003 Ironman and then got heavily into cycling. So I created a club for financial types. Which they reluctantly let me back into when I got out of jail. That's how I met Chayefsky."

Chapter 102

RYLAN WAS ON A roll now, I sensed. All I had to do was listen.

"Chayefsky was richest guy in the bike club by far," he continued. "He's a genius. MIT advanced math degree, got his fingers in the aerospace industry, Silicon Valley, biotech. He made his money off his hedge fund, where he developed this high-frequency trading algorithm that insiders call the crystal ball.

"Some say he cleaned up in the 2010 flash crash and others say he caused it on purpose. His software is a literal printing press. I mean, the man laid his own private transatlantic fiber cable to his offices in London! He also played soccer for MIT and is an incredible athlete. The dude's a winged demigod."

"How did you hook up with him, then?"

"I would be lying if I said I didn't work to get in his good graces. He'd heard I'd doped during the Ironman and wanted to know about it, so I helped him with that. Then I helped him buy some drugs through some of my old Staten Island connections, helped him buy some women.

"Then, after a night of debauchery where he watched me beat the shit out of a Twenty-Third Street club bouncer who'd mouthed off to him, he approached me to help him with a problem he had. One that if I helped him fix, he would set me up with a desk on his fund. We're talking two and a half billion in assets. He was offering me an opportunity to make my life whole again, a seat back at the table."

"What was the catch?"

"Someone was blackmailing him," Rylan said. "He told me someone had a video of him having sex with a girl who wasn't his wife. That it was the daughter of a colleague, and she was apparently seventeen at the time, so he was looking at a lot of trouble at his office, plus a rape case, and an extremely messy divorce all wrapped up into one. He couldn't have it coming out, and he was willing to pay to make sure it did not. The guy who was using it was hammering the shit out of him for millions."

Rylan closed his eyes and balled his fists.

"But I saw the video, Mike. It was on a phone that I took from the vault. It's not what he said... My God..."

His whole body started trembling. He grasped his skull in his hands.

"Why did I watch it? He told me to hand it over. Shit, why did I do any of this?"

"It's OK," I said, putting my hand on his shoulder. "You're doing the right thing here. Just get it off you."

"It wasn't of him having sex, OK?" Rylan said, his eyes bugging with stress. "It was... sick... evil. It starts with this girl standing in a fancy kitchen. She looks like a high school kid, like a babysitter or something, has her little purse, puts it on the counter. Then Chayefsky comes through the swinging door, six-three, ripped, and buck naked.

"He has a crowbar in his hand, and he just hits her, smashes her right in the face with it... He... ties her up and brutally tortures this girl to death. Her screams. I had to turn off the sound. Then after she's finally dead, he ties on a chef's apron, puts on some classical music, and starts to... cut her up like a chicken. I fast-forwarded it, but the last scene I saw was him frying something, Mike. Standing there bare-assed in the blood splatter, swirling butter around something in a copper pan."

It was my turn to stare at the floor tile as he broke down, sobbing and sniffling. It all clicked together. Luminous Properties. Cannibalism. Naomi Chast's murder.

"I'd heard rumors that Chayefsky was into sick, twisted stuff, but I've peeked into the window of hell, Mike. I keep seeing the expression on this girl's face as she's sitting there. So screw it. Put me back inside. I don't want it anymore. Keep the money, Wall Street, everything. I don't want anything anymore. I'm done swimming in this river of shit."

I stood to leave.

Rylan suddenly wiped his nose and stared at me.

"But that's not why I'm telling you. I sent him a girl. He said he needed a hooker, so I sent him this girl I know for some special party he's having tonight. He kept asking all these questions about her that I realized were attempts to see if she'd be missed. Don't you see, Mike? You have to find them. This maniac is going to kill her."

Chapter 103

A LITTLE BEFORE SIX that evening, Lopez and Doyle and I looked at each other nervously as I sped us off Exit 3 from Interstate 95 near Long Island Sound in the part of Greenwich, Connecticut, known as Old Greenwich.

We had reason to be tense and alert. We'd recovered the smartphone from where Rylan had stashed it in the Brooklyn–Battery Tunnel and had seen the video on it. It was exactly what Rylan had said. The billionaire mogul was indeed some kind of serial killer, and we had to find him and Rylan's associate, Iliana, before Chayefsky killed her.

After ten minutes of weaving our way through a neighborhood of winding private roads, we stopped at a gate call box. I told the tinny voice we were police and were there to speak to Mr. Chayefsky. I had to show my shield to the video camera above the box before we were buzzed through the heavy iron gate onto the driveway of Chayefsky's estate.

We drove up a curving, wooded rise. At its crest, a little past a rock formation, an inlet suddenly came into view, a ruffling wilderness of salt-marsh cattails against a sweeping, stunning expanse of placid glittering blue.

"How can this be Chayefsky's property or anybody's property?" Lopez said, amazed. "It looks like a state park. Who'd he buy it from? The government?"

"Nope. Jay Gatsby," Doyle said.

The house, when we finally saw it another eighth of a mile later, was even more ridiculous than the grounds. It looked like an English mansion out of a Jane Austen novel, or maybe something a school would take a day trip to. It had two towers and at least four chimneys and a huge antique weather vane with a verdigris copper dolphin leaping from between the waves of dormers in the blue-gray sea of the slate roof.

We parked in the circular driveway and climbed up wide stairs onto a white-on-white covered porch you could have thrown a wedding on. Off the porch to the right was a massive gentle slope of manicured lawn, on which I spotted a fenced-in grass tennis court and a hedge maze and beyond it, a faded dock, where a pristine thirty-foot white sailing sloop bobbed softly.

"So this is what they mean by happily ever after," Doyle mumbled as the Fort Knox-like door swung open.

We stood looking at the woman standing there. It was hard not to.

In the doorway, near the base of a set of *Gone with the Wind*–style stairs, stood a beautiful woman in skintight white yoga clothes. She was about six-one, with a perfect toned body, perfect olive skin, and bright-green almond-shaped eyes in a face that demanded to be looked at. Her lush russet-colored hair was worn up, but it looked like it could easily do that Pantene knot-untying thing with a flick of her pointed chin.

I would have said she was a model, but models weren't as relaxed and elegant and kept up. She looked like she could be anywhere from twenty-two to forty-two. A *retired* model, I thought. An expression popped into my head from nowhere. *Private Viewings Only.*

"Mrs. Chayefsky, I'm Detective Bennett. We'd like to talk to your husband," I said.

"My husband? He's not here. I'm not even sure if he's in New York. In any case, he doesn't come home until quite late. But you can talk to me. Have you found Consuela's car? She's already gone. We had a car service take her home."

"Consuela?" Arturo said.

"Yes. One of our housekeepers. Her car was stolen from the train station," the gorgeous woman said. "Isn't that what this is about?"

No, it's about your husband's proclivity for killing and eating people, I felt like saying.

"We need to speak to your husband. It's urgent," Doyle said.

"Urgent?" she said. "What's going on?"

"He could be in grave danger," I said. It wasn't a lie. He was in grave danger. Of being put into a mental asylum for the rest of his life.

"I demand to know what's going on now," she said.

"Ma'am, there's no time," I said. "This is urgent police business. We need to contact him right now. Could we please have his cell phone number?"

She shook her pretty head vehemently.

"No, I can't hand that out. I'm sorry. He told me never to do it. Never."

“Not even to the police?” Arturo said.

“Especially not to you,” she said.

Arturo looked wounded. Like it was personal.

“He has so many businesses and tax things and partnerships, we get subpoenas all the time. I probably shouldn’t even be talking to you. You need to leave. I’m sorry. I thought this was about my housekeeper’s car. Now that I know it’s not, you have to leave. Contact him through his office. Good-bye.”

Lopez and Doyle stood there seemingly frozen after she closed the huge door.

“You know who she is or was, right?” Doyle said. “She’s that supermodel from the nineties.”

“Dude, he’s right,” Lopez said, elbowing me. “She used to be, like, in music videos and Victoria’s Secret.”

“Well, it looks like Victoria is keeping her hubby’s secrets,” I said as we hurried off the porch. “So pick up your chins and come on. We need to get the hell on the road and find this son of a bitch before that girl becomes his next victim.”

Chapter 104

ILIANA KUZNETSOV HAD been in limos before. Cheesy white superstretches with disco ball interiors. Hummer ones. Even a MINI Cooper one once with a hot tub in the trunk.

But the car that had picked her up from her hotel room at nine on the dot wasn't like that at all. It was a luxury Mercedes Maybach with a spacious and shining inlaid-wood cabin in the back. It was almost like a living room. There was a state-of-the-art entertainment console with a large-screen HD TV, dual headphones, clocks and thermometer dials and switches everywhere like the instruments on an airplane.

The white-leather power chaise seat she lay back in was hands down the softest thing she'd ever parked her butt on, like being sunk into a hammock of piled spa towels.

She smiled as she powered the überplush seat back a little with the control, resisting the urge to kick off her stiletto heels.

For a moment, she imagined that this mogul or whatever he was beside her was her boyfriend, like she was suddenly Julia Roberts in the 1990 film *Pretty Woman.* She hit the seat back another smidge. There. Perfect. She could get used to this.

The forty-something black-haired man smiling next to her as he spoke almost imperceptibly into a Bluetooth headset was obviously as upscale as the ride. He was sexy, handsome, tall and quite lean, and perfectly groomed in a dark European-tailored pinstriped suit. His playful smile softened his hard, sharp face and cool blue eyes. Iliana had been with men like him before. Rich, handsome, horny, hard-charging businessmen who could probably get all the action they wanted for free except they didn't have the time. She smiled. He sure beat some sweaty fat bastard. The nine thousand she would make tonight would be the easiest money ever made.

He finally pulled out the Bluetooth and flicked it into the drink holder beside him.

"Ugh. I hate that thing. How rude of me. How do you do, Iliana? Rylan has told me so much about you. I am Gabe," he said, very deliberately shaking her hand, making a little game of it. "Thank you so much for coming out with me tonight. I love your dress, by the way. It's perfect for the party we're going to. Classy without being boring. I hate boring."

"Me too," Iliana said. "I like your car, Gabe. It is yours, right? I noticed that it had private plates."

"How perceptive of you, Iliana. So you're not just a pretty face, I see," Gabe said, zipping his own chair back until he was almost prone. "Yes, it is my car. You know what I like most about it? The windows. The tint is new. It's literally impossible to see into here. We can see everything yet remain invisible. I mean, we could be doing *anything* in here right now and no one would know."

He toed a compartment under the TV and a refrigerator drawer buzzed out. Iliana felt her breath catch when she looked inside. Half a dozen frosty dark-green bottles of Dom Pérignon.

How much money does this guy actually have? Iliana wondered as Gabe ripped off the foil and popped the cork from a bottle.

"Actually, you can have this bottle. We'll do his and hers," he said, handing it to her.

Iliana hefted it by its long, delicate neck as he grabbed another one for himself. It was like a genie bottle from a kid's book. A cold and heavy and very expensive genie bottle. She took a sip. Bubbles tickled her tongue. So cold and sweet. Like ginger ale.

"I just have one more phone call to make," Gabe said, sipping from his bottle. "But we're going to have fun tonight, Iliana," he added as he grabbed the Bluetooth.

"I can tell."

Chapter 105

"HEY, DO YOU LIKE gadgets, Iliana?" Gabe suddenly said, snapping his fingers after he finished his call. "I want to show you something."

From the pink-silk-lined inside pocket of his suit, he took out a metal ingot. It was matte black, about the size of a matchbox. He placed it carefully on the inlaid wood console between them.

"Check this out. This runs on Wi-Fi," he said as he pressed a button on his phone. Suddenly six legs sprang out of the ingot with a tiny click and it immediately began moving forward, just like an insect. It stopped at the rim of a drink holder, its little wire legs probing. Then it began to travel nimbly around the right side of the holder.

"Weird. A little toy robot bug?" Iliana said. "Is it remote control?"

"It can be," Gabe said, smiling proudly. "Or it can just crawl around on its own. The artificial intelligence it has can make it learn and remember things. It also has an audio-video feed. I can send it places. Boardrooms. Ladies' rooms. Only kidding. I wouldn't do that.

"One of my tech companies came up with it. We have a big one we're working on for the government, about the size of a deer, that can carry five hundred pounds. I love robotics, don't you? I call this little guy Willis because he has a will of his own, get it? Look at Willis go."

Willis actually gave her the creeps, but she nodded politely as she took another sip from the bottle. Was this guy some kind of inventor? Definitely an odd duck.

"Hey, how do you like the champagne? Not bad, huh?" Gabe said, rolling his neck.

"It's very good. It's like soda. Dom is French, right?"

Gabe nodded quickly as he zipped down the black glass divider that separated them from the driver. *God, this guy is restless,* she thought. *Or coked up, maybe?* The driver was a very smooth-skinned black man who, even seated, seemed to be very tall.

"You hear that, Alberto?" Gabe called up through his big cupped hands. "Look at me. I'm living the American dream tonight, baby. German car, French champagne, and a Ukrainian beauty!"

"Yes, you are, sir. Yes, you are," Alberto said, grinning.

They both stared at her then for a long awkward moment. The driver from the rearview, Gabe from the left. Both with the same unblinking expression. Flat and patient and rapacious. Iliana thought of a picture from the frayed fairy-tale book at the orphanage in Dnipropetrovsk where she'd grown up. They both looked like the wolf seeing the first of the three little pigs.

There was something between them, she realized. Like they were friends. More than employer–employee. Something weird.

She glanced at the little bug thing as it made the rim of the console and probed and turned around. It suddenly stopped and turned and seemed to stare at her as well. She held her breath, suddenly extremely scared for some reason she couldn't name.

Rylan had assured her that his friend knew she didn't do weird. Sometimes men forgot, though. She had been hurt by very cruel, sadistic men her whole life. That was why she carried the stun gun in her purse. The bodyguard she could handle, and this soft American, too, no matter how much money or ego he thought he had. She stared at the metal thing, resisting the urge to smash it with her fist.

Pretty Woman, she thought, disgusted with herself. She wasn't even alive in 1990. Get over on this weird bozo and move along.

That was when she started to feel light-headed. She zipped the seat to upright, and when she looked forward at the driver, he was still staring, which didn't make sense.

The car is moving. How can he drive and keep staring at me at the same time?

"Could we put up the divider, Gabe?" she said, setting the bottle down.

"Alberto, Alberto, Alberto. How many times do I have to tell you? Ladies don't like it when you undress them with those big eyes you have," Gabe said as he hit a button and the tinted divider started to rise again like a dark tide.

When it was up, she tried the button for the window to get some air, but it kept clicking uselessly.

"Gabe, could you pull over? I think I'm going to

be sick," Iliana said as she slumped against the white-silk-lined, vaultlike door.

Gabe leaned over and put his long fingers to her neck just below the jawline.

"You're going to be fine, Iliana," he said as he stared at his watch. "Take a little nap now, OK? I'll wake you up in a little bit."

Iliana's heavy eyelids began to droop. The last thing she saw was the metal bug on the floor, pausing briefly before it began to climb up her white stiletto heel.

Chapter 106

BY 10 P.M., WE WERE speeding down a dark street in the Wakefield section of the Bronx near the border of Mount Vernon. The block of row houses flying by off to my left would have been charming if every single one of them hadn't had plywood windows.

We were now down to the chicken-with-its-head-cut-off strategy in trying to pinpoint Chayefsky. Robertson, back at the Harlem office, had gotten a list of Luminous Properties holdings and was feeding us addresses.

We were concentrating on the ones in the city's poorer neighborhoods where Chayefsky might be hosting one of his sick parties. We'd been to three properties already, one in a run-down section of Yonkers and two in the northern Manhattan neighborhood of Inwood. But they had all been abandoned.

I got a bad feeling in the pit of my stomach as we came under the rusted hulk of an elevated subway track on White Plains Road. Chayefsky and the girl could have been in Tahiti for all we knew. I had the sinking feeling we were running out of time.

"There's Two Hundred Thirty-Ninth Street right there. Make a right," Doyle said to Arturo behind the wheel.

Half a block east of the elevated track on East 239th, we slowed before a four-story brick tenement that looked abandoned. It had cinder-block-sealed windows and was completely saturated with decades of graffiti.

"Welcome to another fine abandoned crack house brought to you by Luminous Properties," Arturo said, shaking his head.

"Wait. Look," Doyle whispered as he flashed his Maglite into the garbage-strewn lot beside it.

There were two cars parked there. Doyle swung the light onto the cars' hoods to show a BMW symbol, then a Mercedes three-pointed star.

"Go around the block to the back of the lot by that fence," I said to Arturo.

We circled around and got out on foot. Through a gap in the fence was an obstacle course of random discarded crap. Tires, a drawerless chest of drawers, a bunch of baby clothes in a torn white plastic bag.

As we approached, we saw that parked next to the Mercedes and BMW were three motorcycles, two Suzuki crotch rockets, and a bright-red Denali. We could also hear something now. It was music from somewhere. A rap thump, faint and unrelenting like the working of a giant, distant heart.

The music was coming from an open doorway to the right of the vehicles. I skirted the cars and stayed close to the wall as I took a quick peek inside. A set of stone steps descended into darkness, and as I stood there trying to let my eyes adjust, a bright light came on at the foot of them. Then a person stepped out from the right onto the bottom step. A jacked-up, scary-looking Hispanic guy in a leather jacket with a lot of gold chains stopped in his tracks as he saw me.

"Police! Freeze! Hands! Don't move!" I yelled at him, pointing the Glock I was already holding in my hand.

He didn't listen to me. Instead, he turned and bolted back into the corridor whence he'd come, hollering in Spanish at the top of his lungs.

I hit the bottom of the steps just in time to see the big guy slam a door at the end of the rough stone-walled corridor. The rap music cut as I was halfway to the door, replaced by a sudden rabid barking.

Barking!?

I finally arrived at the slammed metal door. There was even more rabid barking. It sounded like there was a kennel on the other side of it.

There was no knob, so I pushed against it. It moved, but only a little. There was something heavy blocking it. I cursed as the barks grew fainter and fainter. *No!* Whoever was in there was getting away.

A roar of one of the motorcycles sounded behind me as Doyle and I finally managed to shoulder open the jammed door enough for me to stick my head in. It was a garbage-strewn boiler room with a fifty-gallon blue plastic trash barrel behind the door, filled with bricks. On the other side of the room, there were some metal steps leading to another door, another corridor.

My eyes fell to a sunken gravelike section in the concrete that was covered in feces and blood. That was when I realized it.

"It's OK. The girl isn't here," I said. "It's dog fighting."

We'd stumbled upon some kind of pitbull fighting ring or something.

"OK?" Arturo said. "No, it isn't. I have a dog. We need to go get those bastards. They need to be locked up."

"Forget 'em!" I yelled as I pulled him back down the corridor toward the outside. "We just need to hit the next address on the list. We're running out of time!"

Chapter 107

GABE CHAYEFSKY EXCHANGED A pleased nod with Alberto as he took the coat from the junior senator from Pennsylvania in the soaring travertine foyer of the Old Bronx County Courthouse. Alberto exchanged the senator's cell phone for a glass of brandy, then deftly escorted the senator's security detail toward the coffee urn set up by the door.

Gabe nodded as the senator's fit and fiftyish head security guy, Scotty, gave him a little wave. Scotty was clean-cut, just recently retired FBI, but his dolt of a son worked for Chayefsky's charitable foundation's DC office now. Scotty, bought and paid for, knew the drill by this point. Look away, don't ask, don't tell. Gabe grinned. He had Scotty by his aging wrinkled balls.

Senator Bob Plutchik put out his palm and then suddenly lurched forward and tried to get Gabe in a headlock with his free hand. As if. Gabe grabbed the former MIT power forward by the fat pinkie of his right hand and pulled, twisting the laughing, howling senator around until he had him in a chicken wing.

"I'm spilling my drink, you dirty bastard," the senator said, laughing. "Scotty, you seeing this? Shoot this asshole, would you?"

They laughed and hugged for real. Senator Plutchik, Chayefsky's old roommate at MIT, was the youngest senator in Pennsylvania's history. He was snotty, sometimes pushy to the point of being aggravating, but there was an undeniable aura of genius about him, an uncanny intuitive awareness of people. He also had the quickest, keenest nose for human weakness and vulnerability Chayefsky had ever seen.

If it hadn't been for his nontelegenic horselike features, he might very well have made it into the White House already, Chayefsky thought. Bob was a player, all right, not to mention Gabe's oldest and closest friend since they'd killed the three girls on their business class trip to Prague in '93.

It was ironic, really, Gabe thought, that with all

his money, he actually had a senator in his pocket for free.

"Sorry I'm late," said the senator, "but as I'm leaving the house for the chopper, that bitch of a wife of mine demanded that I actually change Amanda's shitty diaper."

"No apologies, Bob. Relax. Unwind. You haven't missed anything. She just came around."

"Oh, shit, don't tell me that," the senator said, his cold gray eyes shining like metal in his long, sharp-featured face as he took a sloppy hit of his drink. "You know how much I love standing there when they wake up. The look on the face. Like that cute little black one in the Bahamas when she figured it out. That one was a classic."

Gabe smiled at the memory from two Christmases before. Classical music and the taste of cool, dry Riesling as he sat on the still-warm sand with his friend before the huge bonfire on the private island's rocky beach. Alberto, in his pristine, glowing chef whites, sweating as he turned the roasting black girl on the spit.

"You and your theatrical ruins," Bob said, looking up at the foyer's crumbling rotunda. "What the hell is this place, anyway? A school?"

"An old courthouse," Chayefsky said.

“What? How much you pay for it?”

“It was a steal. One dollar. Actually, my foundation bought it.”

“What? A dollar? I know this is the Bronx, but—”

“I promised to turn it into a preschool.”

“You? That’s hilarious. When’s that gonna happen?”

“Never,” Gabe said, and laughed as he put his arm over his friend’s shoulder. “Enough grab-assing, Senator. This way. We’re set up in one of the holding cells downstairs.”

“A holding cell? No effing way, man,” Bob said, slamming him a wide-eyed high five. “Now that’s what I call a hardcore setting. If the holdin’ cell’s a-rockin’, don’t come a-knockin’!”

They were halfway down the candlelit basement stairs when there was a chirp from Chayefsky’s Bluetooth.

“What is it, Alberto?”

“A car is at the fence. Three men in it. They look like cops.”

Gabe fidgeted with his antique cuff links as he thought. He was not nervous. He was as incapable of nervousness as he was of compassion. Everything was a matter of thought. The speed of his thought, his ability to stay several steps ahead.

He considered the heist earlier today, the fact that he hadn't heard from Rylan yet. But he wasn't supposed to hear from Rylan for another two days anyway. He had people at the networks and two of the city's rags, and there hadn't been the hint of an arrest. And if Rylan had been arrested and had decided to cooperate with the police, why send only three men?

It was nothing, he decided as he continued down the stairs. No need to hit the panic button. Just a coincidence. He had spent a year setting this up. It was time to reconnect with his old friend.

"Send O'Brien out to deal with them. That fat bastard is NYPD, isn't he? I pay that asshole enough. But stay alert, Alberto, as I know you will. If there's further interference, we simply go to abort mode."

"As always, sir," Alberto said.

Chapter 108

"CAN I HELP YOU, GENTLEMEN?" said a big-gutted white-blond guy in a black Windbreaker behind the chain-link gate as we got out of our unmarked.

The fence surrounded the Luminous Property next on our list, a massive, beautiful old square building at 161st Street and Third Avenue in the South Bronx. Behind the fence, parked next to a crane in a cleared-off lot beside the building, were two vehicles, a dark-gray Ford Expedition and a dark-blue Mercedes limo.

Doyle, who was a car nut, had already pegged the Merc as a Maybach, a half-million-dollar billionaire's car. I took a breath as I stared through the fence up the steps of the templelike old building.

Chayefsky was in there. I just hadn't thought there would be a security team protecting him.

"Yeah, hi," I said, smiling as I showed the blond guy my shield. "What's going on here tonight? Why are those cars here?"

"Hey, chief. How's it going? I'm on the job, too," said the guard as he flashed his own shield back at me. "There's a private party here tonight by the property owners. A discreet party. A lot of rich folks and celebs will be here, I'm told. I actually just got here. I'm working security."

"A celebrity party in the middle of the Melrose section of the Bronx?" Arturo said.

The large, pudgy cop smiled, rolled his eyes.

"I guess the upper crust are slumming or something tonight. Who knows?" he said. "It's all legit, so don't worry. Where are you guys from? You're not out of the five-two."

"Your boss know about this? You moonlighting?" I said.

The guy frowned.

"Now, come on. Why you gotta be busting my horns, man?" he said. "You know the drill. My precinct captain knows but ain't gonna say so. Hell, you didn't hear it from me, but the job actually came through him. Somebody who knows somebody in the mayor's office, probably. Do I ask questions? I just pocket the cash."

"Well, that's funny, chief," I said. "Because I don't pocket the cash, I only ask questions. I need you to open the gate."

"That isn't going to happen," said a voice from behind him.

A new guy walked over. Taller, neat brown hair, clean-cut, about fifty. He showed a badge as well.

"Homeland Security?" I said.

"He reads. Bravo," the fed said, eyeing me with disdain. "This is a private function. All you need to know is this is an issue of national security, and you can't come in. I suggest you call your boss."

"The only thing I'm going to do is arrest Gabe Chayefsky for murder. I know he's in there, because that's his car. Now, open this gate."

"Gabe Chayefsky? Who the hell is that? Where are you getting your information?" the fed said coldly, not moving an inch. "What's your name?"

"He's Detective Open This Fucking Fence," Doyle yelled, shaking the chain-link, "and I'm Sergeant I'm Going to Kick Your Fucking Ass. Open this fence now!"

That was when it happened. There was a bunch of yelling; then several figures came out of the side of the building. One had a coat over his head. We watched open-mouthed as half a dozen men piled into the SUV and the SUV screeched across the lot to the other side of the construction site. A man got out and unlocked another fence, and then the SUV peeled out into the street.

"Arturo! Go around and block that gate! And call in backup now!" I yelled as I drew my gun.

I pointed my Glock at the cop's chest. Doyle drew and aimed his between the fed's eyes.

"Open this gate or I'll shoot you where you stand," I said. "I won't say it again."

Chapter 109

THE MOONLIGHTING COP AND the fed looked at each other and then turned and ran for the front of the building.

Doyle and I hopped the fence. We could see Arturo screech into the breach of the other gate as we landed on the other side.

We heard the roar of an engine as we were running for the steps, and around the back of the building came the Maybach. A tall black guy behind the wheel gave us the finger as he gunned it straight toward us.

I raised the Glock in my hand and fired at him. The windshield in front of the driver's face starred, but only barely. It was bulletproof.

I emptied the Glock at the car anyway as it kept coming. Doyle joined me. We stood there shoulder-to-shoulder shooting until the windshield was a huge spiderweb. Still the car kept on coming. Doyle actually threw his empty gun at it as I pulled him to the left and out of the way at the last second.

The speeding Maybach went past us and ripped through the construction site fence like a sprinter through finish-line tape. Tires screeched as it braked and tried to turn at Third Avenue's sharp corner. It didn't make it. There was a tremendous smash as it slammed against and then through the parked cars on the opposite side of the street. Then the tanklike beast flipped as it crashed into the front wall of a pizza parlor.

"Doyle, take Arturo and get inside the building! Find the girl!" I said, running at top speed across the street toward the crashed limo.

The long Maybach had landed on its side halfway inside the pizza parlor. There were glass and debris everywhere. The whole front wall of the pizza joint was caved in. Beyond the destruction, a Mexican guy behind the counter stood in slack-faced shock as a soccer game continued to play too loudly on the battered TV above him.

"Call nine-one-one!" I screamed as I climbed over the rubble and shoved aside the shattered bench from a booth, trying to peer through the cracked glass of the tipped car. Its wheels spun stupidly, the engine still roaring.

I was up on the side of the car, reaching for the handle, when there was a muffled pop from inside. I immediately hopped back down. It was a gunshot! It was followed quickly by another.

I hopped up again and finally got the door open. At the other side of the flipped-over car was a man in a suit, a gun beside him, blood leaking from a hole in his temple. Through the lowered driver partition, I saw the side of the black driver's motionless torso.

They killed themselves, I thought as I stared, shocked, into the car. *How can this be happening? How can Chayefsky and his driver have just committed suicide?*

My radio blooped as I staggered in a daze through the debris back onto the sidewalk.

"Doyle! Did you find the girl?" I called into the radio. "Tell me you found her!"

"We found her. She was in the basement. We just brought her out."

"Is she OK?" I said.

There was a pause. It was too long. Way too long.

"I thought we could save her, but she's dead,

Mike. They killed her. Two to the head. The bastards. They killed her."

It took seven minutes for the first fire truck to come. The cop and the fed and whoever else had been there were long gone. Arturo had grabbed a tablecloth from a dining room table set up inside, and we covered Iliana's body with it.

Arturo and Doyle, staring down at the body, looked a little shook up but were hanging in there, holding it together. I was proud of them. They were both going to be really great cops.

That was when I saw the limo approach the gate. I ran toward it, my hand on my holster, as squad cars began to pull up behind it.

Inside, behind the driver, I spotted a famous man, a television personality, along with a group of smiling, laughing, rich-looking men and women.

"What's going on?" the driver said. "These guests are here for the party. They're here for the underground dinner party."

I shook my head back and forth. At the driver, the city lights, at Iliana now being wheeled into an ambulance. I didn't think I'd ever stop.

"Sorry," I finally said sadly as I fished out my gold shield.

"Party's over."

EPILOGUE

Chapter 110

AFTER THE LAST PRAYERS had been said and the last pints had been lifted, Mary Catherine found herself alone back at the old farmhouse where she'd been born. Her brother, Timmy, and Uncle Jerry, who'd come in from London together, were staying until Wednesday, but they had gone out with some old football friends who had come to the funeral.

It seemed like just about everybody in the town had come to see Mrs. Flynn off into the great beyond, but it wasn't so much her they were honoring as Mary Catherine's father, dead these last ten years, who had been a famous footballer in his own time and a town leader. The first to tell a joke or to tip a hat or to pitch in if any of the neighbors needed help with a lost calf or cutting the hay in August.

Mary Catherine looked out through the drizzle at the farmyard. Her mom had put up a good fight in keeping the old homestead together, but her age and illness had left their mark in the weeds in the vegetable garden, the holes in the henhouse roof by the apple orchard.

She thought of her mother standing at this very window as the six of them ran about like packs of wild geese. They were a rambunctious family, at least when Da wasn't nearby. When her father was home, a calming solemnity came home with him.

She went into the parlor. It was as if she'd just left it on the day she left for America. The same photos on the wall, the ribbons for her father's prize horses, her mother's collection of country-western albums.

She sat, sorting through the old records. Eddy Arnold, Jerry Lee Lewis, and Elvis, of course. Her mother had loved American music, country and the early rock and roll. They all did and knew every song by heart.

When she got to Buck Owens, she smiled and slid the record out of its sleeve. Her mother had been right mad for Buck Owens and his sad, jangly cowboy love songs. Even her father had liked him after a few glasses of lager on a Saturday afternoon, singing along in a perfect American country accent in his good tenor voice.

She had just put it on, the first strains of "Together Again" ringing through the empty old house, when she heard the tires on the gravel driveway. She thought it might be her brother and uncle home early from their homecoming pub crawl until she looked out the window and saw the florist van up from Clonmel.

More flowers. Probably some long-lost cousin in Australia; her mom's family from County Down had been massive. A long-lost relation only now just hearing the news, she thought, going back to the albums in her lap.

"Just come in and put them in the kitchen, please," she said to the knock on the mudroom door.

The screen door creaked open at the same time she heard the van suddenly pull away.

"Hello?" she called.

Then there was a footstep in the doorway, and she was looking up as all the albums spilled out of her lap like cards in a fallen deck.

"I'm so sorry, Mary Catherine," Mike said. "I wanted to be there for—"

But she was in his arms by then, the stress of

the last weeks breaking like a dam, and she was bawling, unable to talk, unable to breathe, unable to do anything but hold him.

This man who she'd never stop loving, impossibly there for her now at the precise moment she needed him. Like a miracle come across the ocean for her at her time of greatest need.

He sang along with Buck Owens as he took her hand and they began to sway.

"Nothing else matters," Mike whispered in her ear.

"We're together again."

Turn the page for a sneak preview of

TRUTH OR DIE

Coming June 2015

"WHERE EXACTLY did it happen?" I asked.

"West End Avenue at Seventy-Third. The taxi was stopped at a red light," said Lamont. "The assailant smashed the driver's side window, pistol-whipped the driver until he was knocked out cold, and grabbed his money bag. He then robbed Ms. Parker at gunpoint."

"Claire," I said.

"Excuse me?"

"Please call her Claire."

I knew it was a weird thing for me to say, but weirder still was hearing Lamont refer to Claire as Ms. Parker, not that I blamed him. Victims are always Mr., Mrs., or Ms. for a detective. He was supposed to call her that. I just wasn't ready to hear it.

"I apologize," I said. "It's just that—"

"Don't worry about it," he said with a raised palm. He understood. He got it.

"So what happened next?" I asked. "What went wrong?"

"We're not sure, exactly. Best we can tell, she fully cooperated, didn't put up a fight."

That made sense. Claire might have been your prototypical "tough" New Yorker, but she was also no fool. She didn't own anything she'd risk her life to keep. *Does anyone?*

No, she definitely knew the drill. Never be a statistic. If your taxi gets jacked, you do exactly as told.

"And you said the driver was knocked out, right? He didn't hear anything?" I asked.

"Not even the gunshots," said Lamont. "In fact, he didn't actually regain consciousness until after the first two officers arrived at the scene."

"Who called it in?"

"An older couple walking nearby."

"What did they see?"

"The shooter running back to his car, which was behind the taxi. They were thirty or forty yards away; they didn't get a good look."

"Any other witnesses?"

"You'd think, but no. Then again, residential block . . . after midnight," he said. "We'll obviously follow up in the area tomorrow. Talk to the driver, too. He was taken to St. Luke's before we arrived."

I leaned back in my chair, a metal hinge somewhere below the seat creaking its age. I must have had a dozen more questions for Lamont, each one trying to get me that much closer to being in the taxi with Claire, to knowing what had really happened.

To knowing whether or not it truly was . . . *fuckin' random.* But I wasn't fooling anyone. Not Lamont, and especially not myself. All I was doing was procrastinating, trying hopelessly to avoid asking the one question I was truly dreading.

I couldn't avoid it any longer.

"FOR THE record, you were never in here," said Lamont, pausing at a closed door toward the back corner of the precinct house.

I stared at him blankly as if I were some chronic sufferer of short-term memory loss. "*In where?*" I asked.

He smirked. Then he opened the door.

The windowless room I followed him into was only slightly bigger than claustrophobic. After closing the door behind us, Lamont introduced me to his partner, Detective Mike McGeary, who was at the helm of what looked like one of those video arcade games where you sit in a captain's chair shooting at alien spaceships on a large screen. He was even holding what looked like a joystick.

McGeary, square-jawed and bald, gave Lamont a sideways glance that all but screamed, *What the hell is he doing in here?*

"Mr. Mann was a close acquaintance of the victim," said Lamont. He added a slight emphasis on my last name, as if to jog his partner's memory.

McGeary studied me in the dim light of the room until he put my face and name together. Perhaps he was remembering the cover of the *New York Post* a couple of years back. *An Honest Mann*, read the headline.

"Yeah, fine," McGeary said finally. It wasn't exactly a ringing endorsement, but it was enough to consider the issue of my being there resolved. I could stay I could see the recording.

I could watch, frame by frame, the murder of the woman I loved.

Lamont hadn't had to tell me there was a surveillance camera in the taxi. I'd known right away, given how he'd described the shooting over the phone, some of the details he had. There were little things no eyewitnesses could ever provide. Had there been any eyewitnesses, that is.

Lamont removed his glasses, wearily pinching the bridge of his nose. No one ever truly gets used to the graveyard shift. "Any matches so far?" he asked his partner.

McGeary shook his head.

I glanced at the large monitor, which had shifted into screen saver mode, an NYPD logo floating about. Lamont, I could tell, was waiting for me to ask him about the space-age console, the reason I wasn't supposed to be in the room. The machine obviously did a little more than just digital playback.

But I didn't ask. I already knew.

I'm sure the thing had an official name, something ultrahigh-tech sounding, but back when I was in the DA's office I'd only ever heard it referred to by its nickname, CrackerJack. What it did was combine every known recognition software program into one giant cross-referencing "decoder" that was linked to practically every criminal database in the country, as well as those from twenty-three other countries, or basically all of our official allies in the "war on terror."

In short, given any image at any angle of any suspected terrorist, CrackerJack could source a litany of identifying characteristics, be it an exposed mole or tattoo; the exact measurements between the suspect's eyes, ears, nose, and mouth;

or even a piece of jewelry. Clothing, too. Apparently, for all the precautions terrorists take in their planning, it rarely occurs to them that wearing the same polyester shirt in London, Cairo, and Islamabad might be a bad idea.

Of course, it didn't take long for law enforcement in major cities—where CrackerJacks were heavily deployed by the Department of Homeland Security—to realize that these machines didn't have to identify just terrorists. Anyone with a criminal record was fair game.

So here was McGeary going through the recording sent over by the New York Taxi & Limousine Commission to see if any image of the shooter triggered a match. And here was me, having asked if I could watch it, too.

"Mike, cue it up from the beginning, will you?" said Lamont.

McGeary punched a button and then another until the screen lit up with the first frame, the taxi having pulled over to pick Claire up. The image was grainy, black-and-white, like on an old tube television with a set of rabbit ears. But what little I could see was still way too much.

It was exactly as Lamont had described it. The shooter smashes the driver's side window, beating the driver senseless with the butt of his gun. He's wearing a dark turtleneck and a ski mask with holes for the eyes, nose, and mouth. His gloves are tight, like those Isotoners that O. J. Simpson pretended didn't fit.

So far, Claire is barely visible. Not once can I see her face. Then I do.

It's right after the shooter snatches the driver's money bag. He swings his gun, aiming it at Claire in the backseat. She jolts. There's no Plexiglas divider. There's nothing but air.

Presumably, he says something to her, but the back of his head is toward the camera. Claire offers up her purse. He takes it and she says something. I was never any good at reading lips.

He should be leaving. Running away. Instead, he swings out and around, opening the rear door. He's out of frame for no more than three seconds. Then all I see is his outstretched arm. And the fear in her eyes.

He fires two shots at point-blank range. *Did he panic?* Not enough to flee right away. Quickly, he rifles through her pockets, and then tears off her earrings, followed by her watch, the Rolex Milgauss I gave her for her thirtieth birthday He dumps everything in her purse and takes off.

“Wait a minute,” I said suddenly. “Go back a little bit.”

LAMONT AND McGeary both turned to me, their eyes asking if I was crazy. *You want to watch her being murdered a second time?*

No, I didn't. Not a chance.

Watching it the first time made me so nauseous I thought I'd throw up right there on the floor. I wanted that recording erased, deleted, destroyed for all eternity not two seconds after it was used to catch the goddamn son of a bitch who'd done this.

Then I wanted a long, dark alley in the dead of night where he and I could have a little time alone together. Yeah. *That's* what I wanted.

But I thought I saw something.

Up until that moment, I hadn't known what I was looking for in the recording, if anything. If Claire had been standing next to me, she, with her love of landmark Supreme Court cases, would've described it as the definition of pornography according to Justice Potter Stewart in *Jacobellis v. Ohio.*

I know it when I see it.

She'd always admired the simplicity of that. Not everything that's true has to be proven, she used to say.

"Where to?" asked McGeary, his hand hovering over a knob that could rewind frame by frame, if need be.

"Just after he beats the driver," I said.

He nodded. "Say when."

I watched the sped-up images, everything happening in reverse. If only I could reverse it all for real. I was waiting for the part when the gun was turned on Claire. A few moments before that, actually.

"Stop," I said. "Right there."

McGeary hit Play again and I leaned in, my eyes glued to the screen. Meanwhile, I could feel Lamont's eyes glued to my profile, as if he could somehow better see what I was looking for by watching me.

"What is it?" he eventually asked.

I stepped back, shaking my head as if disappointed. "Nothing," I said. "It wasn't anything."

Because that's exactly what Claire would've wanted me to say. A little white lie for the greater good, she would've called it.

She was always a quick thinker, right up until the end.

NO WAY in hell did I feel like taking a taxi home.

In fact, I didn't feel like going home at all. In my mind, I'd already put my apartment on the market, packed up all my belongings, and moved to another neighborhood, maybe even out of Manhattan altogether. Claire was the city to me. Bright. Vibrant.

Alive.

And now she wasn't.

I passed a bar, looking through the window at the smattering of "patrons," to put it politely, who were still drinking at three in the morning. I could see an empty stool and it was calling my name. More like shouting it, really.

Don't, I told myself. *When you sober up, she'll still be gone.*

I kept walking in the direction of my apartment,

but with every step it became clear where I truly wanted to go. It was wherever Claire had been going.

Who was she meeting?

Suddenly, I was channeling Oliver Stone, somehow trying to link her murder to the story she'd been chasing. But that was crazy. I saw her murder in black and white. It was a robbery. She was in the wrong place at the wrong time, and as much as that was a cliché, so, too, was her death. She'd be the first to admit it.

"Imagine that," I could hear her saying. "A victim of violent crime in New York City. *How original.*"

Still, I'd become fixated on wanting to know where she'd been heading when she left my apartment. A two-hundred-dollar-an-hour shrink would probably call that sublimated grief, while the four-hundred-dollar-an-hour shrink would probably counter with sublimated anger. I was sticking with overwhelming curiosity.

I put myself in her shoes, mentally tracing her steps through the lobby of my building and out to the sidewalk. As soon as I pictured her raising her arm for a taxi, it occurred to me. *The driver.* He at least knew the address. For sure, Claire gave it to him when he picked her up.

Almost on cue, a taxi slowed down next to me at the curb, the driver wondering if I needed a ride. That was a common occurrence late at night when supply far outweighed demand.

As I shook him off, I began thinking of what else Claire's driver might remember when Lamont interviewed him. Tough to say after the beating he took. Maybe the shooter had said something that would key his identity, or at least thin out the suspects. Did he speak with any kind of accent?

Or maybe the driver had seen something that wasn't visible to that surveillance camera. Eye color? An odd-shaped mole? A chipped tooth?

Unfortunately, the list of possibilities didn't go on and on. The ski mask, turtleneck, and gloves made sure of that. Clearly, the bastard knew that practically every taxi in the city was its own little recording studio. So much for cameras being a deterrent.

As the old expression goes, show me a ten-foot wall and I'll show you an eleven-foot ladder.

The twenty blocks separating me from my apartment were a daze. I was on autopilot, one foot in front of the other. Only at the sound of the keys as I dropped them on my kitchen counter did I snap out of it, realizing I was actually home.

Fully dressed, I fell into my bed, shoes and all. I didn't even bother turning off the lights. But my eyes were closed for only a few seconds before they popped open. Damn. All it took was one breath, one exchange of the air around me, and I was lying there feeling more alone than I ever had in my entire life.

The sheets still smelled of her.

I sat up, looking over at the other side of the bed... the pillow. I could still make out the impression of Claire's head. That was the word, wasn't it? *Impression*. Hers was everywhere, most of all on me.

I was about to make a beeline to my guest room, which, if anything, would smell of dust or staleness or whatever other odor is given off by a room that's rarely, if ever, used. I didn't care. So long as it wasn't her.

Suddenly, though, I froze. Something had caught my eye. It was the yellow legal pad on the end of the bed, the one Claire had used when she took the phone call. She'd ripped off the top sheet she'd written on.

But the one beneath it...

WINNER OF THE EDGAR™ AWARD FOR BEST FIRST NOVEL

The Thomas Berryman Number

James Patterson

One of the classic novels of suspense by the world's bestselling thriller writer.

It begins with three terrifying murders in the American South. It ends with a relentless and unforgettable manhunt in the North.

In between is the gripping story of a ruthless assassin, the woman he loves, and the beloved leader he is hired to kill with extreme prejudice.

'*The Thomas Berryman Number* is sure-fire!'
New York Times

CENTURY

THE *SUNDAY TIMES* BESTSELLER

Hope to Die

James Patterson

I am alone, I thought. Alone.

Pain knifed through my head. I sank to my knees, bowed my head, and raised my hands towards heaven.

'Why?' I screamed. 'Why?'

Detective Alex Cross has lost everything and everyone he's ever cared about.

His enemy, Thierry Mulch, is holding his family. Driven by feelings of hatred and revenge, Mulch is threatening to kill them all, and break Cross for ever.

But Alex Cross is fighting back

In a race against time, he must defeat Mulch, and find his wife and children – no matter what it takes.

THE END-GAME HAS BEGUN.

CENTURY

Also by James Patterson

ALEX CROSS NOVELS

Along Came a Spider • Kiss the Girls • Jack and Jill • Cat and Mouse • Pop Goes the Weasel • Roses are Red • Violets are Blue • Four Blind Mice • The Big Bad Wolf • London Bridges • Mary, Mary • Cross • Double Cross • Cross Country • Alex Cross's Trial (*with Richard DiLallo*) • I, Alex Cross • Cross Fire • Kill Alex Cross • Merry Christmas, Alex Cross • Alex Cross, Run • Cross My Heart • Hope to Die

THE WOMEN'S MURDER CLUB SERIES

1st to Die • 2nd Chance (*with Andrew Gross*) • 3rd Degree (*with Andrew Gross*) • 4th of July (*with Maxine Paetro*) • The 5th Horseman (*with Maxine Paetro*) • The 6th Target (*with Maxine Paetro*) • 7th Heaven (*with Maxine Paetro*) • 8th Confession (*with Maxine Paetro*) • 9th Judgement (*with Maxine Paetro*) • 10th Anniversary (*with Maxine Paetro*) • 11th Hour (*with Maxine Paetro*) • 12th of Never (*with Maxine Paetro*) • Unlucky 13 (*with Maxine Paetro*) • 14th Deadly Sin (*with Maxine Paetro*)

PRIVATE NOVELS

Private (*with Maxine Paetro*) • Private London (*with Mark Pearson*) • Private Games (*with Mark Sullivan*) • Private: No. 1 Suspect (*with Maxine Paetro*) • Private Berlin (*with Mark Sullivan*) • Private Down Under (*with Michael White*) • Private L.A. (*with Mark Sullivan*) • Private India (*with Ashwin Sanghi*) • Private Vegas (*with Maxine Paetro*)

NYPD RED SERIES

NYPD Red (*with Marshall Karp*) •
NYPD Red 2 (*with Marshall Karp*) •
NYPD Red 3 (*with Marshall Karp*)

STAND-ALONE THRILLERS

Sail (*with Howard Roughan*) • Swimsuit (*with Maxine Paetro*) • Don't Blink (*with Howard Roughan*) • Postcard Killers (*with Liza Marklund*) • Toys (*with Neil McMahon*) • Now You See Her (*with Michael Ledwidge*) • Kill Me If You Can (*with Marshall Karp*) • Guilty Wives (*with David Ellis*) • Zoo (*with Michael Ledwidge*) • Second Honeymoon (*with Howard Roughan*) • Mistress (*with David Ellis*) • Invisible (*with David Ellis*) • The Thomas Berryman Number • Truth or Die (*with Howard Roughan*)

NON-FICTION

Torn Apart (*with Hal and Cory Friedman*) •
The Murder of King Tut (*with Martin Dugard*)

ROMANCE

Sundays at Tiffany's (*with Gabrielle Charbonnet*) •
The Christmas Wedding (*with Richard DiLallo*) •
First Love (*with Emily Raymond*)

OTHER TITLES

Miracle at Augusta (*with Peter de Jonge*)

FAMILY OF PAGE-TURNERS

MIDDLE SCHOOL BOOKS

Middle School: The Worst Years of My Life (*with Chris Tebbetts*) • Middle School: Get Me Out of Here! (*with Chris Tebbetts*) • Middle School: My Brother Is a Big, Fat Liar (*with Lisa Papademetriou*) • Middle School: How I Survived Bullies, Broccoli, and Snake Hill (*with Chris Tebbetts*) • Middle School: Ultimate Showdown (*with Julia Bergen*) • Middle School: Save Rafe! (*with Chris Tebbetts*)

I FUNNY SERIES

I Funny (*with Chris Grabenstein*) • I Even Funnier (*with Chris Grabenstein*) • I Totally Funniest (*with Chris Grabenstein*)

TREASURE HUNTERS SERIES

Treasure Hunters (*with Chris Grabenstein*) • Treasure Hunters: Danger Down the Nile (*with Chris Grabenstein*)

HOUSE OF ROBOTS

House of Robots (*with Chris Grabenstein*)

HOMEROOM DIARIES

Homeroom Diaries (*with Lisa Papademetriou*)

MAXIMUM RIDE SERIES

The Angel Experiment • School's Out Forever • Saving the World and Other Extreme Sports • The Final Warning • Max • Fang • Angel • Nevermore • Forever

CONFESSIONS SERIES

Confessions of a Murder Suspect (*with Maxine Paetro*) • Confessions: The Private School Murders (*with Maxine Paetro*) • Confessions: The Paris Mysteries (*with Maxine Paetro*)

WITCH & WIZARD SERIES

Witch & Wizard (*with Gabrielle Charbonnet*) • The Gift (*with Ned Rust*) • The Fire (*with Jill Dembowski*) • The Kiss (*with Jill Dembowski*) • The Lost (*with Emily Raymond*)

DANIEL X SERIES

The Dangerous Days of Daniel X (*with Michael Ledwidge*) • Watch the Skies (*with Ned Rust*) • Demons and Druids (*with Adam Sadler*) • Game Over (*with Ned Rust*) • Armageddon (*with Chris Grabenstein*)

GRAPHIC NOVELS

Daniel X: Alien Hunter (*with Leopoldo Gout*) • Maximum Ride: Manga Vols. 1–8 (*with NaRae Lee*)

For more information about James Patterson's novels, visit www.jamespatterson.co.uk

Or become a fan on Facebook

WHO IS DETECTIVE MICHAEL BENNETT?

PERSONAL LIFE

Michael Bennett lives in New York City with his ten adopted kids: Chrissy, Shawna, Trent, twins Fiona and Bridget, Eddie, Ricky, Jane, Brian and Juliana. His wife Maeve worked as a nurse on the trauma ward at Jacobi Hospital in the Bronx. Maeve died tragically young after losing a battle with cancer in December 2007. Also in the Bennett household are his Irish grandfather Seamus and their nanny, Mary Catherine. Bennett's relationship with Mary Catherine is a complicated one and they have an on-off romance.

HOBBIES

Bennett doesn't have time for hobbies. He spends his spare time looking after his kids.

EDUCATION

Bennett graduated from Regis High School and studied philosophy at Manhattan College in the Bronx.

WORK

Bennett joined the police force to uncover the truth at all costs. He started his career in the Bronx's 44th Precinct before moving to the FBI. After his time with the Bureau, he rejoined the NYPD as a senior detective.

Bennett is an expert in hostage negotiation, terrorism, homicide and organised crime. He will stop at nothing to get the job done and protect the city, even if this means disobeying orders and ignoring protocol. Despite these unorthodox methods, he is a relentless, determined and in many ways incomparable detective.